Stuck with the Anesthesiologist

Daphne Dyer

Skyway Creative Endeavors

For my favorite Anesthesiologist. Love you forever.

Other Titles

Contents

Three Years Ago

Theo

THE BLUE, RED, YELLOW, and green loading ring spun and spun on my phone's little screen. Destiny waited for me, but my snail-like connection speed ratcheted my adrenaline. Sweat built under the collar of my scrubs.

Where was the promised 5G?

I relaxed my grip. Breaking the phone wouldn't make my email account load faster.

The phone quacked with another text message.

Walter:

Headed to Seattle suckers! Pedi Anesthesia for the Win!

That made six out of twelve anesthesia residents matching into fellowships. It was normally unheard of for so many to pursue additional education after residency.

By twenty-nine years old, most residents are ready to ditch the classroom, work forty—not eighty—hours per week, and earn a real physician's salary.

My class was different.

We yearned to be the best of the best. If I match to one of my top choices, I'll re-earn my dad's respect. Be a son he's proud of.

My email page loaded. I scrolled through the junk to the message from the National Fellowship Matching Committee and clicked the subject line.

Again, the loading ring spun and spun. This was worse than the old days of dial-up. At least then, you knew you could start the next case while you waited for the web page to load.

As it was, my attending caught my eye, tapped his watch, and pointed to OR 5. Time to start the next ACL reconstruction, but I needed to swing through the PACU and check on our previous patient first.

I split my attention between the phone and my coworkers wheeling their patients through the busy hallway.

Another attending and his resident pushed an elderly woman toward me in a wheelchair. I pressed my back against the wall and glanced at my phone.

The NFMC logo greeted me. I read.

Dr. Theodore Sanchez IV,

Congratulations. You have matched into an Anesthesiology Subspecialty Fellowship. Click the link below to learn which program you will be attending.

I pumped my fist. *Yes!* Finally, it was my turn to show my parents what I was capable of.

My fingers flew over the keyboard to enter my log in information.

"Sanchez!" my attending barked.

I held up my phone. "I got in! But I don't know where."

A gigantic smile split his face. "There wasn't a doubt. I'll get started. Get in here as soon as you can."

"Thanks, sir."

The screen blanked to white. The operating rooms needed better Wi-Fi or more repeaters—something. This was ridiculous.

I squeezed my hands into fists and scurried toward the PACU. Our patient, Angela Mendoza, a fifty-four-year-old day care worker from Palo Alto status-post right meniscus repair, was awake. Vitals normal. "Pain?"

"Like I didn't have surgery." She rubbed her hand along the bandage. "The nerve block was a good idea."

I added a note to the sweet woman's chart. "If anything changes, please tell Nurse Lewis. We should have you out of here within the next hour if everything stays the same."

"Thank you, Dr. Sanchez." She squeezed my hand but didn't release me when I tried to pull away. "Are you married?"

"Just to my job."

"I have a granddaughter ..."

"I'm sure she's as lovely as you are." I winked. "She'll make someone really happy someday. I'll see you in a bit."

Mrs. Mendoza blushed, and I jogged into the hallway. Tucked myself into the corner next to OR 5.

The page illuminated, and my eyes scanned the text.

Welcome to the Pain Medicine Fellowship based out of the Department of Anesthesiology and Critical Care Medicine at Johns

Hopkins University. We look forward to extending your training and cultivating leaders in pain medicine.

"Yes!" I shouted, startling the nurses at the charge desk.

I wagged my phone toward them. "Johns Hopkins. My first choice!"

"Congratulations, son. You've earned it." The charge nurse's motherly smile warmed me to my toes. I couldn't wait to hear those words from my mom and dad.

My ten-year plan unfolded before me. Graduate from residency at Stanford. Spend the next year in Baltimore honing my skills and learning how to help patients manage their chronic and acute pain. Certificate of completion in hand, I'll join Physicians Worldwide, return to the rural part of central Mexico where my grandfather was born, and provide lifesaving medical care to those who couldn't access it any other way.

Mission accomplished, I'll step into my dad's shoes as CEO of Sanchez Biotech and usher our family business into its next era of productivity and service to the world.

I imagined the pride on my father's face and the satisfaction I'd finally feel making him—the founder of one of the world's leading biomedical technology manufacturers—proud to have a son using the technology he created.

He hadn't been excited about me pursuing medicine instead of a business degree initially—especially since my future as his successor is a foregone conclusion—but he warmed to the idea quickly.

Investors loved when he introduced me as *Dr. Sanchez*, and I could speak intelligently with them regarding the company's opportunities.

I didn't want to wait to call my parents, but I had to. Patient care always came first. I added my good news to the residents' text stream and entered the operating room.

At the end of the day, I rested my head against my locker. Our last patient had tried to die on us. Luckily, I'd spotted the dropped tidal volume trends, and we'd averted a catastrophe. The relief didn't keep my hands from shaking.

This was exactly why I wanted to complete a fellowship.

I needed to make sure the outcomes for people in small towns were just as good as those treated by level I trauma centers like the one where I trained in the San Francisco Bay area.

I dialed my parents' home in Houston. Mom answered on the third ring. "Theo?" She sounded surprised to hear from me.

"Hi, Mom. I've got great news. Is Dad around?"

"I believe he's on a call. Can we call you back?"

My heart sank. I should have texted earlier to arrange an appointment with him. "How much longer do you think he'll be?"

"I don't know, dear." *We never interrupt your father on a work call* didn't need to be said. After almost thirty years competing for his attention, I knew today wouldn't be any different.

"It's okay. This is important, but I want to tell you both at the same time. Please call me as soon as he's done."

We hung up, and my excited energy sent me pacing from one end of the locker room to the next.

It was only a ten-minute walk to my studio apartment on the other side of campus, but I was unrealistically optimistic. I didn't want to yell over rush hour traffic if they called back quickly.

Please let it be a short phone call.

I could call my sister, but even at seven p.m. she was most likely in the pool for diving practice.

While my dream had always been to work in medicine, hers was the gold medal variety. If it hadn't been for me, she would have made the Olympic dive team a few months ago.

My stomach squirmed and writhed as badly as it had the day I'd caused her to miss the meet which would have birthed her Olympic ticket. The day I lost Dad's respect.

Never again.

With our parents' support—and me staying away—she was home-schooling her senior year of high school, allowing her to double her training.

I knew she'd make the team next time.

I'd have to figure out how to get time off to see her compete, but that was a problem for another day.

The clock ticked fifteen minutes.

Then thirty.

The locker room emptied.

I looped my backpack over my shoulder. I could have been home by now. No point waiting any longer. My dad probably wouldn't call until tomorrow.

The elevator took me to the first floor, and I pushed into the glow of the streetlights. The city was too bright to see any stars, but I gazed at the inkiness for a moment anyway. Baltimore would be the same, but maybe I'd have a weekend off here or there to visit the Allegheny Mountains and see real stars.

I crossed the street and entered Stanford's campus.

Might as well start apartment hunting. I tapped the real estate app on my phone and entered my search criteria. The smaller the better. No roommates. No chances for distraction. Close to the hospital, but in a safe neighborhood. The app retrieved seven complexes with studio apartments in my budget.

My phone rang with my dad's picture lighting up the screen. My nervousness made the phone slip. I juggled it, caught it before it smashed on the ground.

I shook my head. "Calm down, Theo." A steadying breath filled my lungs, and I pushed the button to answer the call. "Thanks for calling me back. I have great news."

I paused by Terman Fountain. The grass rolled down to the shallow body of water where little kids and college students cooled their toes on hot days. I was half tempted to strip off my shoes and socks, wade in, and celebrate with a splash or two.

"Well?" My dad's gruff voice sounded far away.

I sat on the staircase instead.

"We're listening, dear," Mom said.

I sucked in a calming breath. "I matched into the Pain Fellowship at Johns Hopkins."

A beat passed. Two. Something shifted on their end.

"You've worked hard." Mom's voice held tentative pride.

"It's one of the best programs in the country." I bit my lip. "I wanted to make you guys proud."

I heard whispers and a small scuffle. I imagined Mom elbowing Dad in the side so he'd say something. He cleared his throat. "We are, but it's unfortunate timing."

I straightened my posture. "What do you mean?"

"The family needs you." My dad's voice rang clearly. He'd picked up the handset, so I wasn't on speakerphone anymore. "The company needs you. It's time for you to come home and take your place."

Take my place? "We decided I would work for a few years before I—"

"That's not an option anymore."

Dad's gruff voice confused me. We had agreed. "What about Physicians Worldwide?"

"Things change."

"Why?"

"The family needs you." The refrain was as common as water. *The family needs you. The company needs you.* Does it matter what I need? *No.*

That's the point. My birthright is to take over the company and extend our distribution to the far reaches of the world.

It's an honor, but I can do more if I spend time working as an anesthesiologist before I superglue my butt to a board room chair for the rest of my life.

"My fellowship will be great for the family. I'll have better insight into how we can better serve patients. Maybe even come up with new designs and improvements for our devices."

Something sounding like ice cubes clinked in the background. "You already know what you need to about patient care. It's the engineers' responsibility enhance the technology, not the physicians."

"Dad." I tried to sound decisive, but my voice came out as a plea. "I want to complete my training."

I needed his blessing if I wanted to continue. Little else mattered in my life above my parents' approval. I'd already broken their faith when I'd failed Elena.

I couldn't hurt them again. I owed them too much.

"Our investors, the board, and our clients will be confident and proud to see *Board Certified Anesthesiologist* after your name. They don't care about the rest." He sighed. "I'll leave the decision to you, but I counsel you to remember what happened last time you put your whims before the good of the family. I hope you don't repeat history. Call me when you've made your choice." Dad hung up.

I stared at my phone. The burning weight I'd carried in my chest since Elena missed the Olympic Trials intensified.

There was no choice to make. Dad was right.

As much good as I could do completing a fellowship and working with underserved populations, I couldn't abandon my family.

I couldn't let them down.

Not again.

Throughout my childhood, Mom and Dad reminded me the company would be my responsibility someday. I'd sat on my dad's lap during countless board meetings before I even started school.

With medical school and residency over, I didn't have any excuses to keep me out of the boardroom. I would use my medical knowledge to serve where I belonged, ensure our thousands of international employees continued to thrive, and make sure my sister had every opportunity to chase her dreams.

She'd sacrificed for me.

It was my turn to return the favor.

No matter how intense the pain in my chest.

Chapter 1

Present Day

Georgi

NORA BARGES INTO HONEY Beans dabbing her eyes and blowing her nose. Her sun-kissed brown hair flies around her head like she's harboring a personal tornado. "Georgi, he broke up with me in a text message." She shoves her phone in my face and points at the text.

Paul:

> It's been fun, but greener pastures call.

She flops into a chair next to my barista counter. "Who does that?"

"Trolls. The kind who live under bridges and harass billy goats and sweet cardiology fellows." I hand my sister a pile of napkins and the peppermint mocha she ordered via all-caps text message.

It's decaf, but shh, don't tell her.

She's worse than a gremlin if you give her caffeine after mid-after-noon.

Add in a breakup, and nope, she doesn't get any more stimulants today.

"You'll be okay. He wasn't worthy of you anyway." Most of the *men* she *dates*–I use both of those words very lightly—aren't.

Bubee, TX doesn't have a thriving singles population, but some-how my brilliant sister finds the toads. The one-drink, one-lunch, one-text-message-exchange-then-ghost-her toads.

"I have to see him every day at the hospital." She chugs half her drink and returns to mopping the emotion from her face. "I should never have dated another fellow."

Honey Beans is empty. I'm getting ready to close for the night, and she needs to let it all out before we head to the beach for Sangria Under the Pier. The subdued moonlight will only hide so much if she doesn't get the sobbing and runny nose out of her system. She's usually pretty close lipped about her relationships, even among our closest friends. It's a family trait. She won't want the gossip mill getting ahold of this nugget.

At least until the news spreads at the hospital tomorrow.

Time for some clarity. "Did you think he was *The One*?" I ask.

She snorts. "Oh, goodness no. He was too stingy and rude to waitresses, but I deserved a face-to-face break up. Show a lady some respect."

I lift three fingers and tap the ends. "Stingy, rude, and disrespectful. Perfect trifecta for why this is a good thing." I grab a towel, wipe down the tables, and set the chairs on top. I hum Carrie Underwood's "Cowboy Casanova" as I glide through the shop.

Nora cocks her head. "Why are you in such a good mood?"

I lift an eyebrow and spread my arms to encompass the entire coffee shop. "We're alone."

Her face crinkles to figure out what I mean, then her forehead flattens, and she smiles. "He didn't ..."

"Nope." I let my smile spread. "My typical Saturday night nuisance must not be in town, so my heart's light and airy tonight." I scrunch my shoulders. "But I am sorry about your breakup."

It's not right that I'm so happy when she's annoyed and sad, but Nora doesn't know the full history between me and Dr. Theodore Sanchez. My sisters and I share everything, but I never mustered the courage to tell them more than the basic details: Almost every Saturday night for the last year, Dr. Theo Sanchez has paraded his entourage of beautiful people through my shop. He flirts, insinuates, and somehow makes my heart flutter and my skin crawl.

The worst part is the sincerity in his voice and the way his eyes shimmer like he's letting me glimpse his soul.

I fell for his charms once.

In one magical night, he made me feel extraordinary and wanted and precious. I almost thought I was in love.

Then he dumped me like used coffee grounds.

Fool me once, shame on you. Not going to fool me twice.

Now I celebrate the days I don't see Theo, when my heart doesn't long for him to be the guy I thought he was before the entourage showed it's veneered face.

We've watched Mama pine for our deadbeat dad our entire lives. I will not be her. I will not wallow in self-pity when there's work to be done.

Nora grabs the broom and helps me clean. "Maybe if we find you a boyfriend, Theo will get the hint and leave you alone."

"I doubt Theo would care if I was engaged. He'd still act like he's Prince Charming, and I need to be swept off my cowboy boots. He flirts because he hates that I see through his fake charisma, not because he's interested in me." I roll my eyes. "Besides, when do I have time for a high-maintenance man?"

My dating life is stagnant because I'm too busy raising my siblings and cousin. With uninterested or mean parents like ours, someone needs to make sure there's food on the table and clean clothes in the drawers—to be the voice of reason when tempers fly.

"Whatever." Nora finishes her coffee. Tears dry, nose clean, she sighs like peppermint and chocolate have solved all her problems. "You deserve happiness and a break from all the stress you carry."

I wrap her in a hug. "You deserve better than a text message breakup." I release her and untie my apron. "Let's go meet the ladies, enjoy our sangria, and remember how amazing we are without needing a man to validate our existence."

I retrieve the pitcher of sangria from the mini fridge, grab my keys and purse.

Tipsy pushes through the front doors as we reach them and slumps into the booth against the windows. My cousin clings to the sleeves of her oversized grey Bubee Blue Heron high school sweatshirt and buries her face in the crook of her elbow.

I set the drinks down and nudge her shoulder. "What's up?"

"Dad." She spits the word and slams her fist into the counter. "Aunt Imogen convinced the judge to grant him *another* extension, so trial's not until the end of next month. She's trying to get him off with community service."

Icicles run through my veins, my head drops back, and I grind my teeth. The expletives racing through my thoughts are not kind. "She's an idiot."

Last Thanksgiving, my uncle ran over a little boy while he was drinking and driving. It wasn't his first DUI, and the boy almost died.

In a normal world, that earns him fifteen to life, but my aunt, Mayor Imogen Buchanan, can't have her big brother locked up in prison.

Alcoholism is a disease. Putting him in jail won't cure him. He needs medical help.

That's like saying the car made him get behind its wheel and drive it.

She's an enabler and delusional.

He lasted a week in rehab. Refuses Alcoholics Anonymous.

Having him home another month gives him more opportunities to destroy my cousin's self-esteem.

At seventeen, if your dad tells you you're worthless, you believe him.

Yeah, he deserves every expletive in the book. Then to have the book thrown at him.

That's why I still live with my mom and teenage brother in my uncle's double wide.

If his vitriol is aimed at me, it's not aimed at Tipsy. I learned a long time ago not to care what people say about me. Tipsy hasn't grown thick skin—she shouldn't have to—so I do everything in my power to protect her.

I plaster on a smile. "Good thing it's Sangria Under the Pier night. We'll stay out later, so he'll have passed out by the time we get home."

"It's not going to matter." Tipsy lays her head on the table.

Nora and I exchange a look. We haven't seen Tipsy this bad in a while. Normally, she can find a snarky comeback.

Our poor girl. She deserves so much more than this cruddy life.

Nora and I slide into the booth on opposite sides and wrap our arms around her bony shoulders. "You're eighteen in a few more months, then you'll be free."

She turns her head to look at me. "He won't let me move out. He already said so."

"When you're legally an adult, he can't stop you," I say, squeezing her tighter. "If you decide not to go to college, you and I will get a place. Maybe my mom will even let Lee live with us until he goes to college."

My brother got a full ride to play football for Texas Christian University. I lack the vocabulary to describe how excited I am for him to get away and continue my sisters' tradition. Not only are they the first generation to attend college, but my sisters are all going to be physicians. Lee hasn't decided, but he might follow in their footsteps.

I'm the only one who couldn't go. If I'd left, no one would have been around to help them achieve their dreams. To protect them.

Mama can barely take care of herself, let alone five kids. Aunt Sally does whatever Hoyt says, so she's never stepped between him and the kids.

I'd rather be a barista anyway.

Coffee is its own kind of medicine on a crummy day.

"Want something warm before we head to the beach?" I ask Tipsy. March's chill won't help her mood, but fingers wrapped around a steaming cup of creamy goodness will put a smile on her face.

"Chai would be nice."

"One vanilla chai latte coming up." I slide behind the counter and steam the milk.

With a warm beverage for the minor and sangria for the adults, I close Honey Beans, and we head to the beach. We need something good to celebrate.

Theo

Wind whips off the ocean. I pull my beanie farther over my ears to fight the cold as my sister and I jog through the sand. "Only another two and a half months until Olympic Trials. Are you excited?"

Elena groans. "Can we talk about something else? Please." In a long sleeve thermal and running tights, my sister seems impervious to the cold. Her long strides eat up the ground like she's running on pavement, not damp sand.

I do my best to keep up. "Like what?"

"I don't know. Why aren't Mom and Dad having a party this week-end?"

"They are. A few couples at the house in Houston, so I'm off the hook."

This isn't the life I expected to be living when I gave up my fellowship and medical practice. I thought Dad would have me in one of the offices, training, learning the systems. Maybe managing the Bubee factory.

Instead, I'm the party guy.

The bartender.

The DJ.

The bellhop.

The sunscreen-applier.

Every Friday, Saturday, and Sunday, whatever Dad's guests want, Dad's guests get.

Elena leaps a sandcastle. "Nice to have a weekend to yourself, isn't it?"

"Are you reading my mind? Because you have no idea." The rare weekends when I don't have to entertain my parents' work contacts—or their spoiled kids—on our mega yacht are my favorites. I can do whatever I want. Mostly.

I didn't get to Honey Beans today. When Elena showed up, I knew I wouldn't have the opportunity to see Georgi.

She should be on the beach though. I'll at least catch a glimpse as we run by. It will have to be enough to tide my heart over.

Elena knocks into my shoulder. "Should I have stayed home and let you have the boat to yourself?"

I shake off what I'm sure is a tortured expression. Thinking about Georgi and our strained relationship does that to me, but I won't let my melancholy ruin my chance to hang out with my sister. "I'm glad you're here. We don't see each other enough."

"Great, because I'm training here for the rest of the season."

I stop running. "Really? What does Dad have to say about that?" Since she missed the Olympic Trials last time, Dad's been watching her training more closely. A chauffeur drives her to and from practice. Her coach provides detailed weekly progress reports. He won't let anything stop her from achieving her dream.

Especially me.

So why is Dad letting her move in with me?

She circles back and jogs in place. "He's fine with it. I told him I needed to focus and couldn't do it at the pool in Houston."

"That's it?"

She shrugs like her relocation isn't a big deal.

Does Bubee even have a pool with a diving well and a ten-meter platform?

"What about Calum?" I don't hide the disdain in my tone. He coached one athlete to the Olympics, and it put a huge chip on his shoulder. His athlete lost every heat he competed in, so it's not that great of a resume, but he wooed Dad.

Elena tugs on my arm, and we return to our jog. "He's getting an apartment in town, and don't say his name that way."

"Not going to hide that I don't like him." Or his methods.

"You don't have to like him, but you do have to be kind."

"He yells at you."

She makes a nasal chortling sound somewhere between a snort and a laugh. "He's a coach. That's what he does."

"He hit you in the head with a kickboard."

"My positioning was wrong. It's not like I could hear him yelling mid-rotation. It didn't hurt."

"There are better ways."

"Not for elite athletes. And I said I don't want to talk about diving."

Fine. I'll let her deflect, but there's something she's not telling me. "How's school?" She's taking online classes through Houston Community College, but she's never mentioned what she wants to do with her degree when she's done.

"Ugh. Next topic."

"Seen any good movies?"

My sister laughs and shoves me toward the surf. I stumble but regain my balance before my tennis shoes get drenched. Neither of us have time to watch movies, but it's fun to pretend we have lives outside of "work" and training.

"Watch something after our run?" I ask.

"I have to read for my Roman history class."

"We can watch *Gladiator*. That's the same, right?"

"Hmm." She tries not to let her smile reach all the way to her eyes. "Russell Crowe or thirty-five pages of descriptions about how Rome built their roads? I'm not sure which is more appealing."

"Settled." I point into the distance. "Race you to the pier, then we can cool down with popcorn."

"You're on." She takes off in a spray of sand.

My sister is fast. I chase her, but my sides ache and I'm puffing air when I meet her by the pillars.

She doesn't even look winded. "You need to do more cardio."

I brace my hands on my hips and suck air. "Not all of us are trying to be Olympians."

She pats the top of my head. "I'd beat you even if I wasn't training."

I wrap her in a headlock and rub my knuckles in her hair. "Tell yourself that, Pipsqueak."

She squeaks and squirms until I let her go.

"Ready for popcorn?"

She loops her arm around my waist, and I put mine over her shoulder. "With all the butter."

"Maybe we should—" My words clog in my throat at the scene before me.

Worry settles on my sister's face. "Theo? What's wrong?" She follows my gaze.

On the other side of the pier, a group of women sit in beach chairs around a firepit. The glow makes the redhead's hair look like the gleam from a sunset. If I were closer, I'd be able to gaze into her deep, emerald-green eyes or count the dozen freckles scattered like a constellation across her nose.

Don't get me started on her lips

But closer isn't an option. The scowl she's shooting me can't be misconstrued for anything besides loathing.

"Who's that?" Elena asks.

"Georgi Montgomery."

"What'd you do to her?"

"Fell in love."

Ten Months Ago

Theo

I BROUGHT MY HAND to my forehead and blocked the glare from the sunset off the water. Standing at the stern of my parents' mega yacht in the Bubee Yacht Club, I gazed out at the bay. Over the last week the crew and I had prepared the yacht to host weekend parties for my dad's friends and their kids. Next weekend would be my first group.

Party host seemed like a strange task after the past two years serving as a courier, assistant assembly line technician, and inventory specialist, but it was what my dad said we needed next.

Fine. Okay. I'd host parties.

It was an opportunity to get to know the men and women Mom and Dad worked with, our investors, and their families. According to Dad, at least. I wasn't sure how karaoke would help me learn to run a billion-dollar company.

"Sir, a moment?" the captain asked. His stiff posture and perfectly pressed uniform left no question that he was the man in charge.

I dropped my hand and stepped onto the bridge. "Yes, Captain Timmons."

"We're done for the day, sir. Is there anything else I can get you?"

"Take the rest of the night off. You guys have done amazing work this week."

Moving the boat to Bubee, cleaning and repairing every nook and cranny, making the yacht as glamorous as a boutique hotel on Park Ave hadn't been easy, but they'd made the jobs seem effortless.

Timmons nodded. "Would you like the chef to prepare your dinner?"

"No. I'm going to explore. Have you ever been to Bubee before?"

"No, sir." With no inflection in his voice, I couldn't tell if he was happy about the move from Houston.

Guess only time would tell for both of us.

"Good evening, Captain Timmons." I tucked my hands in the pockets of my khaki pants and wandered up the dock toward Camino del Mar.

Even though my dad had built the factory here six years ago, I'd never been to Bubee before. My mom would call it *a cute little town worthy of a Hallmark movie*. That's probably why she and Dad picked this yacht club to park their boats and host their parties.

It was close enough to Houston for people to easily access, but far enough to feel like a minivacation.

The distance allowed me to continue my weekday work as the Employee Satisfaction Liaison. Treating employees to five-star meals, asking how they're doing and how the company can serve them better, then fixing any problems they identified far outweighed being a courier. It gave me a glimpse into the lives of our employees and allowed me a deeper appreciation for how vast our company was.

I'd have to talk to Dad about including employees in the weekend party schedule.

Bubee's beachfront street was full of the typical restaurants and souvenir shops you expect in a town with an economy based on tourism. Lots of beach-themed housewares, T-shirts, and bathing suits decorated front window displays.

The stores had an added Victorian charm. Gabled roofs and intricate scroll work decorated the doors and windows. Flowers bloomed in window boxes and under magnolia trees. The ambiance was almost charming enough to make me forget spring's sticky, hot air clinging to my skin.

I wandered the streets looking for entertaining locations to take our guests when they arrived. It was unlikely they would want to stay on the boat the entire weekend.

Our chef would provide the majority of our meals, so I didn't need to try the restaurants just yet. They smelled good, though. Especially Jake's BBQ and Sobre las Rocas Mexican restaurant. Later, after I wandered a bit, I'd grab a bite.

I turned onto Tiburon Ave, and a glowing bee carrying a coffee bean caught my eye.

I could use a cup of coffee.

Even though my years as a physician were behind me, I couldn't kick my craving for a cup of coffee before dinner.

Honey Beans Coffee was empty except for a redhead sitting in the corner with a teenage boy. He had the look of a one-year-old chocolate lab puppy. With a sparkle in his eye, he hadn't quite grown into his body yet, but his feet and hands told you he would be huge. Textbooks and a calculator filled the little table.

"Be right with you," the redhead said.

I wasn't in a hurry, so I wandered to the back of the store. One long booth ran under the front window with tables and chairs waiting for patrons. A chalkboard menu behind the registers listed specialty lattes. Novels filled the shelves along the back wall, along with a display of T-shirts and coffee mugs with the bee logo.

I picked a book at random and thumbed through the pages, but the words didn't have the same draw as the redhead's lilting voice. She spoke with a familiar Texas drawl, but her words held a sweeter note. Gentle and subtle. Almost homey, if a voice could be described that way.

I couldn't help eavesdropping.

"This is a vector function. In order to find the location on the curve, we use this equation." She tapped the tip of her pencil to the textbook. "We need to solve for x."

The teen's pencil scratched across the paper as he worked the problem.

"Don't forget this," she said.

He shook his head and erased something. "I don't get it."

"Try this." She lowered her voice so I couldn't hear what she said. His pencil started moving again, and he typed information into his calculator.

"Good. X is eleven. Now, what's next?"

"I need to find where the vectors meet."

"Show me."

He muddled through the concepts, but she was patient and precise in her instructions. When one technique didn't work, she tried a different method to help him understand.

After the third attempt, his eyebrows bounced to his hairline. "Oh, wait. I got it. Then check the exponent." His pencil scribbled across the page like he was completing simple addition and subtraction instead of complex quadratics.

The redhead squeezed his shoulder and rose from the table. "I knew you'd get it. You don't have the Montgomery smarts for nothing. You'll ace your test next week."

She unwound her bun and her hair cascaded down her back. Her dark flowered romper made her skin look like porcelain. Stepping behind the counter, she tied an apron around her waist. "Thanks. He was too close to quit. What can I get you?"

"Just a small coffee, please."

She pointed to the menu. "I make an amazing latte, if you want something a little sweeter. The cinnamon hazelnut is the newest favorite."

"No, thanks." After years of stale black, anything with cream or sugar made coffee taste wrong.

"Your loss. Stayin'?" She pressed her finger to a ceramic mug with the glowing honeybee on the side. "Or do you want a walkin' cup?" She lifted a paper cup.

I could have taken my drink to go and continued my tour of the town, but I was intrigued by this woman. You don't expect a coffee bar barista to have mastered vector polynomials, but she had.

I sounded like a jerk when I thought that, but I didn't mean to be offensive. We make assumptions about people based on their professions. As a small-town barista, no one expected her to grasp exponents, polynomials, and limits.

She defied expectations. I wanted to know why. "For here, please."

She plucked a ceramic cup from the pile and filled it from the carafe behind her.

I nodded toward the boy. "Is he taking calculus?"

It was a dumb question based on what they'd been talking about and the book on the table, but it was the only thing I could think to ask. I didn't want her to get back to him just yet.

She gave him a proud smile. "Looks like it, doesn't it?"

"I loved those classes in high school. Sounds like you did well."

She made a face like she'd sucked on a lemon. "Ha. I never made it past trigonometry."

"Then how do you know how to help him?"

She shrugged. "I read ahead."

I almost spat my coffee across the counter. "What? You didn't already know the information you taught him?"

She rocked back on her heels and squinted at me. "You ask a lot of questions."

"Sorry." I ran my hand down my face, the heat from my cheeks evident against my palm. "I'm amazed. You're amazing, and I've lost my manners."

A hint of pink brightened her cheeks. I wasn't the only one who was nervous.

"Where did you leave them? Your manners, I mean." She removed her apron and hung it on its peg, turning her back to me so I couldn't see her face anymore.

"I'm not sure. Will you help me find them?"

She peeked over her shoulder. Her gaze moved over my dress shoes, khakis, and light blue polo shirt. When she reached my face, she turned around and crossed her arms over her chest. "You seem self-sufficient. I think you can manage on your own. Good luck." She wiggled her fingers, sending me on my way, and rejoined the boy at his table. "How's y'all's practice problems?"

Her accent thickened when she spoke to him. They dove back into the textbook and worked their way through the chapter.

I grabbed a table by the window and watched her teach the boy a subject she hadn't known until he needed her help.

Who did that?

Only someone with a heart of gold.

I sipped my coffee. Her eyes found mine. I winked, hoping for another blush. She let her hair fall in a curtain in front of her face.

My skin buzzed like lightning skittering across the sky. I counted the seconds like waiting for thunder to rumble, hoping to see the next glorious strike in her smile or blush.

She burrowed her hand through her hair and offered me a slight view of her cute upturned nose, full lips, and the rosy blush-highlighted cheeks I craved.

What would it take to brighten her cheeks like that again and again? I had a visceral need to get to know her.

Call it attraction. Call it infatuation.

I didn't care. She was a rare gem, and I wanted to know every facet of this extraordinary woman.

She snuck glances at me as she continued to tutor the boy but didn't seem annoyed when I didn't leave. The boy leaned his head against the back of their booth and pinched his thumb and forefinger across his eyes.

She patted his arm and closed the book. "Your brain is full. Get home. Hopefully dinner will be waitin'."

The boy nodded at me. "Want me to wait? We can walk together."

Her eyes dashed to me, then back to the boy. "I have a bunch of cleaning to do. You need to eat before Harry and George take it all."

"I'll save you a plate."

She gestured to the case next to the register. "I'll have one of the leftover sandwiches."

My heart thrummed. She wasn't leaving with him. Hopefully she wouldn't kick me out, and I'd have a chance to see if this feeling building in my chest and buzzing under my skin was just me, or if she felt it too.

He packed his backpack. She kissed the side of his head and walked him to the door.

The boy's gaze glued onto me. "I should stay."

She opened the door and pushed him out. "Home. Dinner. Bed. Now." She shut the door and locked it. Propping a hand on her hip, she tapped her tennis shoe on the tile, pointing away from the building.

He frowned but turned and walked away. When I couldn't see him anymore, she unlocked the door. She leaned against it and fixed her pinched-eyed glare on me. "Any particular reason it's taken you an hour and twenty minutes to drink that coffee?"

"Can I buy you dinner?"

She grabbed a sandwich from the case and tossed it to me. "As long as it's a $4.50 turkey on sourdough." She picked another sandwich, filled a cup with water, and joined me at my table. "What's your name?"

"Theo. Yours?"

"Georgi."

"It's nice of you to tutor him."

She unwrapped her sandwich and took a bite. "If he doesn't pass, he can't play football."

"And football is his life?" Pictures of *Friday Night Lights* and Peyton Manning commercials flashed in my brain.

"Football is his ticket out of here."

"Here?" What I'd seen of this town so far made me want to stay, not run away.

She nudged my shoulder. "Come on, everyone knows the cliché. The only way out of a small town in Texas is a college scholarship. Unfortunately, our Mexican heritage is so far up the family tree, you can't see it anymore." She waved her red hair at me. "So, he doesn't qualify for ethnicity-based scholarships. He's smart, so he might make it on academics, but it's safer to have academic *and* athletic scholarships."

I never bothered with scholarships. Why take money from students who need it when my parents can donate buildings and not miss the cash?

I was tempted to ask all the typical get-to-know-you questions: did you go to college, what did you study, is this your hometown, how many siblings do you have?

But I didn't.

Those things told me about Georgi, but they didn't tell me who she was at her core.

I knew she was kind, helpful, and patient.

She was pragmatic, creative, and logical.

I took a bite of my sandwich. She did the same. It wasn't the best sandwich I'd ever eaten, but the company couldn't have been better. Talking about her student seemed easier than talking about ourselves. "Where does he want to go to school?"

She counted on her fingers. "He's contacted the scouts at A&M, Texas, Texas Tech, Baylor, University of Houston, Rice, and TCU. There might be one or two more, but I can't remember."

"Nothing out of state?"

"He's too much of a homebody."

"You too?"

"I've got things to do here."

"Like what?"

"Teaching calculus." She sipped her water. "What about you? Why are you here?"

I didn't buy her answer. If she could teach herself calculus, there wasn't anything this woman couldn't do.

But I didn't want to push her either. My gut told me her deflection was more about her not being comfortable with the answers than with me. If she didn't want to tell me, I had to be okay with that. "Business," I answered.

"What kind of business?"

That was a complicated question. Employee Relations Liaison was hard to describe, and that wasn't why I was here. I wasn't sure what Weekend Party Host meant yet. I didn't want to give Georgi a bad opinion of me.

I wanted to show her she could trust me.

My parents built their factory here for the same reason they docked the yacht. They wanted to make Bubee part of our home.

Sharing sourdough turkey sandwiches, I was finally excited by the possibility as well. "My parents own Sanchez Biotech."

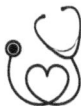

Georgi

I nearly choked on my dinner. I took a sip of water to help swallow, but it didn't relieve the embarrassment raging through me. My cheeks were so hot, they had to match my hair. "I'm in the presence of industrial royalty."

I'd offered this billionaire's son a crappy turkey sandwich. Perfect!

I wrapped the remaining bites of my dinner in their plastic wrap. "Sorry the sandwich wasn't better."

He licked his lips. "It was delicious."

I tipped my chin and stared at him. Theo was handsome. There was no denying it. But he wasn't the kind of handsome that made you stop and stare. Long, toned limbs, deep-hazel eyes, freshly shaved. He smelled salty like the bay with a hint of sweet earthiness.

He was more like the friendly boy next door who grew up to be comfortable in his skin. If you ignored that his front door was gold plated and mine had duct tape holding the screen together.

I drummed my nails on the table. "It's soggy with wilted lettuce and slimy turkey, but thanks for pretending." He was probably used to bread warm from the oven, organic spinach and tomatoes with hand-carved turkey.

He was most likely here to inspect the factory. Here today and gone tomorrow. Not a great situation for flirting.

Or perfect, if you asked my sister, Julietta.

Either way, I wasn't sure what to do with myself now that I knew who Theo was and guessed his normal standard of living.

Theo reached across the table and took my hand. Small callouses on the tips of his fingers scratched my dry skin. "I'm happy you ate with me. You could have shoved me out like your student."

I nodded toward the door. "My brother, Lee. If he doesn't get home soon, our cousins will eat all the Hamburger Helper and he'll starve." Lee worked hard to keep his grades up, but he needed to eat if he was going to grow into a man.

"Your brother. That makes sense. I hear pride in your voice when you say his name." Theo squeezed my hand once and let go. "Thanks for feeding me. I hadn't realized how hungry I was."

I scrubbed the phantom heat from Theo's touch on my thigh. I couldn't get used to him holding my hand. "I need to clean the espresso machines for the morning. It was nice to meet you, Theo." I pushed up from the table. "I'll see you around."

He folded his hands across his lean stomach. "That's how it's going to be?"

"I don't know what you mean." I knew exactly what he meant.

I was acting like a scared chicken, but the discomfort in my stomach didn't care how handsome he was or how nice he seemed. It wanted him gone—so I could breathe again and not worry about embarrassing myself further.

Slimy turkey? Really, Georgi? You couldn't have at least grabbed one of the peach scones or raspberry Danishes everyone loves so much?

"Let me help." He took the garbage from my hand and returned his coffee cup to the sink behind the counter.

I took the soap from his hand. "I'd prefer if you didn't."

He shoved his hands in his back pockets. "Why?"

I gestured between the two of us. "This is awkward." How did I explain my embarrassment to him?

From his slightly-shaggy-on-purpose haircut to his polished shoes, Theo had a look that said he would be comfortable in any situation. Put him in a boardroom negotiating a merger or on a yacht sailing into the horizon, and he'd be in his element.

Me? I knew how to whack the espresso machine three times in just the right spot to keep the boiler working. I only slept three hours last night because I needed to learn Lee's math homework. I forgot to shower this morning because I was too busy buying the previously mentioned Hamburger Helper (clearance sale!) before work, so I knew Lee would have something to eat when he got home.

Theo gestured between us. "This isn't awkward. This is normal get-to-know-you. You want to talk awkward? I spent the last two years counting spools of tubing and driving delivery trucks from Cincinnati to Pittsburg. Please, don't assume because my parents own a big company, I'm not a normal guy."

"There's nothing normal about you."

"Let me prove otherwise. Teach me how to clean the machines, and then let's go for a walk. I'll show you how boring and normal I can be."

I bit the inside of my cheek to keep from returning his smile.

I doubted Theo was boring, but he was right. We'd been comfortable together until I freaked out about his parents. There was no reason I couldn't get my nerves under control and spend a pleasant evening with him.

Besides, an extra set of hands would get me out of the coffee shop in half the time. My motivations were selfish, but he'd offered, right? "Are you sure?"

He pushed off from the counter and spread his arms. "Whatever it takes to spend more time with you."

"We have nothing in common."

"Are you sure? Does me having rich parents tell you everything about me? Because you haven't asked a single question about me besides my name and why I'm in Bubee."

"You think our Venn diagrams overlap?"

He pointed to the table where Lee studied. "We both have smart, athletic younger siblings."

That was something, but not enough. "So?"

He picked up an empty paper cup from the register stack. "We both like coffee."

"Sixty-five percent of Americans fall into that category."

"We live in the same town."

"You don't live here."

He tapped his finger on the counter three times. "As of this week, I do."

My mouth dropped open. "You're that big yacht that takes up more than half the marina?"

Their sailboat and a speed boat had been berthed in the marina since last year, but ... wow! My uncle's trailer didn't look like the period at the end of a sentence compared to the Sanchez's mega yacht.

Why hadn't I put two and two together? *Of course* the handsome billionaire lives on the gigantic boat blocking the view of the water from my trailer's bedroom window.

He scrubbed his hand through his hair. "Yeah, that's us." The strands fell across his eyes but didn't mask his discomfort.

I stepped toward him. "You don't like the boat?"

"It's fine. Conspicuous."

"Do people ever buy a boat that big and hide it?" That would be like trying to hide a forest fire with a wicker basket.

"I guess not. When my parents asked me to move down here, I thought I'd be living on the sailboat and working at the factory. It's weird to have such a big place to myself most of the time."

I didn't expect him to be embarrassed by his parents' ostentatious wealth. His confession made me like him a little more.

Made him a little more real.

I could get to know him ... like him ... and he didn't seem like the playboy, rich kids I'd read about in the tabloids. I'd give him the benefit of the doubt and not stereotype him.

Stepping to the other side of the counter, I pulled the drip pan out of the espresso machine. "Have you ever cleaned one of these before?"

"I disassembled my coffee maker at home once."

"What was broken?"

"Nothing. I just wanted to see how it worked." He pushed up onto the counter (hello arm muscles) and watched me work.

"You're one of those?"

"One of whats?"

"A tinker."

"I am. Is that a problem?"

"Not for this job." I handed him a spray bottle and a towel. It was time to see what those hands could do.

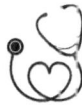

Theo

With the espresso machine cleaned, floors mopped, and fridge restocked, Georgi locked the door to Honey Beans Coffee. Antique streetlamps cast her in a halo of golden light. I wanted to tuck the loose strands behind her ear, but that would be too forward. As much as I was infatuated with her, touching her ear was too intimate.

Not only had Georgi learned calculus for her brother, but she'd mastered espresso machine repair to maintain the class and character of the coffee shop with the vintage machine. She'd talked my willing ear off about how the machine worked and where the owner of Honey Beans had found it.

What new piece of information would our walk teach me about this intriguing woman? I couldn't wait to find out. I held out my hand. "What's your favorite place in town?"

She assessed my hand as if trying to decide if placing hers in mine was a smart decision.

I kept my hand open and relaxed, low pressure, but had to remind myself to breathe while she decided. I wanted to feel her strong, capable hand again.

She twisted her mouth and slid her palm against mine. I tucked our hands against my chest, so we walked hip to hip.

"I have a lot of favorites," she said. "You'll have to be more specific."

"Favorite place when you need to get away?"

Little lines divided her eyebrows. "I'm not ready to share that." She bumped my hip. "How will I get away from you if your only skill is espresso machine maintenance and I don't want to spend more time with you?"

"At least I passed the first test." I took two steps toward the marina. "Favorite place to watch the waves?"

She pulled me to a stop. "Nope. Not that one either."

"Favorite place to … I don't know." We'd already eaten. I didn't want to take her out for drinks because I didn't want to share her with a bar full of people.

I just wanted to get to know her, but she wasn't giving me any clues about how to do that. "This is your town. I want to make it mine, so where should we go?"

She scanned the sidewalks in every direction. "This way." She turned south. We walked the length of the peninsula, past 1940s cottages, Victorian mansions on stilts, and a few homes made from shipping containers, until we reached a rock-strewn beach.

I took off my shoes and socks. "Which favorite is this?"

She shrugged and tossed her tennis shoes on a boulder. "Favorite place to bury a body if you don't want anyone to find it."

I tucked her into a side-hug and laughed. "Is that your second favorite pastime, after tutoring calculus?"

Her arm settled comfortably around my waist. "No, but your reaction tells me a lot."

"That I love your sense of humor?"

"That you don't take life too seriously."

I looked into her eyes. The moon reflected their green back at me like the inside of opal. With so much to learn, I wasn't sure I'd ever know it all, no matter how long I spent studying her. "Do you take life seriously?"

"Sometimes, but I try to let in the silly whenever I can. Otherwise, what's the point?"

"Like this?" I scooped my arms around her knees, lifted her to my shoulder, and spun us in circles.

She grasped the sides of my shirt and giggled. "Put me down. Put me down."

I did as she asked, missing her warmth as soon as she was out of my arms. She playfully swatted my chest but laughed with her whole body. She shot me a wink, and my heart was toast.

Was this what love felt like? I didn't know.

This woman was everything I wanted. Intelligent, playful, loyal, dedicated, gracious.

But was it too soon to label the feelings in my chest and my head?

If it was the first breath of love, how did I prove I was worthy of her? What would it take to earn her affection?

When she caught her breath, she grabbed a handful of small stones and skipped one after another across the water. "Are you any good at this?"

I picked up a flat stone and threw it toward the waves. "Decent. But my question is, which bodies are buried here?"

"The one's not worth mentioning."

"Cryptic."

She lifted her shoulder. "A girl's got to have her secrets."

"Tell me something that isn't a secret."

She tossed a rock into the air as she thought. "I like running."

"On the beach?"

"Sometimes."

"With your brother?"

"No. I usually go on my lunch break while he's in school or at practice."

"What position does he play?"

"Safety. He's fast but doesn't have great hands." She mimed catching a football.

"Not like you?"

"Pft."

I took the rock from her hand and traced my nail along the edge of her palm. "I saw how you took apart and cleaned that espresso machine. You've got skills."

"It's part of my job."

"But you like it?"

She pulled her hand from mine and rubbed it on the rocks in her other hand. "I don't know what else I'd do."

"No bigger dreams?"

"Nothing to write home about. Not like the rest of my family." She sounded dejected when she said it.

I hated the sadness in her gaze. "What do you mean?"

She skipped another rock into the surf, watching it dance across the water three, four, five times before a wave swallowed it. "My three younger sisters are going to be doctors. Lee might go to medical school too, but he hasn't decided yet."

"I'd fit right in."

She scowled. "I thought you said you were a delivery boy, not a doctor."

The words had slipped out. I wished they hadn't. I dug my toe into the sand. "I'm both."

Her arm stopped mid-throw. "What?"

I raised my hands, palms out. I didn't want her to jump to conclusions. Medicine was my past. I didn't talk about it, but it was still part of who I was. "I meant I understand how hard it is to earn attention when your siblings are superstars. You and I have that in common."

She skewered me with a flat glare. "Are you a doctor?"

"Anesthesiologist, but I haven't worked since I finished my residency two years ago.

"Now you're the delivery driver?"

I stared at my feet. "I'm whatever my parents need to help them grow the family business." I didn't understand my current assignment well enough to explain it to Georgi. I also didn't want to further taint her opinion of me.

She turned and walked up the beach. Over her shoulder she said, "I like how you say *family business* like you have a delicatessen on the corner, not like you're worth billions."

"I'm not."

She lifted her eyebrow. "You will be."

"Maybe. I'm supposed to take over the business, but that doesn't mean I'll succeed the way my parents have. Dad has a knack for business that I can only hope to master." Will he train me to be as financially savvy as he is? Will his mentoring include how to merge two companies so the people and the technology flourish?

I don't know. I can only hope.

"I can't even imagine what that's like." She sighed. "All that money, all those responsibilities. My little family is hard enough."

And yet, she learned complex mathematics because she loved her brother. She might be a better fit than me at Sanchez Biotech.

"The challenges are unique," I said.

"Name one thing that's hard about being a billionaire's son." She pointed at my chest. "Something normal. Not like choosing between the Ferrari or Jaguar to drive on a Friday night."

I swallowed hard. The first thing that popped into my head wasn't pretty, but it pressed against my teeth to come out. "I'll never make my parents as proud of me as they are of my sister."

It was the hardest truth I knew. It wasn't easy sharing it with Georgi. She'd judged me for my parents' status, but it was more about being surprised than anything else. Would she judge me for the way I craved what was given to my sister?

"Why's she special?"

"Olympic athletes tend to turn heads."

"That is hard. I'm sorry, Theo." She tucked her arm in mine again.

"I don't want you to think I hold a grudge. I love helping my sister reach her goals. She's an amazing athlete. I want her to compete and win. It's just hard to know I'll never measure up." Not anymore.

"You'll show them ... in your own way. I have no doubt."

"What makes you say that?"

She rubbed her hand across my chest and patted my heart. "A hunch there's gold beating under all that expensive cotton."

She didn't look down on me for envying my sister. She understood it wasn't about Elena but about my parents' reaction to her achievements.

I pressed my lips to the back of her hand. "Thank you."

Could she get any more perfect?

Was this real?

Were my assumptions, the feelings swirling through me first date magic?

I didn't want to wake up tomorrow and realize I was blind to Georgi's flaws, she was blind to mine, and we were incompatible in every way.

I didn't think that was the case. I'd thought my destiny was medicine, but maybe it was here with her

I rolled up my pants legs and we waded into the water until it covered our calves, wandering toward the city's lights.

"No one gets attention in our family," she said. "My mom's too busy stuck in the past, pretending she's not an adult, to care what any of us do."

"But you're an adult."

"Yeah. Bless her heart, she's a little behind."

How did that even work? "And your dad?"

"Disappeared. Dead. I don't know, and I don't care. Even when he lived with us, he wasn't here, so we aren't missing anything."

I stopped and pulled her into a hug. She fit perfectly in my arms, her forehead resting against my chin. "I'm sorry."

She pushed away from me. "Please, don't feel sorry for me. I've survived this long without caring. I'm not going to start now."

I reached for her again. Even if she didn't think she did, she needed a connection. My parents weren't perfect, but at least they were around and involved in my life. "It's not fair to you."

"I'm fine. I love helping my brother and sisters. I'm good at it."

"Who takes care of you?"

She wrapped her arms around her waist and walked out of the water. "Why do I need someone? I enjoy my independence."

I followed like the lovesick fool I was becoming. My reactions sounded crazy in my head. I'd only just met her, but I couldn't deny the pull she'd created in me.

"I'm not talking about independence. If you have a bad day, who do you confide in? Who lifts the extra stress from your shoulders?" I wanted to take on that role for her. I aspired to be a safe place, someone with whom she could share her burdens.

"My sisters and I tell each other everything."

"But what if taking care of them is the hard thing? Do you tell them that?"

She huffed out a breath. "We're back to twenty questions."

"I just ... I want ... you understand my issues with my parents, and I want to be here for you with yours."

She laid her palms on my chest and kept me at arm's length. "Theo, it's okay. I'm happy. I like helping my siblings. I wasn't cut out for the lives they've chosen anyway. Coffee is the medicine I serve, and I have no problem handing it out a cup at a time." She let out a deprecating laugh. "Our Venn diagrams overlap with both of us being underachievers content in our sidekick roles. I just underachieved a little farther down the ladder than you."

I held her hands against my chest. "Nothing about you is under-achieving. Like I said before, you're amazing."

"Hardly."

"Tell me something you aren't good at. Or haven't learned to help the people you care about."

"I can't keep my opinions to myself, and I gossip. What about you?"

The answer on the tip of my tongue was that I was a pushover. I did exactly what my parents told me to because I was so desperate to get back into their good graces.

Who tells a woman they want to date that Mommy and Daddy boss around their personal life? I was thirty years old, and my parents dictated every major decision in my life. That would be the fastest way to end this date.

"I'm not good at doing my laundry."

"That's a copout answer. I bet you haven't had many opportunities to do laundry. Think of something else."

"I can't handle alcohol. One beer and I'm wasted."

"Better, but still not great. Not what I would have thought anyway. I would have guessed you were the frat boy who never volunteered to be the designated driver?"

"I wasn't in a fraternity."

"Too busy studying?"

I'd spent every day since I decided medical school was the best path to my dad's respect living for that dream. "Too busy not having a life." The more time I spent with Georgi, the more that seemed like the wrong way to live.

"We have that in common," she whispered.

I captured her pinky with mine. "And our ability to disassemble coffee machines."

"The foundation of every great relationship." She let go of my hand and found another rock to toss into the waves.

"What makes *you* happy?"

She skipped her rock then met my eyes. "Tonight's pretty close."

I took a hesitant step closer to her and cupped the side of her face in my palm. "Can I kiss you?"

"I'd like that."

I leaned forward until I could almost taste the sourdough from dinner on her breath, but I didn't close the last centimeters. My thumb traced her chin, and I tried to memorize the pattern of greens in her eyes, the texture of her lips, the precise angle of her jaw.

She pressed up onto her toes and pressed her mouth to mine. Her hands dug into the front of my shirt and pulled me closer, until our stomachs met.

I wanted to wrap my arms around her waist and lift her off her feet, deepening the kiss, hungry to show her everything my heart wanted her to know.

But I didn't. I held back.

If I kissed her the way I wanted to, I wouldn't be able to stop. I'd crush her to me, pouring everything I had to offer into these first precious moments.

I didn't want to scare her, overwhelm her with the absurdity of how deeply I already cared.

Instead, I enjoyed her perfect, sweet caress as she led our mouths in the delicate dance of a first kiss. Her lips fluttered against mine. She sucked lightly on my bottom lip and gently opened her lips for a little more.

We weren't all hands and limbs and tongues, groping for everything all at once.

Just a simple, pristine kiss with promises of more to come.

And there would be more.

She was it.

My everything.

One night and I was hers.

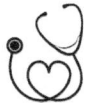

Georgi

My lips still tingled from Theo's kisses. He'd had to meet his parents in Houston the day after our first kiss, but he should have been back yesterday.

His text messages had said his parents were keeping him busy, but he'd promised he'd come into Honey Beans during my shift today.

It'd been hard to concentrate all day knowing I'd see him again.

He was like a tornado destroying every wall I'd built to feel safe in my crazy family.

What would it be like to have someone care if I had enough to eat? Or to ask about my dreams for the future on a regular basis?

What would it feel like to be put first?

Theo made it seem like I'd finally have someone to support me.

My sisters and brother meant well, but they were figuring out their lives. College and medical school took my sisters' attention. Lee was a teenage boy, so it would be too much to expect him to look out for his oldest sister.

I'd taken care of them for so long, they didn't see when I only ate one bite of macaroni and cheese while scooping them full-sized portions. They didn't notice I'd stitched my jeans back together so I could wear them another season while combing the thrift store for stylish clothes for them.

Theo came from a world in which he never wondered if he'd have enough money to buy a pair of pants when his next growth spurt rocketed him five inches in one summer.

Despite our differences, I felt like he understood me. He saw the dedication I had to my family, and he appreciated it. Probably because he had the same dedication.

I mean, who gave up a career in medicine to take over his family's business after he went through all the effort to complete the training?

I didn't think it was about the money.

Theo would be rich regardless of whether or not he took over his parents' company. Doctors weren't known for being poor.

He did it because his family came first.

Was there anything sexier than someone who devoted his life to his family?

Honey Beans's after-dinner crowd wound down.

My heart sighed. I'd expected Theo to be here by now. Maybe his parents wouldn't let him leave. Maybe he had something to do at the factory.

I couldn't be the kind of woman to pine over a man. Not like my mama. I wouldn't start now. Sangria Under the Pier started in an hour. It was time to get ready to close.

I grabbed the cleaning spray and a towel and wiped down the espresso machine.

The doorbell rang, and Theo stood in the entry, backlit by the sunset.

Warring emotions crashed inside me.

He was here.

But he wasn't alone.

The gigantic grin on his face would have melted my heart, but it was aimed at the skinny blonde wrapped around him like bindweed. Three more beautiful women trailed behind him. Each looked like a Victoria Secret model walking the runway in the newest lingerie line.

It wasn't hard to imagine the scene when their clothes barely covered their nipples and their butt cheeks hung out the bottoms of their dresses.

Where was their modesty? They may be in their mid-twenties, but where were these girls' mothers? Why had they let them out in such revealing clothing?

I was being judgy.

I knew it.

But my second-hand Led Zepplin shirt and threadbare denim skirt couldn't really compare. I couldn't have felt more frumpy-small-town if I'd tried.

Theo braced his hands on the bottle-blonde's waist and practically carried her across the threshold. "Hey, Georgi."

Hey, Georgi?

Seriously? That was how he said hi with this woman hanging all over him?

Why was he okay with her using him like the clothing she'd forgotten to put on this morning?

Or was it normal for him to be draped in supermodels like layered necklaces?

It wasn't normal in my world, but maybe that was the problem.

I'd expected the other night and the text messages that had followed to be the start of a relationship.

But maybe it was his PG-version of a one-night stand.

I mean, when you hung out with models, the local barista who didn't let you past first base was probably a turn off.

"Who is this?" I gestured to the blonde.

He readjusted his grip so his hand clutched her hip. "This is Viola. She's not very good at walking. At least not in these shoes on cobblestones. Especially after drinking a bottle of decongestant."

"I see that." Was that a tattoo on her butt? "Is there anything I can help you with?"

Viola ran her finger along Theo's jaw line. "Isn't Teddy pretty?"

Teddy?

I crossed my arms over my chest so I wouldn't snatch her hand away. This was not how I'd imagined our reunion. I wanted to be the one playing with his soft hair and resting my head on his shoulder.

But this nightmare taunted me.

I'd been played. I'd twisted myself around his finger and believed I was special. If I was, he wouldn't let her fondle his face like foreplay.

He ignored her hand ruffling his hair but didn't stop her either. "I'd love another one of your dazzling smiles."

I couldn't find an ounce of kindness in my entire being. "Smiles are reserved for my friends."

Theo's smile slid to the ground. "We're not friends?"

"I don't know what we are." My throat closed.

No, I would not cry. I would not lose it in front of these beautiful women. I wouldn't show Theo how much his behavior hurt me.

Viola draped herself across Theo's chest like a sweatshirt. "Teddy, I want to go to bed."

I wiped my hands and held my palms out. "And I'm done." I stepped from behind the counter and opened the door. "Get out."

Theo chuckled under his breath. "Georgi, I can explain."

"I may not have a fancy degree like you, but I can read the situation."

"Their dads are friends of my dad."

"And that makes this ..." I gestured to her face pressed to his neck. "This is okay?"

His eyebrow lifted. "What do you think is going on right now?"

"Oh, that you brought your entourage to my coffee shop in order to ... I don't know ... to embarrass me? Not sure why you would want to do that, but mission complete. Thanks for the clarity."

"I'm just showing these girls around town. Viola had a runny nose and took too much medicine."

"She just asked you to take her to bed while running her hands through your hair and playing with the buttons on your shirt. How else should I interpret those words?"

"I promise that's not what's happening here. I wouldn't do that to you."

"Then why did you bring them here?"

I wanted him to throw Viola into a chair and sweep me into his arms. If he proved to me he was the guy I'd kissed last weekend, I would give him a chance.

But he tightened his grip on Viola's hip and ran his free hand through his already mussed hair. "I ... I came to see you. They tagged along."

The other blonde—this one taller and able to walk in her stilettos—leaned her head onto Theo's shoulder. "Theo, we need to get her back to the boat. Will you call your daddy's car?"

He shrugged her off. "Give me a minute. Help Viola." He wrapped Viola's arm around the other woman's neck, and they guided her into a chair.

Blonde Number Two ran her fingers through Viola's hair. "She may not have a minute."

He pulled his phone from his pocket and angled it around.

I pointed to the front door. "Reception is better outside."

"Let me take care of this, then we can talk. I'll be right back." Theo gave me a look I couldn't interpret then stepped outside. I shut the door behind him.

Blonde Number Two wandered around the shop. Her fingers trailed the tables to the bookshelves. "Are you a coffee shop or a bookstore? Hmm. Theo spoke highly of this place. He said it was a must see, but I'm not getting the vibe." Her gaze traveled from my scuffed shoes to my unwashed hair. "Not seeing anything special."

I retreated behind the espresso machine. "Please leave." I wasn't about to get into a cat fight with this woman. She'd won. She could take Theo and never come back, for all I cared.

"I will, when the car gets here." She sat on the counter by the register and swung her tanned legs back and forth. "Some friendly advice—"

"Why do I doubt that?"

A sarcastic half-smile pasted itself on her face. "Touché. I'm giving it to you anyway." She circled her finger in front of me. "Based on the mopey look on your face, you had a special night with our gorgeous Dr. Theo. He told you about his sister and his parents, right?"

"Yeah." The word globbed in my throat.

"That's his move." She gave me a *you poor girl* squishy face. "He's one hundred percent devoted to his family. Which sounds sweet but also means he can't be devoted to anyone or anything else. Why do you think he gave up medicine? I'm sorry you thought you were special, but what does a girl like you have to offer a guy like him that would be more important to him than his family?" She hopped off the counter. "Don't let him break your heart."

She glided into the chair next to her sleeping friend and pulled out her phone.

I didn't have a response to her *advice*. Theo had told me himself his family was the most important thing in the world.

Blonde Number Two was right. If he was so devoted to them that he'd given up the career he'd spent years training for, who did I think I was to earn his attention?

My parents didn't even care about me.

Theo's parents ran factories all over the world. When he took over, he'd have to travel.

I had to be here to take care of my family because no one else would.

It hurt my heart, but it was better not to get my hopes up.

Theo opened the door. "Car is two minutes away."

Blonde Number Two ran her arm under Viola's and tried to lift her. "Theo, help me." Her lip pouted.

He lifted Viola into his arms as swiftly as he'd lifted me the previous weekend. "Georgi, these women are just friends."

I opened the door for him. "Sure."

"You believe me?"

"I don't know you well enough not to believe you. I need to get home and help Lee with his homework."

"I'll see you next week?"

Did I have a choice?

Not really.

I was here. Bubee, Honey Bears, and my family were my life.

He could come and go as he pleased.

There was no use pining over a guy who'd flirted with me one minute and then wrapped himself in models the next.

He might think he was just helping out a friend, but I knew better. If he had the kind of boundaries that made Viola's behavior acceptable, he wasn't the kind of man I needed in my life.

Besides, I wasn't special, and the sooner Theo started acting like it, the better for both of us.

Chapter 2

Present day

Theo

ELENA AND I WALK toward the boat yacht as I finish telling my sister the story. I can't get the image of Georgi's hatred on that day with Viola and Lexie out of my mind.

Elena looks at me every couple of steps, opening and closing her mouth like she's going to say something, then she twists her mouth or scrunches her forehead and keeps walking.

She finally stops and stares at me. "Let me see if I've got this straight. You met Georgi and went on an incredible date when you instantly fell in love with her? We're talking love at first sight, like in those princess movies I watched as a kid."

"Yes." I never believed in love at first sight, but it's a close enough approximation.

"Then the next time you saw her, you had Viola, Lexie, and the Gusman twins in tow, but Viola was gorked out of her mind on NyQuil, so you had to carry her?"

"Not my best moment, but yes."

"Why didn't you leave her on the boat?"

"I tried, but the ladies were excited to see Bubee. Dad said nothing mattered except showing them a good time. I'd already had to wait to see Georgi. I didn't want to put it off any longer, so I took them with me. I didn't know Viola had taken a double dose until her words started slurring."

Elena taps her finger to my chest. "And you never explained the situation to Georgi?"

"I tried, but she didn't believe me."

"You couldn't have picked a worse second date." She shakes her head. "Do you still love Georgi?"

"Every time I see her, I want to drop to my knees and beg her to give me another chance, but after a couple of months of her refusing to listen, self-preservation took over. Flirty, ridiculous words come out of my mouth instead."

"You need to fix this."

"It's too late." It's been too late since that first awful night with Lexie and Viola. Georgi made up her mind, and I can't change it no matter how much I try to explain.

Elena doesn't listen. She taps her chin and walks in circles around me. "Kidnapping her so she has to listen would be a bit dramatic."

"And illegal."

She braces her hands on her hips. "Let me think about it."

"Elena, don't. Please." Georgi's not going to listen to Elena any more readily than she listened to me. She's decided she knows the kind of man I am. Whether I like it or not—even if my heart never stops wanting her—I lost her.

My sister skips backward. "What else am I going to do while I'm here?"

"Train for the Olympics."

She lazily lifts her shoulder. "Meh."

"What do you mean, meh?"

"Race you back." She sprints up the beach to the road.

"I do not need a meddling little sister fixing my non-existent love life," I call, but she doesn't hear. More likely she doesn't care.

This is not how my life was supposed to go.

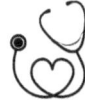

Georgi

I wish I could say seeing Theo flirting with that girl didn't affect me, but lying goes against my very nature. As I pull espresso shot after espresso shot all morning, their embrace is all I see in my mind's eye.

The relaxed way he wrapped his arm around her shoulders, how her hand snaked around his waist. They have an easy affection I envy.

I don't understand men like him.

How can he flirt with me week in and week out as he parades his entourage of beautiful people through of my coffee shop? How does he have the nerve to make my heart race when I know I'm being played?

Why won't my heart read the text message reminding it not to get tangled up with Dr. Sanchez?

It missed the message before and almost broke.

I slide two triple shot carmanilla lattes across the counter to the couple from San Antonio with my best attempt at a smile.

The bell on the door rings. "Welcome to ..." The rest of the words die on my tongue. It's Theo's girl from the beach. In daylight, she's younger than I'd assumed. I'd put her at barely nineteen. Maybe twenty.

Does Theo have no decency? Now he's dating women who are barely legal. She's at least ten years younger than him.

What's weirder is that she's here on a Tuesday. Usually, Theo's guests leave on Sunday, so I don't have to suffer seeing them—or him—on weekdays. I hope her presence isn't a shift in their itinerary.

Bubee does not need to be invaded by the pretty bobble head crowd.

She shines a toothy smile at me. "Good morning! This place is adorable. I love the bookcases in the back." She gestures to the floor-to-ceiling, wall-to-wall shelves.

"It's a lending library, so take your pick." My voice wasn't snarky or mean, was it? I sounded polite, I think. "Can I get you something to drink? Maybe a pastry?"

My eyes sweep over her. It's freezing outside, but her sweaty tank top and capri yoga pants highlight that this girl has muscles on top of muscles. Her traps would give Jason Statham a run for his money, so she probably doesn't eat pastries.

"I'll take a small, non-fat, sugar-free hazelnut latte, please."

"Of course you will." Because none of Theo's women ever order anything with calories.

She tips her head, not missing the sarcasm in my voice. "Did I do something wrong? Are your lattes not great? Theo said they're the best in town."

I grind the beans to get her out of here ASAP. "I'm sure Dr. Sanchez sang my praises." It doesn't surprise me he would send her here to rub his tryst in my face.

She chuckles. "Dr. Sanchez? Wow. I don't know anyone who calls Theo that."

"He earned his title." I don't add the other names I smash in the middle when I say his name in my head. Jerk-face is my favorite. Toad-butt is pretty good too.

Dr. Theo 'Toad Butt' Sanchez. It rolls off the tongue.

She shakes her head. Her stubby ponytail flicks back and forth. "I don't think of him that way. It's too formal."

"I prefer to keep an air of professionalism between myself and my customers."

Her shoulder bobs. "Or you just hate him."

"There's that too."

She sticks out her hand. "I'm Elena. Nice to meet you, Georgi."

I stare at her manicured nails, but don't take her hand. Why is she trying to be my friend? If his record holds, she'll be here this week and then never again. That's the thing about Dr. Sanchez and his gaggle of weekly women: very few ever come back.

If I didn't know any better, I'd think he was a vampire who murdered them when the party ended. But I do know better. The sun hasn't killed him yet, so alas, he's no Dracula.

Still, it's my duty to save any innocent soul I can. They shouldn't end up bitter and angry like me. I spritz three pumps of sugar-free hazelnut into a walkin' around cup. "You seem like a nice girl, so I'm going to give you some unsolicited advice. Steer clear of Theo Sanchez.

He seems charming, but he's using you to pad his overinflated ego. He'll break your heart."

Her bottom lip pouts and layers of compassion fill her eyes. "So he did break your heart?"

"No." *Okay, I need this tiny lie.* One date and I was putty in Theo's hands. I thought it was finally my turn to have something good in my life. He made me feel special and seen and cherished.

I was a fool.

"I won't give Dr. Sanchez the satisfaction of thinking he was anywhere near my heart." The troop of models clinging to him was all the evidence I needed to prove I'd been played. I'd been the weekend fling until he organized his entourage for a trip to their newly minted yacht.

Elena leans in conspiratorially. "But he's not here. You can tell me the truth."

"Why would I do that?" This girl is delusional. I've known her as long as it takes to make a latte and she expects me to spill secrets I only share with my sisters? Nope.

Elena continues to assess me. "Theo's the best guy I know. I want him to be happy. He likes you."

"He likes making me feel like an idiot." Like he needed to get "slumming with the trailer park trash" out of his system, and I fit the bill.

Not that I think of myself as trailer park trash. I'm not Cinderella looking for a prince to sweep me off my feet. I'm good.

I don't need his weekly reminder about how quickly I forgot not to trust anyone but my siblings. I will not be my mother.

I hand Elena her latte, and she clasps her hands around mine. "You aren't an idiot." Her nose crinkles. "Thanks for worrying about me. Theo and I have had our ups and downs, but my heart is safe with him. That's what big brothers are for, isn't it?" She sips her latte. Her eyes widen. "This *is* good. Bye, Georgi. I look forward to seeing you around."

My brain finally decides to catch up.

Big brother.

As in Elena Sanchez, Theo's little sister. The Olympian. That explains the biceps.

I plunk my forehead on the counter.

I was jealous of his sister.

Their affection on the beach was the same kind I have with my siblings. Of course he would protect his sister. Of course he would put his arm over her shoulder after they raced down the beach.

Is it too much to hope she didn't read my jealousy for what it was?

Or that she doesn't tell Theo about our conversation?

I doubt I'm that lucky.

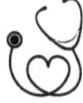

Georgi

My phone dings with Lee's text notification sound.

Lee:

I spin the closed sign, lock the door, tuck my phone and keys in my purse, and sprint from Honey Beans. My heart rate ricochets in my ears faster than if this were a normal run.

Lee only texts me a single letter if Uncle Hoyt's in full-blown bully mode. It's the safety code so Hoyt doesn't realize it's a call for help.

If our uncle ever gets Lee's phone, my brother can explain away the letter as part of an accidental text, an incomplete answer, or the bus he's taking somewhere.

Thankfully, there isn't a lot of traffic on the sidewalks, so I run all the way to the trailer without accidentally slamming into an elderly tourist.

I mop the sweat from my forehead with the corner of my shirt and catch my breath before I climb the stairs.

Hoyt's shouts carry through the door before I open it. "Good for nothing. Wait until I tell your Mama how you're talking back. I gave you one job. Simpleton like you shoulda had no problem."

Time to diffuse this bomb. I take a deep breath and put a smile on my face, then turn the knob and step inside like I have no idea what's happening. "Hey, y'all."

Hoyt stands in the middle of the living room with a beer bottle dangling between his middle and index fingers. Three more sit empty on the table. His face is the same color as a pomegranate. His salt-and-pepper hair is in disarray, like he ran beer-soaked hands through it.

Tipsy hugs her knees to her chest on the sofa and peeks out from behind her arms.

I hang my purse on the hook by the door. "I'm starving. Did anyone start dinner?" Play it cool. Act like I didn't hear the fighting. Distract and move on. That's my job.

"What are you doing here?" Hoyt slurs.

"Makin' dinner. I bought some chicken nuggets the other day." I twist my hair into a low bun and move toward the kitchen side of the room. "Would you rather I make hot dogs and tatter tots?"

Yes, we eat like toddlers, but it works.

"It's Tipsy's turn to cook. Lazy girl won't lift a finger. Been telling her to peel the potatoes." He shakes his head. "Worthless." He takes a long swig of his beer.

Tipsy's tear-filled eyes meet mine. *Worthless* is her dad's second favorite nickname for her. We all feel the stab in our chests when he calls her that.

If anyone's worthless in this family, it's his drunk butt.

But contradicting him or pointing out Tipsy's accomplishments only makes him worse.

With my hand low by my hip, I point to our bedroom. *I'll distract him, you hide.* That's how this works.

"I'll make dinner. She probably has homework."

Lee steps out of the hallway. "Tips, do you have the Physics textbook? I left mine in my locker."

I grab my aunt's polka dot apron and loop it over my head. "You'll jeopardize your scholarship if you fail the test tomorrow." There's no test tomorrow, but Hoyt doesn't pay attention—is too drunk—to know that.

My uncle shifts his body, somehow muscled despite all his drinking, so his full attention is on Lee. "That true?"

"Yes, sir," Lee says.

Hoyt swivels to glare at his daughter. "The boy asked you a question." His voice is a gravel-filled bark.

She flinches. "I do. Daddy, can I get it for him?"

He tosses his hand in the air. "Get outta my sight."

She scampers off the couch, taking the long way around the recliner to stay out of his way, and disappears with Lee into the back.

I make a loud show of rummaging through the cabinets. "Looks like we're out of potatoes. Sorry, Uncle Hoyt. I'll make lasagna instead." I collect the ingredients from the cabinet and fridge and pre-heat the oven.

I may have offered chicken nuggets and hot dogs, but lasagna will take a good hour to bake. I can stand guard and make sure Hoyt doesn't decide to follow Lee and Tipsy into the bedrooms and add more poison to her already dying self-esteem.

If there was a way for me to get us away from him, I'd take it in a heartbeat. I tried CPS, but it was like kicking a hornets' nest with a delayed-release valve.

Hoyt isn't physically abusive, so it was my word against all the "adults": Uncle Hoyt, Aunt Sally, Aunt Imogen, my mom, Grammie. No one backed up my claims.

Once the investigation was over, he was meaner than ever.

Until Tipsy's eighteen, my hands are tied.

So, I do my best to act as a wall. To remind her he's a mean drunk, and she's an amazing young woman with a bright future in front of her.

It's all I can do.

It will have to be enough.

Chapter 3

Theo

I CARRY OUR GUESTS' suitcases from the limousine onto my parents' yacht. The giggling group of women and their boyfriends follow me and our stewards onto the deck. This weekend I'm entertaining the daughters and friends of an investor my dad is courting to throw capital at a new series of ECMO oxygenators he's building.

One of the women—I haven't learned their names yet—drops her chihuahua on the lounge chair, and it promptly poops on the striped, red fabric.

I drop my chin to my chest. *Awesome.*

Elena stands at the railing above me with her nose wrinkled. "Gross."

I shoot her a look I hope translates as pathetic and pleading. "Will you please help me?"

"You do this every weekend?"

"Unfortunately." Four years of undergrad, four years of medical school, four years of anesthesia residency, and two years driving a truck culminated in me as a glorified cabana boy.

Carrying luggage filled with bikinis (even in March), retrieving margaritas and white wine spritzers, rubbing in sunscreen. Most guys would love it.

Not me.

It's demeaning.

I thought my life would be worth more than smiling and being charming while having to hide my room key.

One of the worst nights of my life, an uninvited, drunken visitor snuck into my room in the middle of the night. Her shirt was off, and she had me pinned to the bed before I knew what was happening.

Thankfully Captain Timmons' cabin was next door to mine, and he's a light sleeper.

The embarrassment of him convincing her to leave my room was miniscule in scale to the embarrassment of explaining the incident to my father when the woman's boyfriend paid a visit to the offices.

My sister descends the stairs and takes a suitcase. "Where to?"

"They're all on deck two. I don't care which rooms."

"What's next?"

"Let them unpack and change, then we head to dinner at Sobre las Rocas. Barbara saves us one of the tables in the back and waters down the margaritas to make my life easier." It also allows Judah, our chef, to spend all evening prepping for the beach picnic we'll take them on tomorrow.

When my dad told me I was done with inventory and deliveries, I thought I would move into something like Assistant VP of Project Development. Something that would use my training to improve our company's products.

Instead, I'm scooping dog poop off the furniture and herding celebutantes to my favorite bar.

At least during the week I'm useful. Employee Relation Liaison lunches and helping Mom plan fundraisers gives me a positive working rapport with our staff, and it feels productive.

Elena delivers the suitcases and shoves her hands into her pockets. "As much fun as virgin margaritas sound ..."

"You have to come," I say.

She walks backward toward the stairs. "Calum's on his way over to discuss my training regime."

"Your first party weekend, and you're bailing on me?"

She grits her teeth. "Dad said I don't have to socialize if I don't want to. It's crunch time. I need to focus." Her expression is full of apologies, but it does nothing to lessen the sting.

I'm alone hosting, wrangling, and entertaining. I miss my ORs. I miss the hustle and bustle of the hospital. I miss patient care. "You just don't want to clean up dog poop."

"Does anyone ever *want* to clean up dog poop?"

"I guess not." That's why I do it. It's not fair to our employees to make them clean up dog poop. That's not what they were hired to do. I sit on the bottom step. "I could use some back up, though."

"Call Georgi."

My mouth hangs open. "What? No. Why? She hates me."

Elena juts her chin forward and peers at me with one eye. "Maybe that's because you haven't explained to her what's going on."

I rest my head on the wall. "You mean that Dad basically pimps me out every time he needs to impress a new investor? I'll keep that to myself, thanks."

"I like her. She warned me to stay away from you. You should try harder to win her back."

"Elena, you don't know what you're talking about."

I wanted to be the kind of man Georgi could rely on, but I wouldn't pick the man I've become for her to fall for either.

Who can take a man in my position seriously? I'm the sunscreen-applier and pooper-scooper until Dad decides otherwise.

If I do this well, it will prove I'm responsible and Dad can trust me to put the family and business first. He'll forgive me, take me under his wing, and I'll be a CEO he's proud of.

Maybe it's time to stop worrying about your Dad and live your life on your terms, a little voice in the back of my head whispers. The worst part is it sounds a lot like Georgi.

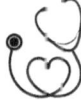

Georgi

The Honey Beans bell rings, and a mass that feels like putrid green slime settles in my stomach.

That may be a tad dramatic.

But Theo's—I mean, Dr. Sanchez's entourage is even bigger this weekend. He holds the door as six statuesque women clippety-clop their stilettos into the coffee shop.

How do they keep getting prettier? Who are his dad's friends, that these are their progeny?

Or maybe they're genetically engineered to be so gorgeous you think your eyes will melt from your sockets if you stare too hard.

That thought makes me feel better. At least people can look at me without risking permanent blindness.

Theo leans on the counter. "Georgi, it's a pleasure, as always." His sagey-salty scent fills my lungs, and my mind wants to link the delicious smell to the memory of his kiss.

Stop it!

I drag my thoughts to an image of him as the eye-melting models' circus director. I try to put him in a funny hat with bright red circles painted on his cheeks, but it doesn't work.

Instead, I'm focused on the way his cheeks are sun-kissed and how he has a small cut bisecting his eyebrow.

I clench my hands into fists to keep myself from tracing it with my fingertip. "What happened to your face?" Did that sound snarky enough? A woman can only hope.

He touches the scab. "Saving a damsel in distress."

I snort. "What do you want to drink?" I don't *need* to ask. He always gets a small black drip coffee. I grab the cup before he answers and turn to the coffee urn.

Why does he come all the way to my humble little coffee shop when I know he has a coffee maker on that floating monstrosity of his? He doesn't need my piddly drip.

He's only here to annoy me. To remind me that he lives his yacht club life and I live mine. That I'll never get to kiss the sweet guy I thought he was ever again.

I hate that I let it get to me.

But it does.

Every stupid Saturday night.

Why don't I leave early? Lock him out? Make someone else take this shift?

Probably the same reason I stop and smell the sage candle in the shop next door on my way in.

I want life to be different than it is. I like the reminder that for one night the possibility existed. In another reality, Hoyt's not a drunk, my mom and dad are happily married, my brother and sisters and cousins are taken care of, and Theo is the man of my dreams.

Someday I'll find a version of that. Just not with Theo.

I let him through the door as my weekly reminder to be more critical and judge people's character before I throw my heart at their feet.

Theo smiles as I fill his cup without him ordering. He turns to his guests. "Ladies, would you like anything?"

One with enough bracelets on her wrist to form her own cymbal section in an orchestra frowns. "Why are we getting coffee before dinner?"

Theo blinks up at me. "It's the only time I get to see Georgi. The love of my life."

I sneer. "Do you hear how obnoxious you sound?"

"Yes."

"And the words still slip past your lips?"

His gaze drops to my mouth. "I like that you're thinking about my lips." His voice is a low, gravelly slide of consonants.

My cheeks pick this moment to heat. "That's not what I meant."

His fingers purposefully brush mine when I hand him his cup. "I'm sure it's not."

I tuck my hands in my pockets and announce to the crowd, "We're closing in five, so if you want something, speak now or forever be thirsty."

The women glance at each other like they need to communicate telepathically for their hive mind to decide they don't want caffeine.

Yes, my internal dialogue is rude. No, I won't say these thoughts out loud. I'm not a monster, but it makes me feel better to be snarky on the inside.

Theo's entourage clippety-clops their way outside, leaving him standing next to the register staring at his dress shoes.

His face drops its swagger to reveal the softened expression I first associated with Theo. The one he wore when he watched me tutor Lee. The one that convinced me a moonlit stroll with a stranger was a good idea.

He shakes his head and glances at me. His gaze darts back and forth between my eyes like he's looking for something. He opens his mouth but snaps it shut before he says anything.

A twinge in my chest wants to know what he was going to say, but I know better than to ask.

I don't know what's real with Theo. We've spent a year in a tango, with him being relentlessly flirty and me trying to forget the way he held me on the beach.

Is he the bravado who confessed to the room that I'm the love of his life? Or is he the loyal family member who lamented being his parents' second favorite child? Is he the sweet gentleman who made me feel like we could be soulmates in one night?

Can any of them be real? Or is it all a show?

Does he even know?

Elena pushes through the door. "Sorry. I couldn't find a parking spot. Where'd the guys go? Why are the girls outside? Hey, Georgi. How are you? Love the cute cardigan. Can I have another hazelnut latte, please?"

This girl doesn't even stop long enough to breathe between thoughts, but she draws my first genuine smile all day.

Her, I love.

I want to put her in my pocket like a good luck charm.

I grab a walkin' cup. "Nonfat, sugar free?"

"And decaf, if you'd be so kind." She hip bumps Theo and takes his spot by the register.

"That can be arranged." I grab the milk from the fridge and pour it into the frothing pitcher.

"No one else got anything?"

"They rarely do. Just your brother," I say over my shoulder.

She squints at him. "Hmm. He does rave about your coffee."

"It's nothing special."

"I'm guessing it's the company, not the coffee."

I nod out the front windows. "Your brother has more company than is good for him."

The women are taking pucker-lip selfies with the sunset in the background. A group of men gather around to get their attention.

Theo spreads his arms. "I'm standing right here."

"I wish you weren't." I can't help that my eyes travel the length of his body. We've already established he's handsome and one hundred percent my type physically. If only the inside of the package was as wonderful as the outside.

He plants his hands on the counter and leans toward me. "You don't always have to be mean to me."

I give him my best pouty face. "If I wasn't mean, you wouldn't know how much I detest these little visits of yours."

Elena fans herself. "Wow. You both have it bad."

Theo's cheeks flush red. "Let's go, Elena." He grabs his sister's arm and drags her toward the door.

"Wait." I chase after them and hand over her coffee.

She wraps me in a hug. "Georgi, do you want to come to the boat tonight? We're having a party."

I extricate myself from her embrace. "I have plans."

"What plans?" Elena's lip puckers.

"Meeting my sister."

"Sangria Under the Pier. They do it every Saturday." Theo grabs Elena's ponytail and drags her backward toward the door. He opens it and tries to angle her through.

She steps back into the shop. "That sounds way better than our party. Can I come?"

I would love to spend more time with Elena. She and Tipsy would be fast friends. After the scene in the trailer the other day, Tipsy needs a night out. "You remember where we were?"

"Yes."

"Don't bring the stiletto crowd or your brother, and we'd love to have you."

Elena pinches her eyes at Theo. "What if I promise he'll be on his best behavior?"

"The answer is still no."

She turns and glares at Theo. "Do you want to tell her, or should I?"

He scoops his sister by the waist and carries her outside. Once outside he puts her down next to their car and they start arguing. She points toward the shop, and he buries his hands in his hair, pulling at the roots.

Should I open the door to listen to their fight?

Theo throws open the driver's door and climbs inside. Elena shakes her head, turns to me, and lifts her shoulders with an expression that looks like, *I'm sorry.*

What doesn't he want me to know?

Chapter 4

Georgi

NORA AND TIPSY HAVE already set up our table and chairs by the time I arrive at the beach for SUP Club. Since they picked the north side of the pier, we can see Elena's yacht.

Tonight, it's fruit punch under the pier instead of sangria, though. Nora's on call—read as: must be sober in case she has to go save a life—and Tipsy's a minor. The rest of our normal complement of women texted to say they are either out of town, working, or on dates. It doesn't make sense to open a bottle of wine just for me.

Nora hands me empty cups. "That's quite the frown."

I fill the cups and take the empty seat next to Tipsy. "I love you both, but I hate when we don't have a good turnout."

"Bridgette might be here in a bit. They had some stuff to do with Jake at the restaurant."

My attention shifts to Jake's BBQ down the beach. The place is a Bubee staple. Raised twenty feet off the sand, the building blazes like a lighthouse. I can't hear the music, but I'm sure a mix of Johnny Cash and classic Bon Jovi pumps from the speakers.

I can almost smell the saucy ribs, spicy briskets, and melt-in-your-mouth chocolate cream cheese pies. People come from miles to eat their food. Since Bridgette and her husband, Keegan, took it over last year when Jake's cancer forced him to retire, its popularity has only grown.

I lick my lips. "See if she'll bring us dinner."

Nora whips out her phone and sends in a request.

I hold up my fingers. "Two slices of Bayou Goo pie, if she can."

Nora's fingers freeze over the keyboard. "It's been that kind of day?"

"It has." The images of Theo and Elena fighting are fresh in my mind. Will she tell me what that was about if she joins us tonight?

"Two sugar comas it is." Nora gives me a flat look. "Have you eaten anything today?"

"Blueberry muffin." At six fifteen this morning.

She types again. "Roast chicken and mashed potatoes for you. Tipsy, what about you?"

Our cousin adds an order of ribs and Nora gets a chopped chicken salad, then we settle into a comfortable silence. The sounds of the waves gently rustling on the shore calms my curiosity over Elena and Theo's fight. I shouldn't wonder—or worry.

I dig my toes into the sand. "Whatever happened with Paul? Did you confront him about the text message break up?"

"No." Nora sips her drink. "When the moment presented itself, I realized I couldn't have cared less."

"Good for you."

"I've learned my lesson: Don't date coworkers. I'll thank him for the education and move on."

"Tipsy, have you thought about college stuff?"

She makes a sound of non-commitment. "The counselor showed me how to apply to the community colleges around here."

"That's a start."

"I don't know what I would do, though." She takes a sip of her drink. "Maybe I'll skip college like you did and work at Honey Beans."

"I didn't skip. I just didn't get very far." A few classes in anatomy and economics and I was done. Life took precedence over dreams. I nudge her foot. "No offense, but do you want to smile at people all day?"

She cringes. "Not especially."

"You like science. Why not pursue something in that field?"

"Be a doctor?" She says it like it's the strangest idea in the world. Like I revealed she's the secret daughter of former Austrian royalty and they want her to take over the country.

"If you want." I shrug. "There are a million choices. Just because my siblings don't have any imagination and took the same path doesn't mean you have to."

Nora sticks her tongue out at me.

I blow her a kiss.

Tipsy laughs.

I've missed that sound. "What's your favorite subject?"

"I don't know."

"Favorite thing to do?"

She points around our circle. "This. Being on the beach."

"If someone paid me to drink wine and gossip all night, I'd be down for that in a nanosecond." Nora snaps her fingers.

"Me too." But that's not true. I wish it was the truth, but I'd get bored. I need to move. That's part of why I love working at Honey

Beans. There is always something to do, even if it's washing coffee mugs.

"Dinner's here," Bridgette calls from the darkness.

We jump to our feet and collect the boxes from her. "You're the best. What do we owe you?"

"Eternal gratitude and a glass of wine."

"You've got the gratitude, but it's a fruit punch night."

"Pour away." She unfolds one of the extra chairs and sighs. "I've been on my feet all day." She slides her feet out of their sandals and wiggles her toes.

"Getting back in the groove?" Keegan's an orthopedic surgeon in Dallas, so they split their time between here and there. They just got settled for their next three-month stay.

"Yeah, slowly."

"We're glad you're back," Nora says.

"Me too. I miss you guys the most when we're gone."

"Time to stay?" I ask.

"Not yet, but that's the five-year plan."

I raise my eyebrow. "That's Keegan talking. Since when do you make plans?" It was a spur-of-the-moment trip that landed her on our doorstep in the first place.

She squeezes my hand. "Good point."

We talk about Dallas and husbands and barbecue.

My attention drifts to the flashing lights on the middle deck of Elena's boat. She must not be coming.

Unexpected heaviness settles in my chest. I wanted her to pick our little party over their flashy one. Maybe she's more like Theo and the party crew than I gave her credit for.

Georgi

Tipsy's exhausted by the time we pack up the fruit punch and camp chairs. I wrap a blanket around her shoulders and dump the rest of the juice in a garbage can so I can put the pitchers in my bag.

Too bad Elena didn't show up. I'll have to find another time to introduce them.

The walk back to the trailer doesn't take long, but Tipsy's sagged against me by the time I unlock the front door.

The TV blares with some racing thing. Hoyt's asleep in his recliner. A case of empty beer cans sits on the coffee table. I gently place the pitchers next to the sink and tiptoe with Tipsy toward our room.

"Where do you think you're goin'?" Hoyt's dark growl snaps out of the darkness.

"To bed."

He glances at the clock on the microwave. 11:03. "My daughter should have been home hours ago. What trouble are you getting her into?"

"None. We were at the beach with Nora."

He pulls the lever to lower his feet to the floor and stands. "Who else?"

"Nobody." Thank goodness Theo and Elena didn't join us. Hoyt hates the yacht club crowd. I would never hear the end of his tirade.

"I don't believe you."

I gesture to the empty hallway. "You don't need to. Ask Tipsy."

"She'll lie for ya."

"We're all tired. I'll talk to you in the morning, uncle."

He stomps his foot like a toddler. "This is my roof. I expect you to follow my rules."

I shake my head and walk down the hallway. "I do." I wish I didn't have to. I wish he would be a responsible, caring father, not a drunken jerk.

"Curfew is at nine," he growls.

I turn toward him and hold my hands up to calm him down. "I'm sorry we were late, but Tipsy is perfectly safe with me and Nora." It doesn't matter that I don't need a curfew.

"Don't talk back."

It's going to be one of those nights. No matter what I say, I won't win, so I'll go to bed and let him sleep it off. I wave over my shoulder. "Good night."

"Get back here."

I stop but don't turn around. "Why? I don't particularly want to listen to you yell at me some more."

He yanks my arm, spinning me to face him. His cheeks are bright red. Snot drips from his nose. His breath smells like he hasn't brushed his teeth in a month. "You always thought you were better than the rest of us, but you're the grown woman who can't afford her own apartment. At least your sisters made something of their lives. They have reasons to be full of themselves. You ain't even good enough to be a waitress like your mama."

After the day I've had, I can't find my filter. I rip my arm free and lower my voice. "You're a drunk and a bully, but I don't parade your flaws in front of you when I'm grouchy."

"What'd you say to me?"

I step toward my room. That was one insult too far. "I'm sorry."

"Get outta my house."

"Good night, uncle."

He grabs the back of my cardigan and yanks me against the wall. He leans in until his breath makes me gag. "I said, get outta my house. You don't get to freeload around here anymore."

"Freeload?" I shove his chest to get his rotting breath out of my face. "Who bought all the groceries while you were in jail? Not Sally or my mama."

Hoyt's hand lashes out before I get a chance to react. The sting in my lip and across my face make me dizzy. He grabs the front of my shirt in one beefy hand, opens the front door, and shoves me down the stairs.

Moonlight reflects on the spittle hanging from his lips. "I see you on my property again, I'll have you arrested for trespassing."

I scramble to my feet and climb the bottom step. "Uncle Hoyt!"

He slams the door in my face. My mom, brother, and Tipsy peek out the bedroom window.

I press my fingers to my stinging lip. They come away bloody.

Lee presses his fist to the glass. I make the universal sign for stop.

He can't get involved. He can't jeopardize his safety or scholarship by fighting with my uncle.

Hoyt's never hit anyone before. I don't want him to get a taste for blood and decide he's not just a mean drunk, but a violent one as well.

I shouldn't have talked back. He'll forget about this by morning once he's slept it off. Makeup will cover the bruises.

But where do I sleep tonight?

My phone, purse, and everything I own are inside the trailer. My shoulders sag. Nora's apartment isn't far.

I mime to my brother to text our sister, tell her I'm coming, and lock their bedroom door.

Hopefully Hoyt's swing got his bad mood out of his system. I don't know what I'll do if he decides I wasn't a good enough target.

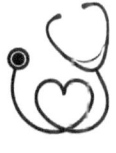

Chapter 5

Georgi

I STARTLE AWAKE. PAIN shoots through my neck and shoulders. My face throbs.

I don't need the mirror to tell me my cheek is purple and my lip's split with a crusty scab.

Nora shuts the fridge and places peanut butter, jelly, and bread on the counter. "Sorry. I did mean to wake you."

I rub my hands around my sore neck muscles. "What time is it?"

"Five thirty."

"Ugh." I flop back on the love seat.

"Life of a fellow." She adds the sandwich to her bag. "There's a possible heart attack I need to check on. Aren't you usually at the coffee shop by now?"

"Thankfully, not today."

She drops her bag by the front door and clicks on the lamp on the side table. "Are you okay?" When I showed up at her door, she doctored me with an ice pack, Ibuprofen, and a hug. She cups my chin and turns my face to the light. "How's your lip?"

I push her hands away. "I'm fine." Sort of, but she doesn't need to hover or worry. I can take care of myself.

She gives me a raised-eyebrow look, saying she doesn't believe me. "What are you going to do about Hoyt?"

"Wait until he's sober and talk to him. He never remembers much after his second beer, so he won't remember me talking back." As long as the bruises don't remind him.

"We can probably get assault charges to stick."

I scoff. "To what end? If Aunt Imogen got him out after he hit that little boy, no way will one tiny slap make a difference. It will make him madder and make it less likely for me to be allowed home."

She pulls out her phone and snaps pictures of my face. The flash blinds me. "What are you doing?"

"In case you change your mind." She tucks her phone in her pocket. "You can move in here. We can be roomies."

I survey her postage-stamp apartment. Twin bed in the corner, love seat and twenty-five-inch TV three feet away. A hot plate and microwave complete her kitchen.

"Thanks, but this place isn't even big enough for you."

She pets her seashell throw pillow. "But it's all mine."

"Lee and Tipsy are by themselves with Hoyt. I have to get back and be their wall."

"Mom's there."

"When has Mama stood up to her brother?"

"Never, but ..."

"There's no but. She might bug him about letting me move home, but when he gets angry, she hides like everyone else." We've been conditioned, trained to run and hide when Hoyt's temper flares.

Why didn't I do that yesterday? Why'd I open my mouth and talk back? It was a dumb move.

I need to do a better job of thinking through the consequences of my actions.

Nora picks at the tassel on her pillow. "I know you think I should have moved into the trailer when I started fellowship to help with them, but I couldn't do it." Her gaze drops to her hands. "He's poison, and it's hard enough when I run into him in town."

My arms slip around her shoulders. "I'm glad you have a home where you feel safe. I just want Tipsy and Lee to have that too."

"What would we do without you?"

"You'll never have to find out."

"Are you going to go over today?"

"The sooner, the better. If I'm lucky, I can walk in like it's home."

Her lips press together like she's going to say something. Instead, she tucks me in for a hug and says, "Good luck."

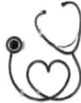

Georgi

Uncle Hoyt and Aunt Sally's double-wide sits in the far back corner of the Bubee Breezes Trailer Park. We moved in when I was ten, right after my dad left. It's soft blue color—like the sky on a spring day—felt inviting and homey to my confused soul.

Since then, the sun has bleached it to a muddy light grey.

It's a pretty good metaphor for the lives we live inside it. What was once a happy, cheerful place is dull and achy. The ghost of what it was.

I pull the door latch, but it's locked. Hoyt tossed me out without my keys, so I knock.

Hoyt opens the door. "What are you doing here?"

I cross my fingers behind my back and say a prayer for amnesia. "I forgot my keys."

He braces his arms against the top of the door frame and leans his bulk forward. "You don't live here anymore."

Dang it. I grasp the door handle. "Hoyt—"

His hand flicks up, and I flinch. He's on the other side of the screen door, and I still flinched.

Way to go, Georgi.

My reaction draws his smile, losing me precious ground in my situation. "I've heard enough of your sass. Get off my porch."

"I'm sorry I spoke out of place. I never meant to imply you can't take care of our family." Even if it's the truth.

"I told you last night—you come back, I'll have you arrested for trespassing."

Snarky Georgi wants to say something like, *Oh really? Go ahead, call them. Let's show the cops my black eye and the busted lip you gave me and see how that goes with your current legal situations.*

But I'm not dumb. He hates the police. They know him too well to put up with his behavior. They'd take him to jail and when Aunt Imogen springs him this afternoon, he'd be more likely to grab the shot gun out of his tow truck and take matters into his own hands than forgive me.

I'd rather not test his aim at close range. I need to use my wits and figure out how to get back in his good graces.

"You can't kick me out."

He straightens and folds his arms across his broad chest. "It's my home. I choose who lives here."

"I want to talk to my mama."

"Lisa's at work." *There's my angle.*

"What about Aunt Sally? She works all day too. She needs my help with Tipsy, and to make dinner and do the laundry. How are the chores going to get done every day if I'm not here to do them?"

"We don't need you."

"You can't just kick me out. Where am I going to live?"

"Don't care."

This tactic isn't working. Hoyt isn't the empathetic type. I'm running out of ideas.

"My phone's in there. I need my wallet. My clothes. Let me get them. Please." I only need to get through the door. One small step, and I'll come up with another idea to ingratiate myself to him.

Hoyt's eyes pinch at the corners like he's going to deny me my property. Can I call the police if he won't let me have them?

No. No police. They'd ask questions. Since everything's in the trailer and the trailer belongs to Hoyt, legally he might own my things as well. I don't know where the law falls.

Hoyt flips the lock. "Five minutes. You take anything that doesn't belong to you, and that shiner won't be nothin'."

"Good to know." I brush past him and scurry into the kitchen.

I don't own a suitcase, so I grab a garbage bag from under the sink and dash into the room I share with Tipsy and my mom. I open my two dresser drawers and shovel my socks, underwear, and pajamas into the sack. I repeat the process with my T-shirts, dresses, and pants from the closet. I don't have much else. A few romance novels. A necklace my brother made me when he was in kindergarten.

I can't leave.

I sit on the bunk bed. Hoyt needs to let me stay. I'm not much, but my family needs me here. Especially when Hoyt's being unreasonable. Especially if he's entering the physical phase of his alcoholism. I don't care if he takes it out on me. I can take a slap. I can hit back if the need arises.

But he might hit Tipsy.

The thought makes me want to vomit. Would he hurt his baby girl?

I can't say no without reservations.

It's not enough.

The only consolation is that Hoyt's less likely to hit Lee. Lee's a big kid. He outgrew me when he was twelve.

And Hoyt loves football. Lee's got a knack for helping Hoyt reminisce about the good old days when he was a football star.

"Time's up." Hoyt calls from the doorway.

I scan the room one more time. I need to be sleeping here by tomorrow night, so I don't worry about missing something.

I step into the front room. "Lee needs help studying for his science test. I'll be back tomorrow to help him."

He grips my arm, shoves me outside. "He'll meet you at the coffee shop. You're done here." He slams the door behind me.

I can't shake the pit in my stomach. Leaving is the worst possible thing for Tipsy, even if it's just for one more night. How will she to survive if I can't find a way back?

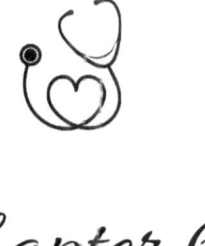

Chapter 6

Theo

"DR. SANCHEZ?"

Very few people call me by my title. The combination of the condescending tone and the use of my moniker curls my fingers tighter around the employee reports in my hands.

Elena's coach is the last person I want to talk to today.

I set my book on the edge of the lounge chair and swing my legs off the side, turning toward him. Calum O'Neil is as tall as I am with the wiry frame you expect on a diver. The premature grey at his temples makes him look older than me by about ten years, even though we're the same age.

I rise and extend my hand. "Coach O'Neil, how can I help you?"

He crosses his arms and tucks his hands into his armpits instead of shaking mine.

That's how it's going to be. Good to know.

"You need to get your sister's butt in the pool." He practically growls the demand.

"Excuse me?" I'm tempted to add, *Who do you think you are*? Or, *You are not her boss, she's yours*, but I don't. Picking a fight doesn't help Elena.

"She's skipped practice three days in a row. She dodges my calls and ignores my texts. She's not here." He gestures to the boat in general. "Even with her injured shoulder, she can dive. Now is not the time for her to develop a rebellious streak."

My neck tenses, and I lift my hand to stop his tirade. "Her injured shoulder? What injured shoulder?" What else don't I know?

He drags his hands down his face. "That girl ..."

"What happened?"

"Two weeks ago, she slammed her shoulder into the platform."

"How did that happen?" Why didn't anyone tell me?

"She got the twisties. Losing their sense of spatial awareness happens to the best of them. Vestibular systems can't keep up with rotation, so they lose their sense of place."

I hate that Calum is giving me the textbook definition like I'm a middle schooler, not an MD.

"I know what the twisties are. Why are you only informing me now?" I should have known the moment she was injured. An injury like this, especially with a psychological component, could derail her bid. She might not even make it to Trials if her injury is bad enough.

Calum holds his empty palm up. "Your parents know. I assumed you did as well."

I clench my jaw. Yelling at Calum won't do any good. "Is this why training moved here?"

His eyes dart out to the bay. "Partially."

I step toward him. "What else?" I need every piece of information in order to help Elena succeed. Being left out of something as important as a significant training accident can't happen. While she's here, it's my responsibility to make sure she trains so she's ready for the Olympic Trials in June.

"She had an argument with one of the other divers training at the pool. We think the mental strain caused the twisties in the first place."

"My sister is the sweetest person in the world. Why would she get in a fight?"

"I wasn't there, so I can only tell you the rumors and Elena's truncated version of the events."

I gesture for him to continue. If something is going on with Elena, she or my parents should have told me. I can't help her if she doesn't tell me everything.

"She hasn't been diving well lately. She stands at the edge of the board for twice as long as she should before she executes her routine. Some of the other divers said she was chickening out and told her to quit so she didn't make them look bad by association." He jabs his finger into his palm. "She needs to train her body and her mind to ignore the critics. If she doesn't practice, she'll never overcome her anxiety."

Anxiety? That's a big word. It leads down the road to psychologists and psychiatrists. Anti-anxiety medication and therapy. That doesn't seem like something my sister needs.

But I don't know. I haven't spent as much time around her as I could have since I made her miss her last Trials meet. I've kept myself scarce, never asked how things are going, because I don't want to remind her of the damage I caused.

I have to get over my hesitation and figure out how to help her. "I am aware of how important practice is, Mr. O'Neil. Thank you for bringing this to my attention."

He continues his speech like I didn't say anything. "We all want the same thing. Elena winning gold is the only acceptable outcome. She won't be ready if she doesn't listen to me. She can't party all weekend, get drunk with her friends, eat donuts and Twinkies if she expects to compete at the highest levels."

"She doesn't do any of those things, and I don't need your lecture." I need to find my sister and figure out what's going on with her.

"If she's done, I have other athletes who value my time."

"What about her shoulder?"

He flicks his wrist like her health is the least of his concerns. "It's fine."

"I'll talk to her." Schedule her an appointment with an orthopedic surgeon I trust first thing. One who sees people as people, not as potential gold medals.

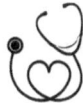

Georgi

I arrive at Love Bug's Tacos and Tamales with my belongings in a garbage sack like I'm Santa Claus.

But there's nothing cheerful or jolly about this situation.

Mama's serving fajitas to a table of Japanese tourists at one of the booths on the side wall. She's a beauty, fine boned and trim, despite the worry lines surrounding her eyes. Her hair's more grey than brown. She always seems smaller than her actual stature when I see her.

My dad ditching her with five kids didn't help. She never got over his rejection. She shrank into herself, not taking it out on us specifically, but she's never been as involved in our lives as I wish she was.

I need her to stick up for me today. She's still my mom. She's still Hoyt's sister. She has a voice. I need her to use it.

Mama waves and points me toward the kitchen. Her boss is at the grill, sizzling up pork adobo and Hatch chili-marinated chicken. The smokey, spicy aroma tantalizes my nose, and my mouth waters.

"Hola, niña. How are ya?" Mona lifts her arm and I give her a side hug, avoiding the grease spitting from the grill. She tips my chin to look at the bruises on my face.

I shrug. "Things have been better."

Mama pushes her way through the swinging kitchen doors and fills three plastic cups with sweet tea. "Hey, Baby. What's in the bag?"

"Everything I own."

She looks at the bag then shrugs like it's normal for me to tote my world around in a garbage bag. "Do you need lunch?"

My stomach pinches. "Probably, but that's not why I'm here."

I haven't eaten since Bridgette delivered the chicken last night. Taking what little Nora had in her cupboards wasn't an option, and I'm used to an empty stomach.

Part of me is optimistic and believes I'll be home soon.

The other part is pragmatic, saving every penny in case I need to rent a room somewhere.

I hold up the bag. "I need you to talk to Hoyt. He won't let me back in the trailer. He barely let me gather my belongings."

Her lips pinch. Her gaze darts to Mona and back to me. Mona knows about Hoyt, so her presence shouldn't keep Mama from talking.

A whisp of hair shakes loose from Mama's bun. "He shouldn't have shoved you out last night."

"Will you talk to him?"

She places the cups on a tray." "Baby, I wish I could. I ..." She adds a basket of chips and two bowls of red salsa.

"Why can't you?"

She holds up a finger and reenters the dining room.

Mona doesn't add her commentary. She's as much of a busybody as I can be, but Mom's worked for her since she opened fifteen years ago. Her half smile gives me comfort. I appreciate the silent camaraderie.

After delivering her tray-full, Mama pushes into the kitchen and continues our conversation like she never left. "You know why."

"No, I don't." I have a guess, but if she's truly abandoning me, I need her to say the words. I need her to tell me to my face why she won't help.

"Baby ... he ... my brother's a hard man like your Daddy was. You have to make allowances for them."

I plant my palms on the stainless-steel counter and glare at Mama. "You mean excuses."

"If he thinks I'm disrespecting him, what will Lee and I do? I can't start over."

"We could get an apartment together." I dismiss the idea as soon as the words are past my lips. That abandons Tipsy to Hoyt's temper. If he would let me move her out of his trailer, that would be one thing. He won't, though. He'll never allow her freedom.

Me assuming she could stay out past curfew put us in this spot in the first place.

Mama sips from the lipstick-stained straw in her water bottle. "You'll be fine. You can live with Grammie."

"I'd rather not." My grandma's form of love and affection typically involves a lecture on the ways I'm living my life incorrectly. Plus, she just got married to her long-lost high school sweetheart. I don't know her husband very well. Small talk at the breakfast table would be awkward.

"What about Mrs. Sullivan's carriage house?" Mona asks.

"Bridgette and Keegan are living there until they go back to Dallas in June."

Mama pats my cheek. "You're a smart girl. You'll land on your feet."

"It's not safe for you, Tipsy, and Lee to live with Hoyt." I point to my lip. "He's escalating."

She rubs her thumb over the bruise on my cheek. "Just with you, Baby. You like to push his buttons."

"Mama!" I stomp my foot. Why won't she listen? Why doesn't she care more about their safety? "This is not my fault. He's a violent alcoholic. Why won't you see that? Why won't you fight to keep our family safe?"

Why won't any of the adults in our lives get their heads out of their butts and see that the kids need them to stick up for us? Protecting us shouldn't be my job. Hoyt shouldn't get away with his behavior.

She shakes her head and mumbles like she's not talking to me. "It's better this way. Too old to live at home." She stops and plants her hands on my shoulders, squeezing gently. "You need to find a nice man to take care of you."

I step out of her reach. "That is *not* the answer." Little Miss Home-maker taking care of her big strong husband has never ever *ever ever* been my dream. I will not be my mother.

"I have to get back to work." Mama kisses my cheek. "It's so nice to see you, Baby. Text me when you get settled, and I'll come visit."

My mouth drops open. She's acting like I'm moving to another city because I feel like it. Mama's a little off, living in her own world, pretending Daddy didn't abandon her, that she isn't a grown woman with kids to take care of, but this ... this is the worst I've ever seen her.

But maybe it's not her refusal to help that surprises me.

My subconscious knew her answer before I walked through the door. She will never stand up to Hoyt. He's her protector and stand-in father figure. He's the voice of authority who tells her who she is.

He has been since she married Daddy—and Grammie and Peepa cut her off.

Live with the consequences of your choices, and don't cry to me when that boy disappears on you again.

No. Mama's actions don't surprise me. Hoyt lets her live in her dream world. She'll never sacrifice that.

What surprises me is the pain building in my chest and the tears burning the back of my eyes and nose.

I didn't expect it to hurt so much for my mom to choose her own comfort and immaturity over me.

It does.

After all these years, I'm not as numb to her apathy as I thought.

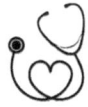

Theo

Elena scrubs a towel against her wet hair as she steps into the living room on the main deck. "Is dinner ready?"

I tried calling and texting her after Calum left. When she didn't answer, I went searching. She wasn't at any of the stores on the main streets. She wasn't at Honey Beans. She didn't take the car, so she couldn't have gone far, but my sister vanished today.

I need to know why.

I place my water glass on the coffee table and pat the sofa next to me. "How was practice?"

"Hard. Calum's not messing around."

I uncross my ankle from my knee and steeple my fingers. "That's funny, because he was here this morning." Her mouth drops open. "He said you skipped practice. Third day in a row. What's that about?" I'm going to start with the easy questions before moving on to her physical and mental health.

She plops onto the sofa. "I thought he'd give me a few more days before he tattled on me."

At least she's not denying the accusations. That would make this conversation infinitely harder. "Talk to me, Pipsqueak. He's ready to drop you."

She scrunches into a ball, dragging her knees to her chest. "Maybe that's for the best."

"What are you talking about? You've worked toward the Olympics your entire life. If I hadn't made you miss the trials last time, you'd already be an Olympian."

"True." Her angry side eye sparks the shame I've carried since that day.

"Do you want to give up?"

"No." The word lacks conviction, but I believe her.

"Then why lie? Why skip practice?"

She rests her head on the back of the sofa and stares at the ceiling. "I went to the pool the other day, and my hand shook so badly, I couldn't open the door. I saw Calum pacing on the deck, and my heart raced like I was doing fifty-meter sprints without coming up for a breath."

It *is* a mental thing. A confidence, anxiety thing. Besides being her brother, I'm not qualified to help her with that. Our relationship hasn't recovered to where it was before the Olympic Trials, so I know she won't open up to me. She needs a therapist she can pour her heart out to.

"You've always handled stress so well before. What's different now?"

She buries her face in her hands. "I'm sorry. I don't know what's wrong with me."

I wrap my arm around her shoulders and wish I could pull the stress out of her like I'm a leech, but she doesn't relax. "Nothing's wrong with you. You're under a lot of pressure."

"I should be able to handle it." The sadness in her tiny voice is like pricking my finger with safety pins over and over and over. Stabbing, stinging, and preventable.

"What you're demanding of yourself isn't normal, Pipsqueak. It's hard work. It's a lot of pressure on a single action that lasts less than five seconds. It's amazing you haven't had issues before." People pressure out of high-stakes situations all the time. They can't handle the mental load. They think they should be able to just take it.

But stress and pressure are things that need to be trained for as well. Have we forgotten to help her with her mental game? I don't know. I should, but I don't.

"Have you talked to Mom or Dad about any of this?"

She pulls out of my hug. "Dad says I need to focus more. Put the stress into my training."

I keep my eyes pinned on her, so I don't roll them. Dad is a *grin and bear it* kind of man. There's nothing you can't muscle your way through. There's no stress that can't be redirected into a tool.

But that's not how the body works. Shaking hands and a racing heart are her body's ways to communicate that Elena is not well. She needs to listen to them and take appropriate steps to decrease her stress and fear.

She might develop an anxiety disorder if she doesn't.

I don't want to plant that seed. It's been a long time since my psychiatry rotations, and I don't want to say the wrong thing and make Elena feel worse about her stress levels. Giving her a clinical diagnosis could work against her.

We'll find another way through this. "How can I help?"

"Help me relax."

I squeeze her hand. "More movie nights. Check. Do you have more reading to do for your ancient history class? He's not Roman, but we can watch Gerard Butler in *300*?"

She fans herself. "I can get behind Leonidas defending Sparta."

"And your shoulder?"

She rolls it forward and back. "I've had worse."

"I have a friend who's an orthopedic surgeon. We'll have him take a look at you." Thank goodness Keegan is in town. He's a fantastic physician and an even better friend. He'll happily do this favor for my sister.

She scoots away from me. "I don't want to go to another doctor."

"He's a friend. He's talented. He'll treat you with respect."

Her forehead bunches, and she sticks out her bottom lip like a toddler pouting. "Do I have to?"

"Yes." I tap her forehead. "Your health is your most valuable asset. You don't want to be a forty-year-old who's unable to put her suitcase in the overhead bin because of stubbornness."

She stands and holds her hand out for me. "Sometimes I hate when you're such a good brother." I clasp her hand, and she pulls me to my feet.

"I owe it to you." If I hadn't screwed up her dreams in the first place, she'd already have her medal. She could have moved on to her next dream instead of being stuck in the one she's pursued since she first bounced on a springboard in our backyard.

She wouldn't need to compromise her physical and mental health to prove to the world something I already know—she's a superstar.

"How about some Milk Duds and popcorn with that movie?" she asks, steering me toward the kitchen pantry.

"Only if it won't mess with your training."

"Ugh, fine. Only popcorn."

"No butter."

She pinches my side. "I should have gone to practice. Now over-protective brother is on the boat."

"I'm getting you to the trials this time, so you'd better be ready."

Chapter 7

Theo

THIRD COAST REGIONAL MEDICAL Center's glass façade is as inviting as the clear blue sky it reflects. Calum agreed to a half-day practice so Elena and I can meet with Keegan during his lunch break.

And by lunch break, I mean the twenty minutes while the hospital staff turns over an OR and he shovels a chef's salad in his face.

Elena completed an MRI earlier.

Keegan logs into the computer in his office and looks at the imaging. "You don't have a tear, but the ligament on your supraspinatus isn't happy. You're developing arthritis in your acromioclavicular joint." He turns to her. "Did you have cortisone injections?"

"Yeah. The last doctor I saw said it would help."

His eyebrow lifts. "Did they?"

"For a little while." She fiddles with the hem on her sleeve.

"Did you rest your shoulder after the injection?"

"No. I had a meet."

He slides in front of her and palpates her joint, taking her arm through various tests to determine her shoulder's condition. "The cortisone drops the inflammation by calming your immune system. If you don't give your body an opportunity to rest, all you've done is taken away its ability to heal while you continue to break the structures. You do more damage than good."

She sinks on the exam table with a scolded puppy expression on her face.

We can't change the past, but we can make changes and do more to help her take care of her body. "What does she do now?" I ask.

"Flexibility and strength training are your best tools. If something hurts, stop. You shouldn't push yourself so hard that you need daily anti-inflammatories. Does your coach manage your cross training?"

Her gaze darts back and forth between him and me. "I do."

Keegan enters an order into her chart on the computer and hands her the card for the rehabilitation department. "I'll set you up with Debney, one of our physical therapists. She's worked with high-level athletes for years. She's good people. You'll like her."

I tap my fingers on my thigh. Might as well take care of everything while we're here. "Do you know a good sports psychologist?"

She shakes her head. "I don't need one. I'm fine."

I give her a look that I hope translates as, *taking care of yourself isn't a weakness.* "Doesn't hurt to ask. Besides, they can tell you after one visit if you need their services or not. If things change, having names and numbers is a good place to start."

I'm not going to let anything slip through the cracks. It's time I take an active role in her wellbeing. I've let our emotional distance keep me out of some aspects of her life.

Not anymore.

Worse things than hitting her shoulder can happen if she gets the twisties again. I won't let her risk her life when one phone call, one appointment can make the difference.

Keegan makes a note in his phone. "I'll ask around and text you."

"Thanks." We say our goodbyes, and Elena and I leave the office.

Within twenty minutes, she has an appointment with Debney for a physical therapy evaluation and Keegan sends me the contact information for two psychologists.

I hold my phone up so Elena can see the names. "Which do you want to try?"

"I don't need that." She pushes my hand down. "Moving here, movies with you, running on the beach, that's all I need."

"I don't agree."

"Let me try it my way. If in a couple weeks, I'm not in a better headspace, I'll make the phone calls. Okay?"

I tug her to my side. "I'll hold you to that."

And add a twist of my own.

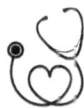

Theo

I gave up visiting Honey Beans during the rare weekdays I'm in town long ago. I could only grovel and apologize so many times without Georgi changing her mind before I learned the actual definition of insanity.

But today is different.

I need her help.

Elena smiles when she talks to Georgi. She's happy and carefree when they gang up on me.

I'll swallow my pride and ask Georgi for help if it relieves Elena's stress. I've seen Georgi help people navigate stressful moments, so I know she's the one for the job.

Plus, I don't mind the excuse to see her more often.

Georgi's at her usual place behind the counter when I enter. Her lip is puffy, and makeup poorly covers a horrid bruise on her cheek.

It's on the tip of my tongue to demand she tell me who hurt her, to run and cup her face and kiss away the pain.

But she won't tell me. I'm the guy she loathes.

I hate that I screwed everything up with her, but like I told Elena before, I'm too embarrassed to tell her the truth about our dad's dictates. Watching the hatred in her eyes morph into pitiful disdain would kill me.

Too bad my heart is pounding in my chest and my visceral need to take away her pain makes it hard to breathe.

Who would hit Georgi? Why? What don't I know about her life? Could I have prevented this?

Her smile evaporates when the door closes and she realizes it's me. "Are you going to start harassing me on weekdays too?"

There's the venom I expect. "I'm still convinced you look forward to seeing me."

I took a chance at Keegan and Bridgette's wedding and flirted with Georgi. I'll never forget the pretty blush on her cheeks or how she gripped my shirt. Even though her words said she hated me, her lips and her eyes disagreed.

I saw a glimmer of the passion we had the first time we kissed.

It gave me the hope I cling to and savor like the last drops of water in a marooned man's canteen.

She pops her fist on her hip and glares at me. "The only part of you I look forward to seeing is your backside as you walk out that door. I love the peace in knowing I might never see you again."

"That's going to make this a little more difficult, then." I knock my knuckles on the counter. "I need a favor."

Her arms make an X in front of her chest. "No."

"You don't know—"

She grabs a rag and wipes the counters. "I don't care. I'm not helping you."

"It's for Elena."

"Still no." She strides through the swinging doors into the back of the shop.

My sister is too important for me to give up on the first volley, so I follow Georgi. "Please—"

She shoves her palm against my chest. "You're not allowed back here."

"I need you to listen." I want to hold her hand to my chest, but I press mine together like a prayer instead.

"Go away, Dr. Sanchez."

"Please, call me Theo."

"How many ways do I have to say no? No. Não. Nee. Nein. Nac Oes. Kahore." Her finger jabs into my chest with every iteration of the word.

I rock back on my heels. "How many languages do you speak?"

"That's not the point." She fists her hands at her sides. "Get out."

I grab the garbage sacks next to the back door. "I'll do whatever you want if you'll help Elena. Want me to take out the trash? I'll take out the trash."

Her cheeks blanch, and her hands wave frantically in front of her. "Stop. Put those down."

I press my hip against the bar and unlatch the back door. "I can take out the garbage. I can scrub the coffee pots. I'll mop the floor. Anything you want."

She snatches the bags from my hands. "That's not garbage. It's my life." She spins away, catching the bag on the corner of the counter, and rips a hole in the plastic. Confetti-colored clothing litters the floor. I purposely avert my eyes from the panties and bras.

I fall to my knees and scoop the clothes into my arms, making sure a sweatshirt covers her lingerie. "What's going on, Georgi?"

She pulls the bundle from my arms and turns her back to me. "Nothing. I asked you to leave." Her shoulders shake like she's trying to hold in her tears.

I tentatively reach out and cup her shoulder, stepping around the pieces I missed to face her. "Talk to me."

She blinks rapidly. "Please, Dr. Sanchez, just go."

I point at the fluffy pink socks next to the floor drain. "Why are your clothes in garbage bags?"

She sniffles. "Because I don't own a suitcase."

Heaviness digs into my chest. "Where are you going?" I keep my tone soft and low, masking the terror in my heart that Georgi might not be at Honey Beans the next time I come visit her.

"Nowhere," she whispers.

If only that made me feel better. She's not leaving, but something is obviously wrong in Georgi's world if her clothes are in garbage bags and she's sobbing in the back kitchen.

I slide my hands up and down her arms, relieved she doesn't shake off my touch. "It's not normal to carry clothes around in a garbage bag."

Her eyes harden. "I know that."

"Then why—"

She jerks out of my grip. "I got kicked out of my trailer, okay? Are you happy now? Have a good laugh. Then climb into your Beemer, go back to your billion-dollar yacht, and tell your spoiled, rich friends that the girl from the trailer park has hit an all-time low. They love laughing at me. They'll think this is hilarious." She buries her face in the sweatshirt on top of the pile in her arms.

There are so many things wrong with what Georgi just said. About herself—and about me.

She's more than a woman from a trailer park.

I take no joy in seeing her like this.

If I could, I'd take away her pain.

I'd put a roof over her head, provide everything she needs, even if she doesn't want me.

But that's how she sees me.

I'm spoiled.

Selfish.

Heartless.

Because I'm the idiot who can't find a way to ditch the party guests who tag along like toilet paper on the bottom of my shoe every Saturday night.

If I ever hope to earn her forgiveness, I need to start by fixing her opinion of me.

I pick up the rest of the clothes that fell from the bag and hand them to her. "I'm sorry."

She presses them to her chest. "Please leave."

"I still need a favor."

"Why would you want a favor from *me*?"

"Because my sister loves you." I do too, but that's never mattered before. "She's having a rough time getting ready for Olympic Trials. She needs a friend. I hope you will be that person for her."

"You don't have to bribe me to be her friend. She's a sweet girl." She steps to weave around me.

I block her path.

If I'm doing this, I'll go all in. For Georgi and Elena. I'll solve both of their problems with one request. And maybe fix Georgi's opinion of me in the process.

"That's not the favor. Will you move on to the yacht?"

She scoffs. "I'm not living with you. I don't need rescuing."

"That's not what this is." Not entirely. Besides, what's wrong with being chivalrous? Aren't gentlemen supposed to help the people they care about? This isn't any different.

"I'm not a charity case."

"Your stuff is in garbage bags in the back of the coffee shop."

She bristles.

Shut up, Theo. You're not helping your cause.

"I ... I didn't mean ..."

"Not that I owe you an explanation, but I'm moving in with my grandma temporarily. I didn't want to walk all the way back to Nora's and get my stuff after work."

Time to try a different tactic.

"What about Elena?"

"She can come to SUP club. All of us will be her friends."

I run my thumb over my chin. "That's not going to be enough. Her training schedule's crazy. She likes to pop into my room at midnight to talk and blow off steam."

Georgi's forehead crinkles into a scowl.

"I don't mean that I don't want to talk to my sister. I'm not pawning her off on you. She needs both of us. It will be easier to help her with her stress and anxiety if we're close by. We have plenty of space on the boat. You won't have to see me if you don't want to."

"No." She fishes a new garbage bag out of a box and dumps her clothes inside.

I swipe my hand through my hair and bite the inside of my lip to keep from shaking sense into her. "Are you being stubborn because I'm asking? If Elena asked, would you move on to the yacht?" If I was in Houston and Elena asked, I have no doubt Georgi would move right aboard.

I know she hates me, but this borders on ridiculous. She needs a place to stay, and I have one. Why does it have to be so complicated?

The bell out front rings.

"I have customers." She brushes past me, but I grab her arm.

"It's okay to ask for help."

"I am asking for help." She pulls her arm free. "Just not from you."

Georgi

Theo slides his sunglasses over his eyes and leaves Honey Beans while I serve iced coffees to a group of elderly motorcyclistas.

"This is the most adorable little town." The woman wearing a faded orange scarf sets her helmet on the bar.

"We like it." I run their credit card.

"We were surprised by the number of gigantic boats in the marina. Y'all are so far from Houston."

Why wouldn't they start talking about the boats when I want nothing but to forget about Theo and his offer?

Move onto his mega yacht?

Never in a million years.

I can't be just down the hall from him. I don't want to be within two hundred miles of him.

He makes me remember things—his arms around my waist, his breath on my cheek, his mouth caressing mine—things I want to forget.

If I lived on the yacht, I might as well sign up for daily paper-cuts with lemon juice. It would have the same effect. Adding tender, painful, avoidable injury to already ailing body parts. I'll pass.

The woman in a leather jacket with unicorns stitched on the back pats her friend's arm. "They're called yachts, Kathleen."

"Oh, I know that. Did you see the really big one? I didn't catch its name."

Unicorns turns to me. "Honey, who owns the biggest one?"

"The Sanchez family owns the *Midnight Star*." The haunter of my dreams.

"Are they part of the mob or something?"

I giggle. "No." The idea of Theo as part of a mob family is beyond ridiculous. He's too pretty for other gangsters to take his threats seriously. "They make machines for hospitals."

"Ah. That explains why my last flu shot cost a thousand bucks." Kathleen sips her drink. "Are there any good shops we should visit while we're in town?"

I sigh with relief as they turn the conversation away from Theo. "Head east and you'll run into stores with almost anything an independent woman might want."

"You have a store full of handsome men who know how to curl a woman's toes?" Kathleen bats her eyes.

Unicorn just rolls hers.

"'Fraid not. But we do have some good restaurants and bars that might help with that. Jake's BBQ and Sobre las Rocas are my favorites."

"Thanks, hon." Unicorn lifts her cup. "Great coffee by the way."

"It's my calling."

"Glad you picked up that phone."

It's not like I had much choice in that matter. Not a lot of employers in Bubee would hire a fifteen-year-old with my family's reputation, but Honey did.

I wouldn't change it for all the *Midnight Stars*.

I probably should have saved more instead of pouring every paycheck into my family, then I'd have a deposit for an apartment.

I honestly never thought Hoyt would kick me out permanently.

While the opportunity to live on Theo's yacht is intriguing, it's not realistic. I can't forget who I am.

I won't end up like my mother, reliant on a guy for my every need.

Grammie's big house has several empty rooms. I can put up with her crankiness while I figure out how to convince Hoyt to let me come back.

Georgi

I sling my garbage bags over my shoulder and walk up the stairs to my grandma's front door. Her two-story pink and white Victorian sits on stilts over the carport. After a steadying breath, I press the doorbell.

"Come in," Turner calls from inside.

My grandma and her new husband are sitting on the sofa playing Scrabble. They had a courthouse wedding a few months ago after a five-decade separation.

Absence made the heart grow fonder, I guess.

I set my bags down in the hall. "Thank you for letting me stay with you."

"Stay as long as you need." She places her tiles on the board. "*Elemental*. Eleven points, but it's on a triple word, so thirty-three points." She scribbles her score on a piece of paper. "Georgi, will you please make spaghetti for dinner?"

While it sounds like a request, it's not. This is how I'll earn my room and board. Wash the windows, sweep the stairs, and then the laundry and the mending. And don't forget the tapestries. At least she doesn't have a cat for me to bathe.

I smile at my ridiculousness. I watched too many princess movies with Tipsy when she was little. Grammie opened her home to me. Helping out is the least I can do.

My encounter with Theo put me in a bad mood. I didn't need the reminder that my life isn't champagne and caviar. It would be wrong for me to live in such extravagance when I should be earning my way back into Hoyt's trailer.

I won't ask my grandmother to speak to him. She won't. Her mantra is *clean up after yourself*.

At least Grammie's will be just uncomfortable enough that I won't want to stay.

"Spaghetti sounds great, Grammie." I put my stuff in the spare room and grab two cans of San Marzano tomatoes, fresh basil, onion, garlic, a bottle of cabernet sauvignon, and everything else I need from her pantry.

The rest of the evening is easy. I cook. They play. We eat. I clean up.

"Good night, Grammie."

She squeezes my hand and kisses my cheek. "Sleep well."

I flop on the bed. "This is better than expected." The bed is soft. The pillows are perfectly plump under my head.

Normally, Grammie's a difficult woman to get along with. She's exacting and doesn't offer a lot of grace, as evidenced by her refusal to help my mom after dad split.

She's been different since Turner came back into her life, though. He mellows her. Hmm ... maybe he can convince her to speak to Hoyt for me. I'll ask tomorrow.

I put my clothes in the dresser and closet, shower, and change into my pajamas. I type a quick text to Nora.

Georgi:

> Grammie's letting me stay in her guest room.

Nora:

> Is that wise?

Georgi:

> It will be fine.

At the very least, the bed is more comfortable than Nora's sofa, but I won't tell my sister that. She's knee-deep in medical school bills. She doesn't need to worry about her lumpy love seat.

This has been the longest forty-eight hours of my life. I switch off my light and snuggle under the fluffy duvet. Tomorrow will be better.

Squeak squeak squeak. Bang bang bang.

Squeak squeak squeak. Bang bang bang.

Grammie's headboard smacks the other side of the wall from mine. I shove my pillow over my head. This can't be happening.

I hum to drown out the sound of my Grammie and her husband … I don't want to think the word … but denial doesn't help.

Canoodling is happening on the other side of the wall.

I'll never get that image out of my head.

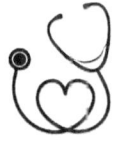

Chapter 8

Theo

"Mr. Sanchez?" Our ship's captain waves me onto the bridge.

I stare longingly at the sunrise for another half a second before steeling my expression and stepping inside. "What can I do for you, Captain Timmons?" Do I sound as weary to him as I do to myself?

He holds up an iPad. "Your father sent the guest list for this weekend. Would you like a copy?"

"Forward it to me, please. Anyone we've had before?"

He shifts the device and reads the names. "The Gusman twins, Viola Rothchild, and Lexie Carmichael."

I nod. Of course it's them. I don't want to host this weekend. There are too many important things going on in our lives to take a break and entertain people for my parents.

Unfortunately, I don't get a say.

Add that I don't know how Elena will react to these particular guests and knowing Georgi's history with them, and the pit in my stomach isn't just a marble of discontent, it's a boulder smashing my intestines to rubble.

I run my hand around the back of my neck.

What do I do?

Hopefully Elena will be at practice, so she'll take care of herself. I'm holding out hope I can help Georgi.

It's not that I don't want her to be comfortable at her grandma's house. I want that to be a warm, inviting home where she feels loved and welcome.

It's more that I also want her here. I want to be the one to provide her a warm, inviting home. I want her to look at me the way she did that first night on the beach when she thought I'd hung the moon and my heart gave itself completely to her.

That look won't happen if Lexie and Viola are here.

Lexie was part of the first group of guests I brought to Honey Beans, when I lost Georgi's respect. Ever since, she's been rude to Georgi. She'll insist on going to Honey Beans just to one up Georgi again. I try to distract Lexie, stop her from going, but my ability to convince Lexie not to do something is on par with my ability to convince Georgi to forgive me.

Most likely, I don't have to worry. I haven't seen Georgi since she refused my help on Monday. She was conspicuously absent from Honey Beans when I dropped in on Wednesday and Thursday. She wasn't even hiding in the back.

Lexie knows Saturday at Honey Beans is part of my routine. She won't want to let me go alone. I have to risk Lexie following me if I want to see Georgi.

"We'll stick to the usual itinerary." Dinner tonight. Beach Saturday. Brunch Sunday.

"Yes, sir. I'll notify the staff. Would you like them in the regular rooms?"

"Don't put anyone on deck one with Elena and me, but please have them ready the room next to Elena's for another guest. She's having a friend stay with us."

It's a lie, but better to be prepared just in case, somehow, I change Georgi's mind.

"Of course, sir." Captain Timmons twists his mouth but doesn't ask who the mysterious guest is. He shakes my hand and disappears back onto the bridge.

I understand his curiosity. Elena and I have never had personal guests on the yacht before. Georgi will hopefully be the first.

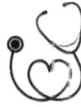

Georgi

I poke my head out of my room and peer into the kitchen. It's blissfully empty. Yesterday, while I was eating yogurt and getting ready for work, Turner needed water. He forgot to put on pants before he joined me, so I have the image of his tighty-whities burned on my retinas.

I don't want to repeat that.

It doesn't help that I barely sleep because they barely sleep.

Who knew my puritanical grandma was a sex fiend?

Not me.

I never wanted to know. I was content in my ignorance.

Oh, what I'd give to go back to those carefree days.

I'm trying to be open-minded. This is their home. They can do what they want when they want, but I'm not sure how much longer I can live here.

I'm sleep deprived, jumpy, and irritable.

Three Greek strawberry yogurts sit on the fridge shelf waiting for me to pack my lunch box. An apple, peanut butter, and sparkling lemonade join the party.

"Georgiana?" Grammie says behind me.

I squeeze my eyes closed. *Please be dressed. Please be dressed.* I slowly turn and peek out from under my eyelid. She's wearing her bathrobe. My shoulders climb down from my ears.

It's something.

"Good morning, Grammie."

"I need you to run some errands on your way home." She holds out a piece of paper.

"Sure, whatever you need." I read over the list in her looping cursive.

1. *Three gallons of Benjamin Moore semigloss paint in Thunderbird*

2. *One paint roller frame with extendable arm*

3. *One three pack of 3/8 inch high-density roller cover applicators*

4. *Painter's tape*

5. *Drop cloth*

"What are you painting?"

Her nose wrinkles. "Nothing. You're painting the front room Monday."

"But I have to work."

"It's the least you can do for staying with me. It's a small chore."

I tuck the list in my pocket. "Right. No problem. I'll work it around the coffee shop."

"When you're done, I might have you paint the main bedroom as well. I'm thinking a bright lemon sorbet color will liven things up. Will you be a dear and make us sunny side up eggs? Bacon. There's sourdough in the pantry. Two cups of coffee too. Thank you." She tugs her robe around her neck and walks back to her bedroom without waiting for my response.

I brace my hands on the counter and take slow steady breaths through my nose. I don't have time to make her breakfast. Honey Beans opens in ten minutes.

I don't mind helping out. Doing my share, but I can't be at her beck and call all the time. Painting a living room is one thing, but Grammie is turning me into a servant.

And the tighty-whities.

Never again, Lord. Never again.

I need to talk to Hoyt.

Theo

Elena pulls my beanie down over my ears. "Perfect."

I pull it right off again. "We can't leave." Our guests are on the upper deck with the karaoke machine, belting out Adele ballads.

Too bad they didn't leave the harmonies to the experts. My ears might actually be bleeding.

Their distraction doesn't mean we can sneak off the boat. They're sure to need something, and it's my job to fetch, pour, mix, and generally make sure they're happy.

I can't do that if I disappear.

Elena fists her hands on her hips. "You've been trapped on this boat all day with them. You didn't even get to go see Georgi." She sticks out a sarcastic pouty lip. "We'll be gone an hour, two tops. Those women won't miss us." She puts my hat on my head and tucks the loose hairs on my forehead under the elastic. "I need to run."

It's nine p.m. on a Saturday night, and my sister *needs to run*.

She went to practice every day this week. She's eating well. Sleeping well. No more trembling hands or other signs of anxiety.

By all accounts, she looks like she's back to the Elena I know.

I don't trust it.

Somethings up.

"Elena, is there something you want to tell me?"

"I've been meaning to ..." She bounces on her toes. "You need new running shoes. Yours are starting to fall apart."

I block the path to the dock. "Why are we running so late?"

She shrugs. "I didn't give it my all at practice today, so I'm making up for it." She swats my stomach. "You could use a couple hard miles too."

Someone tries for a high note, and I jam my fingers in my ears. "Two miles."

"Five."

"Three."

"Deal." She walks down the gangway and starts running as soon as her feet hit the dock.

I catch up as she turns out of the yacht club parking lot. "I hope they don't realize we left."

She adds pace to her legs and sprints ahead. "I don't care if they do."

"You won't be the one who gets the phone call from Dad." It takes everything I have to keep up, but I do.

We run along Camino del Mar, taking advantage of the streetlights and busy nightlife for safety. Elena pauses at a red light. "He shouldn't make you babysit those women."

"It's Dad's way of grooming me to take over. I need to know all the players. Those women will take over their parents' companies, so socializing with them now will make it easier to work with them in the future."

Elena grips her stomach and laughs so hard she squeaks. "Those girls aren't doing anything but spending their mommy and daddy's money. Can you picture Avery trying to understand an Excel spreadsheet? Ha. I'd pay to watch that."

"Don't stereotype them. They're smarter than they act." Most of the time.

"You're too nice."

We reach Sobre las Rocas at the end of the beach. I brace my hands on my knees and suck in deep breaths. I haven't run this hard in a long time. My morning swims are hard but nothing compared to this. "We should head back."

Elena stoops and unlaces her shoes. "I want to run on the sand."

Of course, she does.

I follow. We need to get back. Lexie and the ladies will be furious, so the sooner the better, but I can't deny my sister.

Running on the sand will take longer, but Elena's smiling. That's a win. Lexie can yell at me all she wants if Elena's happy.

A band plays on the beach behind Sobre las Rocas. Locals and tourists wave as we run past. We pass Jake's BBQ and get closer to the pier.

Elena points to the group of women around a firepit with a folding table and chairs. "Hey look, there's Georgi. Let's go say hi." Her tone is too forced.

Was this her plan all along? Get Georgi and me together? I wouldn't put it past her. "Elena, no."

"Why not?"

Because I'm not in the mood to fight with Georgi. I'm worried about her, but she doesn't appreciate any attempts I make to reconcile, and I hate how insufficient that makes me feel. Like when I let you down at the Olympic Trials.

Elena lifts her eyebrows, but I stay silent. I didn't tell Elena about asking Georgi to move onto the boat. I don't want Elena to feel like I'm a helicopter brother scheming behind her back ... even if that's what I am.

My sister doesn't need any other tools to embarrass me or make Georgi uncomfortable.

Elena gestures toward the women. "What's wrong with saying hi?"

Georgi's head is thrown back laughing, and her face glows in the firelight. How can she get more beautiful?

Why am I so pathetic? I can't keep living like this. She doesn't want me. She hasn't for a long time.

I wasn't the man she believed me to be. Who I wanted to be for her.

I let her down like I've let everyone else down.

I need to get over my crush and figure out a way to live my life without this infatuation for a woman who will never see me the way I want her to.

When I still don't say anything, Elena drapes her shoes around her neck by their laces. "Georgi invited me, so I need a good reason not to go over there."

I don't have a reason for Elena not to stay. It's me Georgi hates. I want to foster their friendship. "Have fun. From what I hear, SUP club is the best group of women in town. I'll take care of our guests. Meet you at home."

She touches my forehead like she's checking for a fever. "That's it? You're not worried I'll get lost?"

"You'll be fine. Georgi and her sister will help if you need anything." Because that's who she is, someone who never hesitates to help others but refuses to let me help her.

I step around Elena. Skirting the pier and walking along the road is the fastest way home, but that makes me walk directly through Georgi's party. I don't want to ruin the women's night, so I'll go the long way around instead.

Elena holds up her hands. "I don't understand you. You have no problem barreling into the coffee shop and putting on fake bravado, but when you could spend time with Georgi somewhere neutral, without Dad's guests, you don't. Why?"

"She hates me." My voice can't be any more pitiful. If I cared about things like man cards, I'd turn mine in. I'm like a weepy little kid who just realized Santa isn't real. The magic is gone, and I'm left untethered.

"I hate the guy you pretend to be with Dad's guests too."

"I'm not pretending. That's a side of me you don't typically see." Sort of.

"You drop lines like they are coins in an empty vending machine. Do you care that you'll never get anywhere with that strategy?"

"Poetic metaphor."

She turns me to face Georgi. "Where did your courage go? She's right there. Show her the real you."

"A guy can only be rejected so many times before he takes the hint."

"I've never known you to give up on anything."

She doesn't know about my fellowship. I've tried and failed with Georgi. Over and over and over again. I can't try again. "I need to get back. Have fun." I jog away before I tell my sister the truth.

I've walked away from more than she'll ever realize. I have to do my job and serve our family, so Elena can accomplish her dreams.

Yes, I would love to spend the evening on the beach with Georgi. I'd love to watch her laugh with her sister and mine, but that's not going to happen.

Lexie and Viola have probably realized I'm gone. They've probably called their parents, who will call my dad.

I can't disappoint Dad. Earning his respect back should be my only focus.

Georgi's made her opinions clear. She'd rather live out of garbage bags than let me help her.

Message received.

Chapter 9

Georgi

I WATCH ELENA WATCH Theo run away. She shakes her head and crosses the sand to join us by the fire. Was that a continuation of the fight I saw the other weekend? Do I want to know?

Probably not.

Even if my splintered heart hates the anguished look on Theo's face, getting involved will make it fester until I want to do something to make him smile.

I pat the chair next to me, and Elena sits. "Thanks for inviting me."

I point to the half-empty pitchers on the table. "Drink?" We'll avoid the subject of her tiff with Theo. No festering hearts allowed.

"No thanks."

I point to a full mason jar hidden in the back. "We have grape juice. I bring it for my cousin, but she's not here." I haven't seen Tipsy since I moved out. Lee gives me updates when he pops into the coffee shop. I'd hoped she'd find a way here, but Hoyt locked her at home.

"Juice would be great," Elena says.

I hand her the mason jar and introduce her around the circle. Our turnout is much better than last time. "Nora, my sister, is a cardiology resident. Bridgette and Amanda run Jake's barbecue. Rachel's an ED nurse. Sasha's a pathologist, and Debney's a physical therapist. Fallon's a mechanic. Ladies, this is Elena, future Olympian."

Everyone waves and says hello.

Elena looks like she got the wrong end of a fire hose. "Debney?" she asks.

Debney brushes her long bangs out of her eyes and tucks her bare foot under her. "It's a weird name. I know."

"I have an appointment with you next week to check my shoulder." Elena rolls her shoulder backward. It moves smoothly, but Olympians likely need to be more fine-tuned than normal people.

"I hope I can help," Debney says.

"Dr. Sullivan said you are the best," Elena says.

Bridgette raises her glass. "My husband likes to brag about talented people."

Elena tips her head in confusion.

I point at Bridgette. "She is Mrs. Sullivan, as well as being a barbecue goddess. She loves saying *my husband*, so she does it whenever she can."

"My husband." Bridgette wiggles her face toward me.

"The honeymoon phase looks good on you," Nora says.

Elena's eyes widen. Her mouth gaps like she wants to add something but doesn't quite know what to say.

"It's okay if you don't remember all of our names," Sasha says.

"Maybe we need embroidered jackets like the Pink Ladies in *Grease*?" Fallon flicks up the collar of her jean jacket.

Nora fans herself. "What about when it's 104 in the shade? We're not going to want jackets then."

"Bikinis?" Sasha says.

"I don't want my name on my butt," Fallon says.

"You wear it on your breast every day," I say.

"On a baggy jumpsuit that hides my skin. The only people I see are your cousins and uncle, along with Mateo and Luke, and all of them know better than to let their eyes drift." She wags her finger. "I'm not inviting anyone to drool over my backside."

My friends continue to debate the virtues of nametags on clothing, and the fire crackles away.

Elena sighs, and a small, blissful smile drifts onto her face.

I nudge her foot. "Having fun?"

"I've never done anything like this before."

I lift my glass. "Sangria Under the Pier is a novelty."

"I mean hanging out with friends. No curfew. No expectations."

"You hung out in high school, right?"

"No. Freshman and sophomore years, I was laser-sighted on the Olympics. When I missed qualifying, my parents hired tutors so I could train harder. No time for friends."

"How tragic." I shake my head. "Wow. That sounded judgmental. It probably wasn't if you were following your dream." My sisters have given up parties and acquaintances in the pursuit of medical degrees. Being an Olympian is even more rewarding.

"It just was. Not good or bad." A frown settles on her face.

"And now?"

Elena's head rests on the back of the chair, and she stares at the cloudy night sky. "I did an interview a few weeks ago." Her voice is wistful. "*Olympic Hopefuls*, that kind of thing. The reporter asked what I'll do if I don't make the team. I said I would try again. I'm only twenty. I've got plenty of time to compete. Then she asked about when I retire, and I didn't have an answer. I've never thought about life after diving."

"Do you have to?"

Her head bobbles halfway between a nod and a shake. "I have answers for everything else, so why don't I have one for this? I envy Theo knowing he'll take over for Dad."

He's getting his wild streak out of his system before he has to act like an adult. Sounds like some other "adults" I know.

"Is that why you're in Bubee? To figure it out?" It would make sense for her to escape her normal routine to gain perspective on her goals.

I hate being away from Tipsy and not knowing how she's doing, but there's something to be said for being forcibly removed from my routine. My perspective is different. Relationships are cast in a unique light.

Did I realize how much of my life I devote to fixing other people's problems? Not really.

Do I regret it? Absolutely not.

But the revelation opens my eyes. What do I do next year when Tipsy and Lee go to college? Will I stay in Hoyt's trailer with Mom? Will I want my own place?

I don't know.

I'm a little like Elena in not looking past this season of life. I don't have answers either, but I feel like I'm supposed to.

Elena chews on her bottom lip. "I needed a different pool. I could only stare at the chipped tile for so long before it messed with my head. I need to find that laser focus again if I'm going to win."

I sip my sangria and let the sweet, tangy wine warm my body. "You and your brother are so different."

Elena shifts in her chair like a curious bird on a branch. "You think so?"

"You devoted your life to becoming an Olympian." My fingers and thumb make L-shapes to frame her muscular body. "He parties with models and actresses every weekend." I flick my hands toward the yacht club. "You're serious, and he's pretentious."

Her knuckles whiten on her cup. "You don't know him."

"The last year has given me a good idea."

She swivels her cup into the sand at her feet, turns and faces me with her hands clasping her knees. "You know the parties aren't his idea, right?"

"He seems to enjoy them." He definitely enjoys flaunting the women in front of me.

"He doesn't."

"Maybe you've got rose-colored glasses where he's concerned."

"Or you're heartbroken and want any reason you can find to push him away."

I scoff. "He didn't break my heart." He shattered it, but I'm not confessing that to his sister.

Besides, who falls in love in one night? Love at first sight isn't a real thing. It takes years of getting to know someone to decide if they're the person you're supposed to spend the rest of your life with.

My mom was with my dad on and off for thirteen years and never realized he was worthless.

There's no way I'll make that mistake.

Elena's face fills with empathy that makes my stomach cramp. Why is she looking at me like that?

She clasps my hand. "Theo wasn't kind to your heart. He deserves for you to be mad at him, but he also deserves a second chance."

"What did he tell you?"

"About your first date. And the aftermath."

I grind my teeth together. "He shouldn't have."

"Why not? As his sister, I have a right to know why he's sad."

"He's not sad." I yank my hand from her grip and shove it under my thigh.

Theo loves his parade of women and champagne. He's always happy-go-lucky. Flirty. A modern-day Casanova. Like the Carrie Underwood song I can't get out of my head, except a doctor instead of a cowboy.

Elena shrugs and sips her grape juice. "You should give him a second chance. Spend time with him. You'll realize he's not the man you accuse him of being. Come over after everyone leaves, you'll see."

"I already told him I'm not moving onto your yacht, so give it a rest."

Her cup stops halfway from her mouth. "What?"

Oh, please. I scowl at her. "You had to know. He pretended you need a friend to lure me onto your boat. Like a kidnapper with a puppy."

"He ... he did that?"

"Right? Can you believe it?"

"I can. He's sweet like that."

I don't have the words to explain to Elena how wrong her opinion is of her brother.

It's not my place. He's probably always been her hero. She doesn't deserve to have her illusions crushed, even if I know differently. He's not hurting her by hiding his true self from her, so I'll mostly keep my mouth shut.

I fold my chair and grab the empty sangria pitchers. "I like you. I want to be your friend, but I'm not moving in with a man I can't stand." This was supposed to be a peaceful, carefree evening. If I stay any longer, I'll say something I regret. "See y'all next week."

Nora grabs my hand. "You're leaving already?"

"I haven't been sleeping well."

"Isn't Grammie's house comfortable?"

I wrinkle my nose. "Let's just say Grammie and Turner's nocturnal activities make them not the quietest roommates."

Nora grimaces. Yep. I painted that picture for her. I'm sorry I did it, but she has to know what I'm dealing with.

"Come back with me. We have plenty of space." Elena pops up next to Nora.

Why did I tell her about Theo's offer? If I'd known he hadn't told her, I wouldn't have said anything. I will not live on their yacht. "We've been over this."

"If this is about my brother, Theo is driving Dad's guests to Houston tomorrow and won't be back for a few days. You won't have to see him or them at all. Let me apologize for my behavior."

"You have nothing to apologize for."

"Why not go?" Nora asks. "You have been *extra* grouchy. More so than your overly opinionated self usually is. Do us all a favor. If you can't sleep at Grammie's, give Elena's a try. One night won't hurt."

Elena nods. "The rooms are soundproof. You can sleep as late as you want. I make the best pancakes."

I point from one to the other. "This tag team attack is not cool."

Nora loops her arm through Elena's. "Georgi has a hard time accepting help, so let me answer for her. She would love to spend the night on a luxury yacht, be pampered a little, and have breakfast with you. Do you have a toothbrush she can have?"

"Like all the best hotels" —Elena's voice sounds like an infomercial host—"we supply every toiletry you need—and several you don't. Bamboo linen pajamas, a steam shower, and the gentle lapping of waves to lull you to sleep."

"It's settled." Nora unthreads her arm and replaces it with mine, taking my chair and pitchers.

"I'm not going." I try to take them back, but she spins out of the way.

"If you won't stay, will you walk me back? I'm not sure how to get there in the dark." Elena clutches my arm.

Nora's eyes widen with a grave, somber expression that almost makes me laugh it's so fake. "Theo will blame you if something happens to his baby sister."

The boats are lit up like Christmas trees in the distance, but there's a section along the beach that can be treacherous if you don't know what to look for. "Fine, but I'm just walking you."

Elena squeals like I promised her a new Porsche.

I'll walk her home, do my good deed, and get home. Hopefully before Grammie and Turner need a glass of water in the middle of the night.

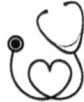

Theo

Lexie sits on a lounge chair at the top of the ramp when I get back to the boat. Blonde hair piled on top of her head, arms and legs tucked inside her pullover sweater like it's a blanket, her eyes bore into me. "Have a nice night?"

Fighting is the last thing I want to do right now. I'm exhausted. I'm heartsick. I'm over pretending I care about Hermes scarves and Michael Kors shoes.

I stop halfway up the ramp. "Do you need something?"

"Did you have a nice night?" Her tone is a low growl.

"Not especially."

"Where'd you go?"

"Elena wanted to go for a run."

Lexie does an exaggerated stretch to look over my shoulder. "I don't see her. Did you leave her behind too?"

"Come on, Lex. It's been a long day."

"We thought you left. Like, *left* left."

Because I would leave a ten-million-dollar yacht and never return. "Where would I go?"

"I don't know. That's not the point. You left without telling us." She shrugs her legs out of her sweater, and it drops off her shoulder, revealing that she's not wearing anything underneath.

Ugh.

It's on the tip of my tongue to say, *I don't have to report my movements to you.*

But that comment would lead to an argument of epic proportions. Lexie's twitching eyebrow and firm-set mouth tell me she wants to fight. She enjoys the power struggle of a good argument. I won't give in to her.

If she were Elena, I'd offer her popcorn or a cookie to smooth everything over.

Lexie's not that kind of woman, so I need to appease her. Calm her down and get her to her bed.

"Did everyone else go to sleep?"

"Why didn't you tell us you were leaving?"

"You were having fun singing. We didn't want to interrupt. Elena gets this way sometimes. She needs to train, and I can't let her run around after dark alone."

"You always put her first, don't you?"

No. "Yes."

Her eyes soften and her mouth turns down into a frow. "What do *you* want, Theo?" She stands from the lounge chair. Her sweater slouches lower, barely holding on to the one covered shoulder. Half an inch of satiny pink shorts are visible below the lower hem.

At least I know she's wearing shorts. The look in her eye sets off warning bells in my head. I need to get to my room and lock the door.

"Why do you do this?" she asks.

"This?" I walk up the ramp and slide around her toward the door to the stairs.

Her hands slip up my chest. "Give everything you have to your family when they don't appreciate you."

I grip her wrists and remove her hands from my body. "Lex ... don't do this."

"Answer me."

"They appreciate me."

She shakes her head. "Teddy. Elena walks all over you. You could have been singing with us, but she pulled you away."

"I'm not a singer."

"But you have fun with me?" There's so much vulnerability in her tone. I hesitate. I don't run like my gut tells me to.

"You are a wonderful person ..." *some of the time.*

I can't tell her the rest of my thoughts. She's the daughter of one of Dad's biggest investors in Boston.

She's here for the boat. The party. The escape.

I wish she wouldn't pretend otherwise. She's only upset I left because I wasn't at her beck and call. "I'm glad you enjoy the boat. Tomorrow we'll have brunch and commemorate another fun weekend." I place my hand between her shoulder blades and turn her toward the stairs. "Sleep well."

"You won't leave again, will you?"

"No."

"Did you know Daddy's giving me the Albuquerque office?" She sticks her tongue out.

Envy jolts through me like a bee sting. What? Party girl Lex is going to manage one of her dad's subsidiaries? While I'm paying my dues pouring margaritas?

She chews her bottom lip and locks up at me from under fluttering lashes. "I asked him for the one in Houston, but he said I'm not ready. Isn't that silly? How will I come hang out with you if I'm stuck all the way over in New Mexico?"

Because New Mexico might as well be Australia to her. "I'm sure you'll find a way."

If Lexie's dad thinks she's ready to take a managerial role in his company, why aren't I?

I'm older, more mature, with more life experience. It's time I stop waiting for my dad to think I'm ready.

If I start small, he's more likely to agree to let me take on an active role. Instead of returning to Houston every week, I can shadow the Bubee factory manager. I'll continue to host parties on the weekends while I devote my weekdays to learning our company from the people who make things happen every day. I won't just take them out to lunch like a once-a-year doctor's visit. I'll partner with them every day like a mentorship.

Dad can't say no to that.

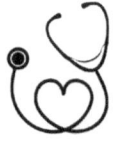

Chapter 10

Georgi

Bubee is beautiful at night. It reminds me of the descriptions of
people going for invigorating strolls in a Regency novel.

Stars peek out from behind the clouds like pictures in a frame.
Melodic waves soften the harsh nip from the breeze. Couples prom-
enade along the main road under antique lanterns.

Even as Elena and I pass the crowded restaurants and bars, the
gentile effect doesn't lessen. Maybe it's the intricate scroll work on the
architecture or the bands crooning classic country songs. Either way,
the angst I felt arguing with Nora and Elena earlier is gone.

Yes, they manipulated me, but so what? The walk is nice.

"Theo wasn't lying when he said I need a friend," Elena says to
break our silence.

"He didn't need to ask. I am happy to be your friend. We'll make
you a Bubble yet."

"A Bubble?"

"A Bubee Bubble. A local. An integral part of our community."

"Kind of embarrassing having your brother ask people to be your friend like we're in kindergarten or something."

"I bet he's been like that your whole life. You just didn't know it."

"That's even worse." She scrunches her face. "How many of my friends were only my friends because he begged them to be? Ugh. I don't want to know."

"For all his faults, it's sweet how he looks after you." It's his one redeeming quality. I never thought I'd find one, but there it is. It makes me reevaluate some of the conclusions I've drawn about him.

Not enough to stop hating him, but enough to see Elena's better with him as her brother.

Her shoulder bumps mine. "He's a keeper."

"Ha. I wouldn't go that far."

We get to the yacht club, and I tuck my hands in my back pockets. "I'll see you later."

She grabs my elbow and tugs me toward the docks. "Come have hot chocolate."

I shrug out of her grip. "I should get home."

"You never say yes to anything, do you?"

"Not really."

"Seems to me like you need a friend just as much as I do."

She's not wrong. We spent all night with women I consider my dearest friends and I didn't ask any of them if I can stay in their homes.

Part of it is logistics. Amanda lives on a ranch outside of town, and I don't own a car. Fallon lives in the apartment above my uncle's shop, and he would never let me stay there.

But the other part is the embarrassment.

My uncle kicked me out of our home because I was a sassy busybody.

I don't regret sticking up for myself or Tipsy, but I don't need to air our family's dirty laundry around town. There are enough rumors about what happens in our trailer. I don't need to confirm them.

Elena loops her arm through mine. "No is not an acceptable answer." She drags me onto the dock.

The *Midnight Star* is massive. It's got to be, what? 200 feet long? 250? When they call it a luxury yacht, they're not lying.

The hull is the same black as the night sky with white and silver detailing on the finishes. There are four layers of windows, so at least four levels ... err, decks? A pool and two hot tubs. There's an open space for sunbathing on the nose of the boat.

What else is hiding from public view?

We go through a door—or is it called a hatch? Down a set of stairs into a stainless-steel kitchen. Elena grabs two ceramic mugs from a cabinet and retrieves milk and chocolate syrup from the refrigerator. "I hate the powdered stuff." She sets a pan on the induction cook top and adds the ingredients.

"What can I do?"

She waves away my offer and points to a barstool. "Sit. How did you become a barista?"

I climb on the seat and lean my elbows on the counter. "That's a quick story. I needed a job. There weren't a lot of options for a fifteen-year-old that didn't involve food service. I figured making coffee would be easier than waiting tables."

"Did you ever think about doing something else?" She pours the milk into the saucepan and then swirls in what has to be half the bottle of chocolate syrup. Where is her Olympian diet of kale and cucumbers?

My mouth waters with the rich chocolaty aroma. "Nah. I like working with people, and it pays the bills. Why change if I'm happy?"

"Kind a like me. You pick a thing and stick with it."

"Loyalty and dedication to the things we love are important." I'm comfortable. I've never seen a reason to look for anything else.

Sure, I've had wild hairs about this or that—like the time I thought I'd open a museum dedicated to the indigenous people of South Texas or when I wanted to grow and sell vegetables behind the trailer—but nothing ever stuck.

Honey Beans Coffee has always been at the center of my days.

I got into a routine, kept my head down, got things done. Somehow fourteen years passed me by, and I don't know what I did with them.

That's not true.

I know exactly where they went.

Helping my sisters get straight As, study for SATs and MCATs, and researching medical schools and residency programs. Getting everyone out of the house when Hoyt was in one of his fits.

That's how Sangria Under the Pier started. Hoyt was drunk, so I took everyone to the beach. I bought a $1.50 bottle of grape juice, clearance strawberries, and birthed a tradition.

When Elena's done, she pours the hot chocolate into mugs and leads me to a set of lounge chairs on the top deck. She flicks a switch, and all the lights go out, gifting us an unpolluted view of the stars.

My mouth hangs open. The clouds have cleared, and this far away from the street we lose just enough light pollution to see most of the galaxy. It's breathtaking and awe-inspiring. "This is amazing."

She shrugs like it's no big deal. "You should say *yes* to fun stuff more often."

"I should, but I can't. Too many people depend on me."

"I depend on you, so you should stay."

"Easy as that?"

"Yep."

Can it really be that easy? I don't want to go back to Grammie's. The rocking headboard has scarred me for life. I can't look Turner in the eyes.

I could ask our other friends for a place to stay, but then I'd have to explain why I need a bed in the first place.

Elena doesn't care why I need a bed. She just wants a friend to hang out with.

I can be that.

"How much is rent?" I sip my drink to cover my nerves. Am I really considering this? Where is my iron resolve from the beach?

I can't do this. Can I?

Elena considers my question with a serious divot between her eyebrows. "A conversation a day. Maybe a run. Theo said you're a runner."

I nudge her. "How much money?"

Her head rocks side to side on the lounger. "Do we look like we need your money? Let this be a friendly gesture, my thank you for letting me hang out with you."

"But you don't need to thank me. I like hanging out, and I would feel better if I paid something."

"Can you cook?"

"Probably not up to your standards, but I'm not half bad with Italian." Noodles and tomatoes go a long way to fill empty bellies.

"How about you have to provide a meal for me and Theo once a week?"

Because of course she'd throw her brother into the mix.

But this is his boat. I can't get away from him if I live here.

Can I handle that?

Can we exist in the same space without my duct-taped heart breaking again?

I have to try.

Maybe being around him more will help me see how wrong we were for each other from the start. It will be the final nudge I need to get over the last vestiges of my crush.

The man I have a crush on isn't even real. This will help prove that the Theo from the first night never existed.

I hold up three fingers. "Three dinners."

She pushes my ring finger down. "Two."

I hold up one finger on my other hand. "Two dinners and one breakfast."

She squeals and wraps her arms around me. "Deal." She scrambles to her feet and extends her hand. "Let me show you to your cabin."

"I get a whole cabin?"

She winks over her shoulder. "And en suite."

"How long can I stay?"

"As long as you'd like."

Is this girl for real?

I follow her down the stairs to the main deck. We pause at the landing, and she points down the hall. "Mom and Dad's suite is up here with the living room, dining room, and game room. There's a hot tub as well."

She continues the tour as we wind down the levels. Level two has six guest suites, currently occupied by this weekend's models. I will avoid them at all costs until they leave tomorrow.

Level three is the kitchen, another living room, tech stuff, and crew quarters. On level four, she leads me down a hallway and points to the first door on the left. "This is you." She points to the next door on the left. "That's me." Then to the door across the hall from hers. "That's Theo's."

"Why are you down here?"

"It's where we hide. These used to be the crew quarters, but when we refurbished the boat, since Theo knew he'd be living here most of the year, he asked to have a smaller room farther from everyone else."

I nod along, but it doesn't make sense. Why would he want the little room in the bottom of the boat? Doesn't it get claustrophobic?

She opens my door, and I take it back. This room is bigger than the room I shared with my mom, sisters, and Tipsy in the trailer. No claustrophobia here.

A soft blue and green tropical fabric covers the bed and shades the window. There's a desk in the corner, a closet and two dressers in the wall. There's even a purple orchid on the bedside table.

Elena opens the top drawer and pulls out peach pajamas. "Here. Toiletries are in the drawers in the bathroom." She gives me a hug. "Thanks for staying. I need this."

She closes the door, and I sink onto the bed.

Who lives like this?

Me apparently. But only tonight.

Because even as luxurious as this is, I need to find a way to get home.

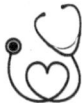

Theo

The predawn hours are my favorite on the ship. With no one else awake, I don't have to fetch a mai tai or find a sun hat.

My time is mine for these few brief hours.

I slip into the flume pool and turn on the jets. Nothing crazy, just a warmup swim. I pull my first freestyle strokes and let my mind wander. Our guests. The run with Elena. The fight with Elena. The fight with Lexie. Worrying about Georgi.

Even if she doesn't want me to, I care what happens to her. I said I'd walk away, but I need her to be taken care of and safe.

I can't believe Elena tried to get me to crash Georgi's beach party. I didn't need to ruin their night with our fight. Elena knocked on my door when she got home, so I knew not to worry. I hope they had fun.

I swim for another forty-five minutes until my muscles are tired and my stomach growls. It's interesting that the pool is my stress relief, but it's the boulder on my sister's back. We both love it, but she's naturally more talented than I am.

Maybe her time with Georgi last night helped lessen her anxiety.

I scrub the towel against my head and wrap it around my waist. I don't need to accidentally run into Lexie while I'm feeling this relaxed, so I take the crew stairs in the bow and weave toward the kitchen.

I freeze in the galley's doorway.

Georgi's standing at the counter with her back to me. A cup of coffee in her hand. Wearing peach shorts and a tank top, her skin glows. Her hair's a beautiful, rumpled mess I want to run my fingers through.

What I wouldn't give for this to be the sight I wake up to every morning.

What is she doing here? Elena must have convinced her to stay.

It's what I wanted.

She's here. I don't want to startle her or drive her away.

My mouth flaps open. I can't find the right sentiment.

If I were smart, I'd run. Leave her in peace to enjoy her morning routine without getting her hackles up.

But I'm not smart.

I want to pretend for a moment longer that she wants to see me, to talk to me. That she doesn't hate me and she's on my boat because she wants to be.

I step forward and lift my hand like I'm going to wave.

My shoulder slams into the doorway. "Oof." *Smooth. So distracted you can't walk through a door.*

Georgi startles. Coffee spills on her hand. Her eyes widen, and her cheeks flush. She scrubs her hand on her shorts. "Theo." She steps toward the other door. "I didn't know you were up yet."

I step back into the hallway. "Sorry to disappoint."

Her eyes travel across my wet chest, down to my towel. They linger. My face heats at the desire and attraction in her eyes. I don't think she realizes when she licks her lips.

She shakes her head and tightens the grip on her coffee. "I'll let you have the kitchen."

I take two quick steps into the space. "You don't need to run away. I just wanted a banana." I pluck one from the basket on the counter and wave it at her as I step back to the door.

I'd hoped for a full breakfast, but that will have to wait. I'd rather have her be comfortable.

"That's okay. I've got to get ready for work." She slides into the other hallway, speed walking toward the stairs.

I dash after her. "Georgi? Wait."

She slowly turns to face me, fidgeting with the rim of her coffee cup. Her cheeks are the same peach as her PJs, and I want to run my thumbs across them. A million sentiments cross my mind.

You're beautiful.

Thanks for staying with Elena.

Can we be friends?

Instead, I peel my banana. "I'm glad you're here. I promise I'll give you your space. I won't be another thing you have to worry about."

She nods and disappears down the stairs.

Georgi's on my boat.

Georgi is on my boat.

How do I get her to stay?

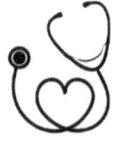

Chapter 11

Georgi

WHEN I HEAR THEO move back into the kitchen, I reverse my direction and climb the steps to the top deck two at a time.

I need to get away from Theo. The plan to see him every day to get him out of my system couldn't have hit a bigger brick wall.

Watching that bead of water drip from his shaggy hair, traverse his well-defined pecs, slope over the valleys created by his ab muscles, and then soak into the towel hanging loosely from his sculpted hips ...

Hello, heart palpitations and butterflies.

Hello, every bad idea I've ever dreamed about falling for Dr. Theodore Esteban Alejandro Frederick Sanchez IV.

I've never seen him without a shirt before.

Heck, I've never seen him in anything but a button-down dress shirt.

Shirtless Theo will send me to the Emergency Department for an EKG if I don't hide.

My room would have been a more logical place to disappear—yes, I'm hiding. No judging—but he might look for me there.

Or I'll run into him when he goes to take a shower and get ready for his day.

Nope.

I'm hiding up here, in the little alcove where Elena and I drank hot chocolate last night, until I have to get ready to leave for work.

I settle onto the lounge chair and curl my knees to my chin. The first sip of my coffee warms my insides. I breathe in the savory aroma until my heart rate is normal.

Living here is an epically terrible idea. I didn't think through every scenario or consequence of my decision.

Never did I imagine running into sexy Theo within the first ten minutes of waking up.

I close my eyes and lean my head back. Elena meant well, but I can't do this. I'll deal with Grammie and Turner's newlywed bliss. Ear plugs are a thing.

"Oh, no. What are you doing here?"

My head snaps up. Lexie—I think that's her name—stands at the top of the stairs with one hand on her hip and the other holding some kind of green smoothie. Her eyebrow twitches higher and her toe taps.

Perfect!

Dr. Sanchez isn't hosting just *any* guests. He's hosting *her*.

The mean one.

The entitled one.

The one who proved to me that Theo couldn't be the man I thought he was.

Ugh. Why didn't I go to my room again?

"Good morning." I use a pleasant tone.

"Did you sneak on the boat?"

"Yep." I point to the railing. "I climbed the hull with a grappling hook right there, snuck into the kitchen and commandeered their coffee machine. The hazelnut creamer isn't half bad. I mean, if you drink things with sugar and calories and nutritional value."

Her knuckles whiten around her cup. "You can't be here."

I squint at her. "Why is that exactly?"

"Because you don't belong."

I agree, but I won't give Lexie the satisfaction of being right. She won't bully me out of here. I have more right to stay than she does.

I think.

I actually have no idea, but I'm going to act like I do.

Fake it till you make it, right? "Elena seems to think otherwise. Last I checked, her opinions count a heck of a lot more than yours."

"We'll see about that." She spins. Her blonde hair flings out behind her.

I don't contain my giggle. Her little temper tantrum reminds me of the way Angelina, Sister Number Three, would rant when I wouldn't let her steal our eggs to throw at Ian Sullivan's car.

Forget everything I said about avoiding sexy Theo. If my presence ruffles Lexie's feathers, I'm staying one more night. She doesn't get to boss me around or decide who can and can't be friends with Elena.

Spoiled, self-righteous twits can't win. I won't let them.

If Lexie leaves knowing I have a more permanent place here than her, my inner avenger will dance a jig. Justice for the little guy has been achieved.

Theo said he'll stay out of my way. I'll take him at his word.

Looks like I'm stuck with the anesthesiologist.

At least for one more night.

Theo

I take as long as possible to shower and get dressed. Georgi doesn't want to be around me, so giving her plenty of time to leave also has the added benefit of limiting my time with Lexie, Viola, the Gusman twins, and the rest of our guests before I have to drive them to the airport.

Elena sits with Lexie and Viola at the outdoor table sipping orange juice.

"How are you ladies this morning? All packed?" I ask.

"Didn't you hear? Daddy's coming." Lexie pops a grape in her mouth. Her toothy smile has an almost vicious quality.

I freeze. They can't stay.

Georgi will hate that.

So do I, but as previously established, it doesn't matter what I want.

My eyes dart to Elena, and she nods. "Check your phone."

My rule is no phone before breakfast, so I haven't turned it on yet. I power it up, a barrage of text messages ringing in. Most from my mom. A few from my dad.

"How did this happen?"

Lexie folds her hands across her stomach. "I told Daddy I was having a marvelous time and didn't want to leave just yet. I suggested we have a little reunion. Sanchezes, Carmicheals, Rothchilds, Gusmans. Everyone. He made some calls, and now we're here for the foreseeable future."

"Where's everyone staying?" The boat doesn't have staterooms for everyone who's already here plus their parents.

I'm not kicking Georgi out, but with this new development, she might leave of her own accord.

Lexie flutters her fingers, like the logistics of hosting upwards of twenty people with no notice aren't a big deal. "Daddy rented a house, but we're staying here." She presses her hand to her chest. "Your mom is such a great hostess. We feel like we're family."

Don't grind your teeth. Don't snarl. Accept your job and make everyone happy. It's for the good of the family.

"I'll work on logistics with the captain." I nod toward the stairs. "Elena, will you help me?"

She follows. When we're out of sight, she grabs my arm. "Captain Timmons already has everything covered. What's up?"

I run my hands through my hair and squeeze the roots to help alleviate my growing headache. "Georgi."

"What about her?"

"We promised her a quiet, stress-free place to live until she can figure something else out. Mom and Dad plus all of them." I jerk my thumb over my shoulder toward the women. "They aren't stress-free."

Elena rests her hand on my shoulder. "She'll be fine. I'll explain it to her."

"She's going to think I set this up to show off." She always assumes the worst about me in every situation.

"Maybe it's the perfect opportunity to show her you aren't like our parents. Show her you don't belong with the Lexies of the world. That you are the man she needs."

"Do you think that will work?" Can I be who my parents need me to be and show Georgi I'm the guy she first thought I was? The desire in her eyes when I saw her earlier was real. It gives me hope.

Elena shrugs her shoulders to her ears and holds her hands out, palms up. "It doesn't hurt to try."

But it will hurt to fail.

Georgi

When I get back to Elena's boat after work, there's a sunset orange suitcase in my room with a note.

> *Garbage bags are so last season. Welcome home.*
> *-T*

I want to be annoyed at his presumption, but the sentiment makes me smile.

Home. He underlined the word twice.

Who knew he could be witty?

There's a knock on my door. I open it, half expecting ... hoping it's Theo, but Elena brushes past me and collapses on the bed. "I need to apologize in advance."

The tension in my chest changes. Why was I hoping Theo's smile was on the other side of the door?

I loathe him.

With every fiber of my being, I loathe him.

I don't want to be disappointed he's not here so I can thank him for the suitcase.

I'm being silly. I sit next to Elena and try to decide what kind of tension her apology deserves. "What are you apologizing for?"

She throws her arm over her face. "Our parents are coming." She says it with the gravity usually associated with invading armies.

The British are coming. The British are coming.

I put the suitcase on the bed and zip it open. I'm not one to turn down a thoughtful present regardless of the giver. "I get it." That's why Theo left the suitcase. It's his way of bidding me goodbye.

But why the *welcome home*? I guess he wasn't calling the boat my home. Maybe he thought I'd convinced Hoyt to let me move back in.

I grab the plastic bags with my stuff. I had to stop at Grammie's house to change before my shift this morning. She gave me a raised eyebrow when I walked in wearing last night's clothes, but people in glass houses and all that.

Elena peeks in the bag at my studiously-folded clothes. "What are you doing?"

"Packing."

"Why?"

"If your parents are coming, I assume I need to vacate the premises."

She grabs my hand. "No. You're my guest. You are welcome to this room as long as you want it. I just need you to know they're … particular? I'm not sure that's the best word. Mostly they're nice, but sometimes they're a lot."

I don't know what an overbearing parent looks like. My mom was always so uninvolved. After dad left, she just didn't know what to do. She disappeared into herself because it was easier. I don't blame her.

Why love anyone if they will leave you? It was safer for her heart to push my brother, sisters, and I away than to watch us repeat Dad's example.

This isn't the time to think about my parents, their disastrous relationship, and its fallout. If I'm staying here, I need to be prepared.

"What should I expect?"

"Family dinner tonight. Just you, me, Theo, Mom, and Dad. They're making Lexie and the other girls eat at the houses their parents rented. We'll be casual. I think Judah is making mahi-mahi."

Elena is a firehose of information. Where do I even start with everything she just said?

What is *casual* to people who own a yacht like this? Trailer life didn't prepare me for dinner with a couple worth more digits in their bank account than I have letters in my name.

The bigger issue is that Lexie didn't leave, and her parents are here. "Those women didn't go home?"

"Unfortunately, no." Elena sticks out her tongue and crosses her eyes. "They're annoying. Anyway, Mom and Dad need to talk logistics for their visit, and it's better to do that without listening ears."

I swallow hard. What the heck have I walked into?

I add my shorts to the suitcase. "I'll go back to my grandma's house. Thanks for last night, but this is ..."

"A lot?"

"Yeah."

She flips the suitcase lid closed. "I'm only going to say this once. If you still want to leave, I'll let you, but first you need to know something. Are you listening?"

I twist my mouth and give a single nod. "I'm listening."

"You owe me."

That wasn't what I expected her to say. I take a step back. "What do you want?"

"Our deal was I give you a room." She waves her hands to encompass our surroundings. "And you make me dinner. You can't cook tonight, so you have to cook tomorrow. But then that earns me another meal, so I guess you're stuck for a couple days."

"Do they teach blackmail to you rich girls?"

"*Us rich girls.*" She flops the suitcase open again. "We have more work to do then I thought." She takes my shorts out of the suitcase, opens a drawer, and drops them in. "This whole *us* and *them* thing is stopping right now. We are friends. If I needed a place to stay, you would let me sleep on your floor in a sleeping bag, so stop pretending like I don't want you here, you're not my real friend, or you owe me anything."

"But you said I owe you dinner tomorrow."

"That was just to get your attention. I don't care if you cook or not. That's up to you. I want my friend to feel comfortable staying in my home. Can you manage that?"

I rub my thumb along the hem of my shirt. She's right. I've never felt like relationships are transactional before, so why am I starting now?

Being a Bubble is a gift not the reward for good behavior.

The boat and its trappings make me uncomfortable. I don't know how to behave. I don't know the manners or etiquette expected of me. I don't want to accidentally bump into a vase of flowers and end up with a thousand dollar bill.

I fill my lungs and hold the air in tight, slowly letting it out to recenter myself.

"Thank you, Elena."

Her arms wrap around me, and I feel lighter. I'm still worried, but I can get through anything. I can adapt and find my way.

She grabs another handful of clothes out of my garbage bag and folds them in the dresser or hangs them in the closet. When she gets to my orange silk dress with tiny pearls along the hem, she holds it up to my side. "Wear this to dinner."

"You said casual."

"I know, but this dress is too pretty to be in a closet. I'll dress up too if that makes you feel better."

"It's not too much?"

"It'll be perfect." Something dances in her eyes that I don't understand. "Be ready at 6:30."

After a shower to wash the coffee smell from my skin, I steam the wrinkles from my best dress. When I'm dressed, hair curled, makeup applied to cover the last traces of my bruises, I admire myself in the full-length mirror. The dress cinches at the waist and then flares to my mid-calf. It makes my hair look like a darker auburn than carrots, which I love.

At 6:30, Elena knocks on my door. "Ready?" Her turquoise sheath dress shimmers.

I step into the hallway and wiggle my toes. "I left my heels at the trailer."

She slides her feet out of her shoes and tosses them though her doorway. "Barefoot it is." She weaves her arm though mine. "You look beautiful. The dress was a good pick."

A door clicks shut behind us. Theo's navy suit and a pale pink tie make his brown eyes look more like Nutella than I've ever seen before. I bite my tongue to keep myself from licking my lips.

He's the kind of delicious that goes straight to your hips. No amount of cardio or squats will take off those pounds.

A slow smile spreads across his face like he's reading my mind. "Aren't you two lovely this evening?"

I ignore the flutter in my chest. I point at his suit "This is what qualifies as casual at Sanchez family dinner?"

His long fingers spread across his stomach and smooth nonexistent wrinkles from his jacket. "Not all of us are naturally stunning."

My cheeks burn, and Elena rolls her eyes. "Mom and Dad are waiting." She tugs my arm, and I fall in behind her. I can't help myself. I peek over my shoulder.

Theo rubs his thumb along his lower lip as his eyes run from the top of my head to my bare feet.

I try to remember that I hate him. I don't want to be objectified because I look nice in a dress.

But when was the last time anyone looked at me with that much desire?

The night you kissed him, remember?

The night I thought his promises were sincere and I let myself get swept away in the magic in his eyes.

Remember the next weekend? Irritating Lexie and handsy Viola? He brought them to the coffee shop like trophies for you to admire. To show you how little you meant to him. Then chose to help Viola instead of talking to you about what was happening. Remember all of that?

The memory sobers me.

I remember.

Theo's eyes tell lies I can't let myself believe, no matter how nice it feels. Feelings are fickle and fleeting.

Besides, I can't get distracted. Staying here is a short-term solution. I need to get home to protect the people I love.

On the main deck, Elena's parents stand by the living room windows holding glasses of champagne —I'm assuming—based on the bubbles.

Sanchez III is handsome in that silver fox kind of way. His hair has greyed at the temples giving him a distinguished air only compounded by his erect posture, broad shoulders, and keen eyes.

I wouldn't want to face him in a boardroom.

And ... crap ... Theo is going to age magnificently.

His mom is no different. In a tailored white suit with three-inch ruby-red heels, she could be a model or the president of the United States. Where Theo's dad is hard angles, his mom's expression is sweet softness. Cotton candy to his Jolly Rancher.

Elena pops up on her toes and kisses her dad's cheek. "This is Georgi." She hugs her mom. "Georgi, these are my parents, Ted and Corine Sanchez."

I'm not sure if I'm supposed to curtsy or shake their hands, so I do a weird little knee bend, partial bow thing that makes Theo chuff out a laugh. Elena backhands him in the stomach.

Ted takes my hand. "Wonderful to meet you. How do you know our children?"

I'm not sure which answer to give. *Theo swept me off my feet and then proved himself a playboy.* Or *I am the homeless barista they showed pity on and let stay on your floating palace.*

Elena grips my elbow and hugs me tight. "Georgi invited me to a get together on the beach with a bunch of her friends when I was feeling lonely."

Corine's hand joins Elena's on my arm and gives a gentle squeeze. "What a sweetheart you are."

"It's nothing compared to you guys letting me stay here."

"Oh, nonsense. We have more room than we have ever been able to fill," Ted says.

Theo runs his hand through his hair and shakes his head, but he doesn't say anything.

I've seen the boat illuminated in the early hours of the morning with what looked like a hundred people partying. Do they not know about Theo's activities?

"Would anyone, besides Elena of course, like a glass of champagne?" their dad asks.

Theo declines. I decline as well.

The taste would be lost on me anyway. If I'm not making sangria, six-dollar bottles of Arbor Mist are more my speed.

Theo's hand finds its way to the small of my back. Tingles shoot up my spine. I step away, but he applies gentle pressure, steering me toward the dining area. "Shall we sit down to dinner?"

He guides me to the table and pulls out my chair then slides into the place next to mine. Elena frowns at her brother but sits across from us as Ted and Corine take the heads.

Plates of macadamia-crusted mahi-mahi with green beans and roasted red potatoes are placed in front of us. The whole table takes their first bites in silence. The contradiction of the fish melting across my tongue and the crunch of the macadamia nuts causes a moan to escape from my chest.

Theo nudges my elbow. "That good?"

"I've never had this before. It's divine."

"What's your favorite food?" Theo draws my attention to his mouth, placing a bite between his teeth and sliding the fork out.

I nibble on my cheek. Sitting at a table which costs more than I make in a month eating a meal which costs more than I make a day, I can't bring myself to tell them.

I drop my gaze to my plate and take another bite.

"What is it? Can't be that bad." Elena points at her brother. "Theo's favorite food is Lucky Charms."

I raise my eyebrow.

Theo points his fork at his sister. "They're delicious."

"Do you eat it all together or do you save marshmallows for the end?" I ask.

He leans closer. His breath rustles the hair on my neck. "I don't like to wait for the good parts. I want every bite to be as delicious as possible."

He's talking about cereal, but his answer feels deeper and more provocative than simply liking his marshmallows mixed with his toasted oats.

Is he talking about all of life?

Is he the kind of guy who, when presented with the Oreo patience challenge, goes ahead and eats the one Oreo instead of waiting for the second?

Being a woman who's never had one Oreo, I'm not sure what I would choose, but his intense stare makes me want to find out.

"Impatience is just one of our son's shortcomings." Ted scoops a bite into his mouth. "I hear you weren't the best host to our other guests this weekend."

Theo drops his gaze to his lap, his jaw tightens, and his ears turn pink.

"Ted, manners." Corine scolds.

"Elena and I went for a run." Theo pushes the food around his plate.

"Where was Calum?"

"It was late. We didn't want to bother him. I needed the workout too."

Ted dabs his napkin to his lips. "You shouldn't abandon our guests, especially at such a late hour. I expect better as we prepare for the gala."

"Gala?" Elena says while Theo says, "Yes, sir."

Silence falls. Silverware clinks on the porcelain plates. I want to break the awkward tension, but this isn't my home. It's not my table.

Why is Theo's dad so upset about one run? Theo can't be expected to be available twenty-four-seven. There aren't many staff members on the boat, but there are enough to help anyone who might need something.

Elena said the parties aren't Theo's idea. Does that mean he doesn't want to be part of them at all?

Elena finally breaks the silence. "Dad, a gala?"

"A fundraiser for cancer survivors. We haven't hosted one at the yacht club yet, so we decided, since Don Carmichael wanted to spend time in Bubee, we'll take advantage of the gathering. Theo, you will help your mother organize a bachelor auction and raffle prizes over the next three weeks. No more lunches in Houston until after the event."

While Elena, Ted, and Corine talk about the party, Theo hunches into himself and pushes the food around on his plate. I pull my phone out of my pocket. Under the table, I type in the notes app.

> *My favorite is macaroni and cheese, so I guess you and I are good company.*

I pretend to be interested in what Ted's saying, leaning my chin on my hand while I press the phone against the side of Theo's thigh.

He frowns. I poke him again and lay the phone on his knee.

He grabs it before it falls and reads the message.

Theo's cheek twitches. He types and hands my phone back. His fingers brush mine. The rough callouses on the tips rasp against my skin like my favorite worn pair of jeans.

I read his message.

> *The best.*

I sit straighter in my chair and will myself not to look at Theo's cloaked smile. He's happier. That's all that matters. "Mr. Sanchez will you tell me more about your business?"

Ted's eyes brighten. "We started making anesthesia machines and have branched out into numerous other biomedical technologies."

"Is that why you're an anesthesiologist?" I ask Theo.

"Partially. I—"

Ted's fork pings against his plate. "An MBA would have served him better."

I blink at Ted. Every time he opens his mouth, he attacks Theo. Why isn't he proud of his son?

I've heard of tough love, but this is ridiculous. What's up with this family dynamic?

Ted's just being mean.

"About that, Dad. I want to shadow the manager in the factory here. Learn more about the management and logistics side of the business. Since Elena's here, it would be better if I stay in town during her training anyway."

"You have enough to do, especially now that you'll be helping your mom organize this fundraiser. You will be the finale of the bachelor auction. Recruit other men who will encourage the highest bids."

Theo dabs his lips and places his napkin next to his plate. "I can balance working at the factory with my other responsibilities."

"You aren't ready." Ted's tone is cutting and final.

Theo turns his attention to his almost full plate. Not eating. Not talking.

I want his smile back. It's not right for such a handsome face to be so weary.

It takes a sheer act of will for me not to yell at Ted. He's my host. I will respect him.

But, gees! What the heck?

What happened for Ted to be so hurtful toward his son?

Why won't he let Theo take an active role in the factory here?

Did Theo do something to lose his dad's respect?

It can't just be his and Elena's run yesterday.

If it were, Ted would be sniping at her too, but he's not. He hasn't said one unkind word to Elena all evening.

His insults are purely, precisely, unerringly aimed at Theo.

Or is Ted a jerk who needs a good talking-to? Like Hoyt needs a stay in prison?

At least with my broken family, I know the rules. Hoyt's in charge. Everyone stays out of his way. We love each other the best we can. We carry each other's burdens however we are able.

Elena hasn't spoken up to defend Theo once. He's alone. That's not how families are supposed to love each other.

I can't let the smile I brought him earlier be the last one I see.

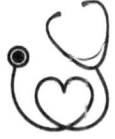

Chapter 12

Theo

LESSON ONE IN *How to Embarrass Yourself in Front of the Woman You Love*.

1. Fall in love on your first date, then subsequently introduce her to the women your dad forces you to entertain, so she hates you.

2. Try to explain what happened over and over to try to win her back, but never make any progress because you can't stop bringing guests to her coffee shop.

3. Find out your love is homeless, but she rejects your offer of help.

4. When your sister convinces your love to move in, have your parents host a dinner in which they insult you and criticize your life choices.

5. Sit in stunned silence because you know they are right, and you will never do enough to earn her love. Just like you lost theirs.

6. When your love passes you a note to lift your spirits, contain yourself and don't start dreaming about running away with her.

7. Fall back into despair when your dad rejects your proposal to play a bigger role in the family business and adds layers to his disapproval.

Thank you for attending my class. Don't repeat my mistakes.

Chapter 13

Georgi

AFTER CHANGING OUT OF my dress and washing the makeup off my face, I knock on Elena's door. I need clarity, and I don't trust myself to ask Theo.

"What's up?" She leans her cheek against the doorframe. She changed into her pajamas—buffalo plaid shorts and a T-shirt from a swimming competition—and braided her hair into adorable pigtails.

Sometimes I forget she's so much younger than me. Right now, she's so much like Tipsy—youthful, innocent ... not naive, but I can't think of the right word, maybe uncorrupted and positive.

Does she see how her dad treats Theo? Or is this about to be the rudest of awakenings?

"Can we talk?"

"Of course." She grabs a sweater from the back of her chair. "Let's go outside. I'm tired of this stuffy cabin."

I grab my sweatshirt, and we climb the stairs to the top deck. She grabs throw blankets from a cabinet by the door, and we snuggle down. "What do you want to talk about?"

Subtlety has never been my specialty, so I don't start now. "Why was your dad so mean to Theo at dinner?"

If you'd asked me before the meal, I would have told you I'd take solace in seeing Theo's confidence ratcheted down.

But watching the scene unfold at dinner made me feel sorry for him.

No one should ever be insulted or demeaned the way he was.

People deserve to be loved regardless of their accomplishments, not because of them. Theo's dad doesn't get that.

Even if we only judged Theo by his accomplishments, he's a freaking physician. He has an MD after his name. That should be worth a heck of a lot.

Elena rubs the soft blanket against her cheek. "Dad hasn't always been. Theo ... well, he ..." Tears spring to her eyes. She takes a ragged breath and thumbs the moisture from the corners of her eyes. "Theo made some bad decisions a few years ago ... he wasn't there for me when I needed him. He hasn't earned back Dad's trust."

"What did—" Elena's face is crumpling, and this was not supposed to be a conversation in which I make her cry. That's not why I'm here. I don't need the details. It's none of my business.

I can't reconcile the overprotective brother I've seen these last few weeks with a man who would let her down so completely that even the memory of the event makes her cry.

Nothing matters more to Theo than Elena, her health, and her success. I can't imagine him letting her down.

Yes, he let me down, but I'm not his sister. He doesn't love me—never could love me—with the depth that he loves her.

Even if he did make a mistake, that's no reason for his dad to be so mean. Kids make mistakes. Families forgive, learn, and move on. Theo doesn't deserve to continue to be punished for something he did years ago.

Even my anger will cool, given enough time.

"Your dad doesn't seem proud of Theo at all. That remark about medical school being a waste of time. Did you see Theo's face?" I wanted to hug him, use my body as a shield against the barbed words, and give his dad a piece of my mind, but my position is tenuous.

It's selfish of me—and so much like my mom not helping me with Hoyt that my stomach turns—but it's the truth.

Maybe I can help his dad mellow out if I spend more time with the Sanchezes. If I can't move home and help Tipsy, I can help heal the rift between father and son.

Elena sits straighter and leans on her fists. "But Dad's right. How does being a doctor help him run our company?"

"I don't know, but when Theo asked about the factory, your dad said no. How does hosting parties, or whatever he's doing here, help?"

"More business happens on this boat than in Dad's office." Her response sounds canned, like she's been trained to say it.

Are their parents here as often as Theo is? I don't watch the boat like I'm the CIA, but I haven't seen them around town once.

None of it dismisses or excuses Ted's behavior toward his son or explains Theo's whipped-puppy reaction.

"Your dad shouldn't talk to Theo the way he does. Why does Theo just sit there and take it?"

She stares pointedly at me. "He's good at brushing off negativity."

"Me?"

"How many times has he asked you out? Begged you to forgive him for a dumb mistake?"

"We aren't talking about me." This is different.

"You can sit in judgement on my dad, but when I hold the mirror up to your behavior, you shy away? How's that fair?"

"It's not the same." We aren't here to talk about my relationship with Theo.

Elena snorts. "Close enough. Theo wants you to like him, but you're rude and condescending when he tries to be your friend."

"He doesn't want to be my friend."

She settles back in her chair. "You're right. He wants so much more."

The vision of Theo in his towel jumps unbidden to my mind. I turn my face to the water to cover my blush. "No, he doesn't." At least my words sound full of conviction.

If Elena's assertion were true, he wouldn't bring the entourage to see me. He'd come alone. He'd talk to me.

Like he used to? When you were too mad, too stubborn to listen?

Shut up, brain.

Elena swings her legs off the edge of her lounger and leans into me. "If he doesn't want to date you, why do you think he keeps asking?"

"Because he doesn't like to lose."

Because he wants to embarrass me and soothe his ego since I didn't fall for his show the second time he came to the coffee shop. Because we're in this time loop, and every weekend we are doomed repeat the worst day of my life.

She points toward the stairs. "Ask him."

"No, thanks."

"You know I'm right."

"Theo's a smooth talker. He knows how to make people think and feel exactly what he wants them to."

Elena's eyebrow cocks. "If that were true, don't you think he'd wrap my dad around his finger?"

My mouth moves to contradict her, but I don't have an answer. I flap my lips like they can come up with a rebuttal.

They can't.

She's right.

Theo should be able to charm his way into his dad's good graces. Why hasn't he?

What's stopping him?

I don't want to consider that I've been wrong about him all along. I want to keep the wall between us.

In what world could Theo and I be a couple? Not this one.

Not one in which being an anesthesiologist isn't good enough to earn Theo's parents' respect. What happens when he brings home the small-town barista and declares his love for her?

Nothing good.

Not for Theo.

Not for me.

But that doesn't mean I can't be kinder to him. Make up for the harsh criticism I've doled out like his dad.

I can be his friend.

How do I do that? Where do I start?

How will he interpret my behavior?

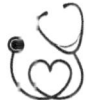

Theo

An hour and fifteen minutes in the flume pool, and my head isn't any clearer than when I woke up.

I don't want to be part of my parents' gala. I don't want to be auctioned to raise money. I don't want to sit through another meal with my dad telling me what a screw-up I am.

I already know I'm not the son he hoped I would be.

I've let him down.

All I ever wanted was to make him proud of me, like he used to be. After dinner last night, I'm out of ideas.

I need a cup of coffee and a hot shower. As I approach the kitchen, mugs clink. Something metal hits something else metal.

It's too early for Judah to cook breakfast. It's probably Georgi again. I don't want to scare her out of the kitchen like yesterday. She should feel at home.

There's no other way to my room, though. Maybe if I'm quick, she won't see me.

I peek around the corner. Yep, Georgi's at the stove. She turns and I whip my head back.

"Theo?"

I grind my teeth. Stupid. I should have slunk past. I step so she sees me through the door and raise my hands. "I was just walking past."

Her face falls. "Oh. Okay."

Is she sorry I'm not stopping?

That can't be right.

I push my luck. "What are you doing?"

She scrunches her nose. "I ... umm ..." She lifts a plate. "I made you breakfast. There weren't any Lucky Charms, but I remember from our walk ... before everything ... you like scrambled eggs, so ... yeah."

I squeeze the doorframe, so I don't do something stupid like gather her in my arms and kiss her until she swoons. Despite everything, she remembered.

And she cooked.

"I love eggs. Thanks." I take the plate from her. There aren't any other plates on the countertops. "Did you make yourself breakfast?"

She refuses to meet my gaze. "No. I'll eat at work."

I don't want her to leave. I can only guess what caused this truce, but I want to savor it. "We can share these. Please, have some."

She reaches up like she's going to touch my shoulder but stops mid-motion. Twisting her hands together instead. "That's okay. I'll see you later." She dashes out of the room.

I stare at the plate.

Georgi made me breakfast.

She made me one of my favorite breakfasts.

I set the plate on the counter and grab a fork. The eggs are light and fluffy with a hint of salt, pepper, and melted goat cheese. The coffee maker is full of warm coffee and a note card has the letters T and H with a hesitation mark scrawled in the middle.

My smile is gigantic, and I don't bother hiding it.

The only thing that changed between yesterday and today was dinner.

Breakfast may have been spawned out of pity, but I'll take it.

I'll take anything Georgi's willing to offer.

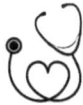

Theo

I'm still on cloud nine when Dad calls me into his office. "I have errands for you to run." He hands me a list of businesses. "Please convince them to donate to your mother's fundraiser."

It's an easy enough task. One I've done a hundred times for Mom's other fundraisers.

Any step away from the blender and the sunscreen is a win.

I can get off the boat and show my dad I'm useful. After last night's refusal to let me work at the factory, I thought entertaining guests would be the sum of my responsibilities. Lexie, the girls, and their parents will be back later, so there are pillows to fluff and margaritas to pre-mix.

None of which teaches me to follow in Dad's footsteps.

How far away is the day when he will call me into the office and open the accounting software to teach me his trade?

Hopefully not too much longer.

Honey Beans is conspicuously absent from my list of potential donors, but I might make a last-minute addition. I'd like to see Georgi before this evening. It will be pressing my luck, but I can't get those eggs—or her kindness—out of my head.

My first stop is Sobre las Rocas. Most people frequent the restaurant and dive bar for their margaritas, but they also make the best chilis rellenos in town.

I have no idea if Georgi likes spicy food. It's not something we covered in our year of her yelling at me to get out of her coffee shop. I'll have to ask. Maybe she'll have dinner with me without my parents or sister present.

Barbara is at the hostess stand wiping down menus when I climb the ramp to the elevated restaurant. The owner spent her formative years in Mexico before her parents returned to Texas. She brought back her love of Mexican cuisine, and thankfully shares it with our town.

"Good morning, Barbara."

She wraps me in a hug. "What are you doing here alone this early? And on a Monday?"

I tell her about the fundraiser and ask if she's willing to donate to Mom's raffle. I would prefer her restaurant cater the event, but Mom and Dad like to serve bland food to their uptight guests. It keeps them circulating, which makes them spend more money on the fundraising items.

By lunchtime, I've secured donations from Sobre, Love Bugs Tacos, Jake's BBQ, the Del Mar Inn, and several of the novelty stores along Tiburon Ave.

The next stop on my list gives me pause. I'm not sure why my dad included Buchanan Automotive and Towing, but he has.

I don't like the idea of coming face-to-face with Georgi's uncle. My opinion of the man can't get any lower. Between what he did to that little boy at Thanksgiving and the bruises and split lip he gave Georgi, I'm not sure I trust myself to hold my tongue.

If I don't stop, Dad will ask why I skipped it. That will lead to a conversation about why Georgi needed a place to stay.

He could get judgmental. I want my parents to love Georgi as much as I do, so I'll go and use it as an opportunity to understand Georgi better.

I pass the hospital on the way to Buchanan Automotive. A twinge in my heart misses the rigor and excitement of patient care.

But that was my old life, one I can never have back.

It gives me an idea, though. Keegan's not single, but he knows the physicians who are. I bet I can find volunteers for the bachelor auction amongst their numbers. I send Keegan a text and ask him to meet me at his earliest convenience.

Buchanan Automotive is a steel building with four service bays and a small office. With Hoyt's reputation, it's amazing he runs a thriving business, but the well-maintained machinery and updated interior tell a tale of prosperity.

If Hoyt can sustain this level of success, it doesn't make sense that Georgi's worried about them having enough to eat and clothes to wear.

Or does Hoyt not share with his nieces and nephew? Could someone else be responsible for Buchanan Automotive's lucrative standing?

Another mystery in the Buchanan-Montgomery family tree.

Harry Buchanan is at the service desk when I enter. Grease stains the coveralls tied around his waist. His white shirt's not as white as the day he pulled it from the ten-pack's plastic.

"How can I help you?" Georgi's cousin asks. Dark brown hair flops across his forehead.

I extend my hand across the counter. "We haven't met. I'm Theo Sanchez."

"Everyone knows who you are." He crosses his arms over his chest, adding an extra flex to his biceps, like that intimidates me. "How can I help you?" he repeats.

I retract my hand and ignore his glare. "My parents are hosting a fundraiser to benefit cancer survivors. We hoped your company would participate and donate services. Maybe a mechanic or two will participate in the bachelor auction."

Harry rests his hands on the desk. "My dad makes those decisions." His fingers grip the plastic like he doesn't like the answer. Is Harry the one keeping this place solvent? That's a question for another day.

"Is your dad around?"

"He's out on a run."

It's on the tip of my tongue to ask if it's a beer run, but that won't endear me to Harry. I don't need to give the Buchanan men something else to hold against Georgi.

"Can I leave my card? Have him call me?" I pull my wallet from my back pocket and hand him the navy-blue business card.

He flicks it with his finger. "No promises."

"How about you? We would appreciate you being part of the bachelor auction."

A humorless laugh dribbles from his mouth. "Waste of time. No one'd bid on me."

"You don't know that. Some of my mom's friends like the blue-collar type."

He rolls his fist, flexing his forearms. "I've got better things to do than embarrass myself in front of your mama's rich friends."

"If you change your mind." I tap the card. "It's for a good cause."

He tosses the card on the desk, grabs a stack of invoices, and pushes through to the back office, dismissing me.

At least I can check them off the list.

In the garage, Tipsy sits on a stool in the corner typing information into the computer. I check my watch. It's not late enough for the high school to have been dismissed already.

What's she doing here?

Georgi told my sister she hasn't been able to contact her cousin since she moved out. I'd love to facilitate a reunion. Repay Georgi's kindness from breakfast.

Harry's not watching, so I let myself in. A couple of the mechanics are working on cars, but none of them pay attention to me. I recognize a woman from their sangria parties changing the oil on an old Chevy.

"Tipsy?"

Georgi's cousin slowly turns in her chair, her eyes wide.

I raise my hand. "Hi, I'm Theo."

Her eyes dart to the door I used to enter the garage. "You shouldn't be back here."

"I know. I just wanted to say hi and invite you to the boat. Georgi misses you."

She chews her lip. "I can't go there."

"Why not?"

"Dad won't let me."

"If you change your mind, the door is always open."

An engine rumbles in the back. Her eyes widen. She slides off the stool. "Dad's back. You need to go."

"I'm here to speak to him."

She grabs my elbow and spins me away from the sound, toward the big garage doors. "He's been in a bad mood all day. Come back tomorrow. Maybe he'll be better."

My desire to please my dad wars with my desire to take Tipsy's advice. If I can cross all the donors off my list in one day, Dad will trust me with the next task. "Are you sure?"

"Yeah." She pushes me toward the door. "Tell Georgi hi for me."

"Tell her yourself." I press another one of my business cards into her hand. "Saturday we're taking a picnic to the barrier islands. Come with us."

"I'll try."

It's something.

And if she can take a risk, so can I.

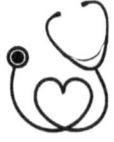

Chapter 14

Theo

MY FINGERS DRUM RESTLESSLY on my steering wheel. Parked outside Sanchez Biotech's Bubee factory, I contemplate my life choices.

My sweaty hand drifts to the door release.

The Bubee factory is like most other warehouses. A hundred thousand square feet of machines, conveyor belts, and people working hard to provide for their families.

I could walk through the front door and ask to see the manager.

Easy.

Jess Tanaka is beloved by the employees and treats everyone like a sibling. She's been the manager for five years. Most of the time she is smiles and laughter, but if a member of this family makes a mistake, she's not afraid to let them know.

She's the kind of leader I hope to be one day.

We've met a handful of times, but none of those were enough to encourage the good opinion I have of her.

How do I know so much about her when Dad refuses to let me shadow her?

The only way I can: HR files and the town gossip mill.

Without a doubt, if I ask to see her, she'll tell my dad.

I slide my hand along my thigh and dry it off, then place it on the steering wheel.

Am I willing to cross Dad to move my career forward? What happens when he finds out I'm searching for new mentors?

Weekday lunches have helped me get to know the employees on a personal level, but I don't know how to run the company. I don't know how to manage people and supply chairs. I can do more for our family than entertain Lexie and her ilk.

Dad doesn't see the difference between the kind of friendship my dad has with Lexie's dad, and I have with Lexie.

Dad would never rub sunscreen on Don Carmichael's back. Mom would never scour the ship to find a missing diamond earring. Dad wouldn't apologize for taking a run after dark while Don had his after-dinner cognac.

Does anyone else see the double standard besides me? Why have I lived this way for so long?

There are better ways to help my family than hosting parties. There have to be.

I open the door and stride toward the front of the building with purpose. Ms. Tanaka will tell my dad, but he'll get over the disobedience—like he got over me going to medical school.

Someday he'll appreciate my decisive efforts to become a true asset to our company and family.

Someday he'll see I've put everything he holds dear before what I want and forgive me for the biggest mistake of my life.

He'll let me be the son I long to be.

Georgi

"Turkey or ham?" Elena holds up two packages of cold cuts.

"Turkey, please." I slice apples into wedges and arrange them in plastic containers with grapes, strawberries, and kiwi. "I can't remember the last time I went on a picnic."

"They're always part of the party itinerary."

The last week on the boat has been enlightening. Elena spends most of her time training and eating. Her level of dedication and the sameness of her days would drive me crazy.

She's in the pool by six a.m., runs, bikes, lifts weights, and practices yoga. Every meal is identical except for slight variations when she eats dinner with her family. After dinner, she and I sit on deck talking about everything and nothing until she can't keep her eyes open.

Theo swims every morning and spends the rest of his day either at the desk in his room poring over paperwork or talking to business owners in the community organizing the fundraiser. After dinner, he disappears into his room and shuts the door.

I've been tempted to invite him on deck with Elena and me, but it feels awkward to invite him to do something in his home. Plus, I don't think he wants to intrude on our girl talk.

There have been moments when I've wondered how he would respond to one of Elena's questions or if he has a silly side note to add to a story.

Lexie, Viola, Avery, and Alexis come and go like this is a five-star hotel. Somedays they're here. Other days they stay in their parents' rentals.

Either way, I avoid them.

After a day behind the espresso machine, I just don't have the energy to deal with Lexie's sneers and upturned nose.

Friday, several new carloads of families, loaded down with three or four suitcases per person, descended on the boat.

Corine never gave Elena a straight answer as to why there are more guests this weekend. I would expect more people for the gala, but why now, two weeks before the party?

I guess it doesn't matter.

Ted and Corine hosted a dinner party with dancing until midnight last night. Elena and I hid in her room. Cars collected the guests with younger children and took them to the Del Mar Inn and Sophia's Bed and Breakfast at the end of the night

Today is beach picnic day. Since there are so many more guests than normal, Judah recruited Elena and me to help pack the picnic baskets.

I'm excited to be invited. Honey Beans doesn't need me today. Elena has a "day off," meaning she doesn't have to be in the pool, even though she still has to run and lift weights later.

Elena holds up two loaves of bread. "How many more sandwiches?"

"All of it." Judah places six bottles of sparkling cider in a cooler.

"She's in here," Theo's voice says behind me. I turn, his voice like a magnet.

But Tipsy's in the doorway.

I drop my knife on the wooden cutting board, squeak like Elena, and wrap my cousin in the tightest hug I can. "What are you doing here?"

Her gaze darts to the empty doorway behind her. "Theo invited me."

I release her from my hug. "That was sweet of him." Where'd he go?

Elena clears her throat.

"Oh, sorry. Elena, this is Tipsy. Tipsy, Elena, Theo's sister." I point to the chef. "That's Judah." He salutes and returns to decorating mini chocolate cakes with white chocolate curls.

Tipsy shyly waves. "Hi."

Elena raises her eyebrow. "Sorry, you need to explain your name. I thought Theo's unending moniker was bad."

"It's a nickname," I say.

"I fell over a lot as a kid," Tipsy says at the same time.

I loop my arm over her shoulder. "Your brothers pushed you down a lot. There's a difference."

"Kids will be kids." Elena removes the loaf of bread from the bag. "Theo calls me Pipsqueak because I used to squeak when I laughed."

I point at her. "You still squeak. And squeal."

Elena holds up the lunch meats. "Tipsy, turkey or ham?"

Tipsy leans on the bar. "Ham sounds good."

I retrieve my knife and resume cutting fruit. Tipsy joins the fun and mixes dips, per Judah's instructions.

To say I'm excited to have Tipsy hip-to-hip with me is an understatement. It's hard to concentrate on the fruit because I keep sneaking peeks out the corner of my eye to make sure she's real.

I need to find Theo, say thank you, and figure out how he got around my uncle.

"I've missed you so much! How are things at home?" I ask.

Her eyes dart to Elena. "Same."

"She knows." There's no reason for Tipsy to keep secrets. I'd rather she feel free to talk. That's the downside of me being gone and not having a way to talk to her. She can't tell me what horrible things are happening that I need to help her with. At least she still has Lee.

"Dad's been in a bad mood. He talked to his lawyer the other day, and I guess the guy had bad news."

"Did Aunt Imogen tell you anything?"

"I only work a couple hours a week for her anymore. Dad needs me to help with the bookkeeping at the shop."

"Isn't that Harry's job?"

She just shrugs. "I'm good with numbers."

I love the pride and sense of accomplishment in her voice. "That's the truth. He couldn't count to ten with his fingers and his toes."

Elena snorts.

I shrug my shoulder. "Not all of us have geniuses in our families. That side of our box is missing most of its crayons."

Theo walks into the kitchen with his arms full of grocery bags. He stops behind me, his breath ruffling the hairs at the back of my neck. "Did you refer to me as a genius?"

My stomach bottoms out. I recover with a winning smile. "I was talking about your mom."

"Perfect." Judah claps and instructs Theo to put the delivery on the counter.

I use the distraction to hide slow, steadying breaths.

Yes, I was talking about him.

No, I do not want him to know that.

Theo sets the bags down and unloads pasta of various shapes and sizes. "Mom is the brains of the operation." But the way he's staring at me makes me think he doesn't believe my line.

It's partially true.

From what I can tell, Corine is whip smart, but her heart is her main attraction. She's the only explanation for why her kids are humble and compassionate.

I wouldn't have attributed those traits to Theo a week ago, but now I see them clearly in how he dotes on his sister, helps his mom, and works hard for his dad.

Judah points from me to the grocery bags to the pantry.

I follow Theo with several cans of tomatoes. "Thanks for inviting Tipsy." I can't believe he invited her. Giddiness is evident in my voice. "When did you do that?"

He leans back on the shelf and crosses his ankles. "The day you made the eggs. Her dad's garage was on the list of donors for the gala fundraiser. I thought you'd like to see her."

"I did." I straighten the tomato can on the shelf. "I do."

He grabs another box from the bag and places it on the shelf. "Plus, I owed you for the eggs."

I nudge his arm. "No, you didn't. I didn't cook so you'd feel obligated to pay me back."

He stands to his full height. I tip my head up to meet his gaze. It darts back and forth between my eyes. "Pity is a better reason?"

I chew the inside of my cheek but will my eyes to stay glued to his.

It was a little bit about pity, but also, Theo deserves to know people care about him. How do I say that without giving him the wrong impression? I don't forgive him for lying to me, for repeatedly parading his entourages through my coffee shop, but I don't hate him quite as much anymore.

I don't hate him at all.

Those words stick in my throat.

Theo continues to examine my face as if he can read me like a book. "That's what I thought," he says. "You felt bad because my dad was a jerk, but you didn't want to apologize for all the times you were exactly the same, so instead you made me pity eggs."

He and Elena must have talked. What he's saying and what she said are too similar for it to be a coincidence. "That's not fair."

"That's how it is. I'm glad Tipsy is here, but if you want to do something for me, do it because you want to, not to make yourself feel better." He brushes past me into the kitchen.

I press my forehead against the edge of the shelf. He's right. I tried to cover my bad behavior with eggs.

I don't know why I care so much, but I want Theo to be my friend.

It's a new revelation. One I never thought I'd want.

But it's there all the same.

In the last week, Theo has gone from my second least favorite person (Hoyt will always be number one) to someone I look forward to seeing every day.

I want to be Theo's friend.

I want him to smile more.

I don't hate him.

I refuse to let him think I do anything out of pity.

We need to have an uncomfortable conversation.

Maybe if we'd had one a year ago, we wouldn't be in this situation.

And that's on me.

Chapter 15

Theo

I HAVEN'T SEEN ELENA laugh this much since she was twelve and shot milk out her nose at our grandpa's birthday party. She sits with Tipsy and Georgi on the beach building a sandcastle.

Asking Georgi to hang out with Elena was the perfect solution to the stress my sister faces. Adding Tipsy—who is closer in age to Elena than Georgi—makes it even better.

Their fast friendship gives me hope for all of us.

Georgi and I have moved out of the Hate Zone—and I couldn't be more thankful for that—but I don't want her to be nice to me because she pities me. I want her to be nice to me because she wants to be.

Georgi was referring to me when she talked about geniuses. Her cheeks don't let her lie. They flamed bright pink despite her fake smile.

The compliment flustered me so much, I picked a fight in the pantry. I shouldn't have. I should have braced my arms on either side of her and confessed I think she's a genius too.

She's the most emotionally intelligent woman I know. She reads people. She understands what they need. She gives wholeheartedly.

Until I know Georgi's motivations are sincere, I can't let my heart hope.

My dad is the way he is. He expects a lot from me, so I strive to make him proud and live up to his expectations. That's what every good son does.

Once I work my way back into his good graces, he'll forgive me. He won't be quick with his judgmental comments. He'll be a dad who is excited to introduce his impressive and trustworthy son to clients and business associates again.

My dad organized an over-the-top armada to Willard Island—one of the barrier islands in the bay—with several other families from the yacht club for today's picnic.

Our guests divided amongst the sailboats, motor yachts, and catamarans. After we picnicked with the families on Judah's delicious delicacies, my parents and their friends eagerly retired to the shade on the boats, leaving the younger generations in my care scattered along the beach.

They've created little groups based on age. The elementary- and middle school-aged kids are flying kites in the dunes. The teenagers are skimboarding in the water. Georgi, Tipsy, and Elena play while Lexie and her friends tan on the sand.

"Lexie, can I get you guys anything?" I gesture to the water bottles and sunscreen in the wagon behind me.

Viola props up on her elbows. "Sunscreen my back."

Cabana boy at their service. I grab the SPF-75 and lather it in my hands. She flips her ponytail off her back and leans forward. "This isn't as fun with all the little kids."

"Too much screeching." Lexie twists the top from a water bottle and takes a small sip. "Not enough daiquiris."

"Mom has piña coladas onboard."

"I don't want to hang out with my dad," says one of the Gusman twins—they're identical, and I can't tell them apart when their faces are buried in their towels.

I finish rubbing in Viola's sunscreen and offer my hands to the other girls. The last thing we need is for them to burn. I would never hear the end of it, and I don't want to spend the rest of the weekend applying aloe vera and cold compresses.

Been there.

Hated it.

Lexie unties her bikini and hugs the material to her chest. "Me too."

I add more lotion to my hands and rub it in. She lifts her arm, presenting me the side of her breast.

I hold in my groan. I will not lotion her chest. She can handle that body part. I wipe the rest of the lotion on my arms and legs, then hand her the bottle. "I'll see about bringing you drinks."

Lexie reties her top and stands. "What's wrong with you today?"

"Nothing."

"Is it your parents?"

"There's nothing wrong with me."

"Last time, you hung out with us all day. Today, it's like we're infected or something."

I gesture to the kids throwing mud at each other. "I have a lot of people to take care of."

"Is it that girl? Your sister's friend? The one from the coffee shop who is always rude to me. Why is she here?"

I'm not sure where Lexie's going with this. I haven't shown Georgi any special attention. I specifically avoided her today so I wouldn't be tempted to play favorites. If I get too close and let my eyes wander over her creamy skin, I'm done for. Her modest one-piece suit is sexier than the bikini's the other women are wearing because she's comfortable in her skin.

She doesn't need her assets hanging out to prove she's gorgeous.

She just is.

Mind, body, and soul.

But Georgi's here for Elena, not me, so none of it matters.

She's firmly trying to put me in the Friend Zone. If it's up to me, we'll move through that phase into soulmates, but I know Georgi. She'll pull the train off the tracks at Friendship Station if I give her a chance.

Not that any of this is Lexie's business. She has an inclination of the depth of my feelings for Georgi and has tried to use that against Georgi before. I won't let that happen today.

I'll play dumb. "You said it. She's my sister's friend."

"But she's mean. Why would your parents let them be friends?" Lexie crosses her arms under her chest in an obvious attempt to drop my focus to her breasts.

I don't take the bait. "You insulted Georgi first."

Months after that first fight with Georgi, I'd been trapped in Houston for over a month. I was dying to see her. Lexie, Viola, and the Gusmans were visiting that trip. Saturday night is the only opening in the schedule to get away, so I'd practically sprinted down the dock after the picnic.

Lexie spotted me, and I made the mistake of telling her where I was going. She refused to be left behind. Dad and I'd had a fight, so I needed her to report back that I was doing my party host job well.

It didn't help that Lexie's outfit looked more like intimate sleep-wear than street clothes, and she was in her influencer moment, when she assumed everyone cared about every second of her life.

Bridgette was new in town. She and Georgi were smiling and laughing until Lexie and I entered.

The rest was bruised egos and sarcastic jibes.

Lexie uncrosses her arms and scowls toward Georgi dribbling sand on their castle. "I asked for a skinny coffee. Anyone with half a brain cell should have been able to make it."

I squeeze the wagon's handle and struggle to keep my tone level. "That attitude right there is why I'm not here. Can you find some-thing nice to say?"

Her mouth drops open. "Are you kidding me?"

"Why would I?"

"Just because your parents are here doesn't mean you can hurt my feelings."

My parents being here is exactly why I *shouldn't* hurt her feelings. Her inner middle schooler might come out to play. She'll pull my hair and tattletale to her dad, who will talk to my dad, who will ground me.

Metaphorically speaking.

He can't actually ground me. I don't think. I've never tested his resolve to that degree before.

Either way, I need to calm Lexie down. "You don't care about my opinions. You're bored, so you're picking a fight."

"No one likes being insulted."

"And yet you accused Georgi of only having half a brain cell. It's okay for you to insult other people, but you can't take a dose yourself?"

Her face turns an ugly shade of purple. "That's not what I said."

"Lexie, you'll get a lot farther in life with kindness." *Kindness like Georgi has in spades.* I keep that thought in my head.

"I want you to take me back to the boat. Now." Lexie snatches her towel, whipping sand in her friends' faces, and stomps toward the Zodiac.

Viola gathers her towel and beach bag. "That wasn't smart, Theo."

"I know, but she can't be mean like that."

"Lexie's had a huge crush on you for months, and now you're drooling over your sister's friend. How did you expect her to react?"

"She does not."

"You are so blind." She pokes my stomach. "You're the only reason she comes here."

I shake my head. "She comes because my parents offered her parents an open invitation to our luxury yacht."

Viola pinches my arm and twists. "You aren't the only rich boy she knows." I yank my arm away. "She could be anywhere in the world, but she hauls us to this little Texas town to see *you* whenever she can."

I rub the sore spot on my arm. "I didn't realize."

Lexie loves attention in every form. Parading around in teeny tiny dresses and pajamas, like the other night, is her standard operating procedure. She's a flirt. I didn't think it was specific to me.

"You owe her an apology." Viola helps the Gusmans to their feet. "You can take us out now."

I help them into the inflatable and start the engine. It takes ten minutes to chauffeur them to the sailboat they rode out on.

Lexie takes my hand for balance to step out of the zodiac. I squeeze her fingers. "I'm sorry I was rude."

Her face contorts into something unrecognizable. "Funny how you preach to me to be nice, but you can't manage it yourself."

She's right. Kindness has never been my strength. Empathy, yes. Kindness, no. I'm too loyal to filter my words when someone hurts or insults the people I love. "My sister and her friends are important to me."

"I see." She sniffs.

I'm not sure what she's reading into my statement, but there's a gleam in her eyes that worries me. She doesn't say another word as she climbs aboard the sailboat and strides to the bow. I untie the Zodiac and pilot it away.

I'm tempted to drive to my parents' boat and explain my confrontation with Lexie.

But that's like ratting myself out before she has the opportunity to do it first. I can already see my father's scowl and hear the dressing-down he'll give me about manners, hospitality, and the importance of our good reputation.

Yeah, I'd rather avoid that.

She might not say anything, so I won't risk getting myself in trouble if I don't need to.

Besides, Georgi's standing in the surf, shielding her eyes from the sun, watching me. I'd much rather apologize for my earlier behavior and spend the rest of my day with her.

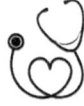

Georgi

Why does Theo have to be so handsome?

When I thought he was a creep, it was easier to overlook.

Now that I know a sweet soul hides under the bravado ... I'm in so much trouble.

I tried not to drool as I watched him push the Zodiac into the water, but Tipsy nudged me, and Elena gave me a knowing smile.

So much so, that I had to walk away before my embarrassment got the better of me and I confessed my changing heart.

His early morning swims have done his body good. He stands at the outboard of the inflatable boat and steers toward me. His light blue board shorts highlight his deep cinnamon tan and the dusting of dark hair across his chest. He runs his hand through his salt-damp hair, and his arms flex and bunch.

I lick my lips because I remember exactly how it feels to have those arms wrapped around me. His embrace was safe and comforting. I hadn't felt that cared for in a long time.

I haven't since.

He tilts the outboard out of the water and lets momentum propel the boat onto the sand. He splashes toward me. "Do you want a ride?"

"No." *Just enjoying the view.* "Is it time to go back?"

The corner of his mouth tips up. "We can stay as long as you'd like."

I tuck my hair behind my ears. "Is forever too long?"

Oh, my goodness! What is this blather coming out of my mouth? Why am I being flirty? I should not be allowed to talk when Theo doesn't have a shirt on.

Theo smirks. "Keegan didn't give me the key to their beach house, but I can grab sleeping bags if you'd like. Camp under the stars."

I shift my gaze to the tall grass swaying on the dunes and force myself not to imagine snuggling under the stars with Theo's arm wrapped around me. "Maybe later. I'm going to walk."

"Want company?"

My inner monologue screams, *Absolutely*. But I manage a more sedate, "Sure."

We're both surprised by my invitation because he stares at me without blinking for a solid minute before shaking his head.

He holds up a finger. "One thing." He jogs over to Elena and Tipsy and grabs something white from his bag. He flaps the sand from the shirt and drapes it over my shoulders. "Don't want you to burn."

I tuck my arms through the sleeves and fasten the middle button. He's taller than me, so the fabric skims the middle of my thighs. "Who brings a button-down to the beach?"

He rests his hands on my shoulders and pulls at the fabric. "I can take it back." His gentle tug rocks me backward so the heat from his chest warms my back.

I gather the material to my neck and step out of his grip. "Too late." I don't hide the way I bury my nose in the fabric. It smells like him. Sage and salt water. A little earthy, a little sweet, a little salty.

He smirks. I stick out my tongue.

This feels like that first night on the beach. Part of me expects him to wrap his arm over my shoulder or around my waist. To pick me up and spin me.

But that's not us anymore.

Even if my flirty side wants to come out and play because I like the way he looks in boardshorts, we fought this morning.

He knew my motivations for making him eggs weren't altruistic, so he reprimanded me.

Last year, he broke my confidence—and my trust.

He's slowly earning it back, but I can't let less than two weeks of seeing Theo in a new light make me forget his behavior.

We walk down the beach, away from the rest of the group. The sounds of kids' giggles are overpowered by the crashing waves. Sea birds ride the air currents. A breeze rustles my hair, and the sun warms my cheeks.

I close my eyes and savor the heat. "This is wonderful. It's been such a cold winter. I'm ready for spring to hit its stride."

He clears his throat. I surreptitiously lift my eyelid. He opens his mouth but doesn't say anything. Instead, he scrubs his hands through his hair.

"What?" I ask.

"Nothing."

"Tell me." Shy is a new look on him.

But maybe that's who he's been all along. Has he faked the flirty, boisterous charm I'm used to?

That doesn't make sense either. He was playful and spontaneous that first night.

Who is this man?

He stops and shoves his hands in his pockets. "I can't decide what to say. None of my ideas sound right."

"What are the choices?"

"I'm glad you're here. We should do this more often." He pinches the bridge of his nose and winces. "You look beautiful."

I poke his shoulder. "You don't want to tell me I'm beautiful?"

His face contorts. "Do you blame me?"

"Not really." I hate that our relationship is too complicated for him to bless me with a simple compliment. I haven't accepted any of the nice things he's said before. I didn't believe them. Maybe I should have.

But that means all those times he called me his soulmate, he actually meant it.

No. I can't believe that.

He was just taunting me. Getting a rise out of me.

We wander closer to the water, and it tickles my ankles. Time to change the subject before we get too deep. "I heard you fighting with Lexie."

His shoulders collapse. "I'm sorry about her."

"Thanks for defending me, but it's not necessary. I'll stick up for myself if I need to."

"She's ... complicated."

"Doesn't seem complicated. She likes attention, and you didn't give her any. Like every popular girl in high school who eventually realizes she's not that special."

"She's used to the spotlight."

"Thank you anyway. I'll stay away so I don't cause any more problems." The last thing anyone needs is for me to stir the pot, as Mama says.

"Please don't."

"It's better for all of us if I hurry up and convince Uncle Hoyt to let me move back."

Theo grabs my hand. "I'm sorry about what I said in the pantry. I was stupid. We want you here."

I pull free and wrap my arms around my waist. "Private chefs, catered beach picnics, and fundraising galas are not where I belong."

I've indulged in this dream too long. Theo and Elena don't live in the real world. Not my real world, anyway. "I can't stay. I should be with Tipsy. I can't help her navigate Hoyt's rollercoaster moods if I'm not home. With his court date coming up, he's angrier than ever."

"Why is protecting her your job?"

"Who else is going to do it?"

"Her mom. Your mom. He shouldn't take the consequences of his behavior out on her in the first place."

"Unfortunately, the other adults in her life aren't responsible. They're just as scared of him as she is, or they're so lost, they don't know she needs help."

His hands rest on my arms. They grip like he wants to pull me in for a hug, but I don't let him. "What can I do?" he asks.

"Nothing."

"You have to let me help. She can move onto the boat too."

I scoff. "Her dad would never let that happen."

"He let her come today."

I give Theo a sad smile. "No, he didn't. She told him she was going to school to work on an extra credit project. When she comes home with a tan, he's going to ask questions."

Theo's hands drop, and I miss them instantly. "I didn't know."

"I know you didn't, but that's the point. You're worried about ice-to-tequila ratios, and I'm worried if my cousin will have a black eye next the time I see her."

"We should call social services."

"They've been by. It didn't help."

"Georgi, there has to be something."

I point at Tipsy and Elena singing Shania Twain into a water bottle. "This is her Cinderella day. The beach is the ballroom. Let her dance and play and enjoy. Tomorrow she'll have the memory of a perfect day to inspire her until she's old enough to be free."

I'll make sure she's taken care of and safe.

He kicks the sand and doesn't say anything. I don't blame him. Our lives don't overlap, so I'm not sure he understands anything I'm saying.

The emotional damage from Theo's dad's dismissive behavior is tragic, but when you add our fear of Hoyt's alcoholism to our situation, they're nothing alike.

I take off Theo's shirt and hand it back to him. This was supposed to be a fun—maybe flirty?—walk, and I ruined it. "We should get her back."

"Sure." The sun's high in the sky, so Tipsy should get away with her subterfuge.

When we dock, I grab Tipsy's bag. "I'll walk you home."

"Georgi?" Corine calls from the big boat. "I need you and Henrietta to come up for a moment."

It's weird hearing Tipsy's given name. I glance at Theo and Elena, but their expressions are as confused as mine.

I hope Lexie didn't get Theo in trouble and is blaming me and Tipsy.

"Gather 'round, everyone." Corine waves her hands like she's herding ducklings. The guests from the beach gather closer. "This has been such a wonderful day. Thank you for joining us and making it so special. It is my hope we can do this again, with a twist. In two weeks, my husband and I will host the first annual Sanchez Cancer Foundation Gala and Bachelor Auction. Invitations with details will arrive tomorrow, but I love a personal touch, don't you? Consider this is your invitation to be our special guests. We would love for all of you to attend."

Corine's guests murmur with excitement. Lexie and her friends wrap their arms around each other, squeal, and bounce like Tigger.

Tipsy grabs my hand and pulls me into the corner. "Me?" She frowns.

"Yes, dear." Corine ushers Tipsy and me to the dining area. "You will be our most special guests. I'm taking you shopping later this week. Let me know what works for your schedules. Elena will arrange everything." She kisses our cheeks and sweeps away to mingle with her other excited guests.

Tipsy face transforms from bewilderment to pure, unadulterated joy. She jumps and giggles with more enthusiasm than Lexie. Elena joins the jumping and adds a little screech of her own.

I love this for Tipsy, but I also hate it. Even though I've been swept away by the luxury and grandeur and magic of their lives, I understand how hard it will be to crash back to reality.

I don't know if Tipsy can handle it. If she can even escape from the trailer for the event, she'll get dressed up, dance until the clock strikes midnight, and end up worse than Cinderella sitting on the broken pumpkin.

Theo's in the corner, running his hand across his stubbled jaw. I weave around the furniture, grab his arm, and yank him into the hallway. "Is this your idea?" I whisper-scold.

He doesn't try to remove his hand from mine. "You knew about the party."

I jab him in the chest. "Inviting Tipsy. Was that your idea?" I never imagined I would be invited, much less Tipsy.

He squeezes my hand. "No."

"You didn't say anything to your mom or drop hints to Elena?"

His hand drifts toward my face. "I thought you would be excited to be included. What's with the interrogation?"

I pull him farther down the hall, so no one hears us. "I just got done telling you how magical today was for her. I used the word Cinderella, and now she's invited to an honest to goodness ball." I throw up my hands. "That's too much of a coincidence for me."

Theo steps close and drops his voice. "Mom saw Elena and Tipsy laughing on the boat and said how nice it was to hear laughter again. I agreed. That's all. I thought you'd be happy."

"Theo, you can't lead her into this life. Someday, yes, she might earn her way here, but until then, she needs to be content where she is."

He braces his hand on the wall next to my head. "Like you?"

"Yes." It's one of the few protections we have from the pain of our circumstances.

Theo shakes his head. "I don't believe that."

I duck out from under his arm and lean against the opposite wall. "That I like my life? Why? Because I'm a lowly barista or because I don't have a big, strong man providing everything I could possibly need?"

He crowds into me again. "No, because when someone offers to love you, you run away. That can't make you happy." His voice is a low growl that twists my insides.

"Better to run first than to be left heartbroken."

His eyes dart to my lips. He leans closer. My back arches, and my legs lift me toward him. He's not touching me, but I can taste the lime margarita on his breath. He whispers against my lips. "You end up heartbroken either way." He storms off, leaving me startled at the yearning in my chest.

Chapter 16

Georgi

Honey Beans is my refuge. Friendly, familiar faces come and go. No one expects anything from me except for a good cup of coffee and yummy pastry.

These are the pressures I can handle.

Theo almost kissing me in the hallway? Can't handle that.

My heart beating out of my ribcage wanting to chase him and forget all the fights we've had over the last year? Can't handle that.

Figuring out how to sneak Tipsy to the gala while simultaneously proving to Hoyt I'm sorry and moving home? Really can't handle that.

I pour coffee beans into the reservoir at the top of the grinder and flick the machine on.

The bell jingles its happy notes.

My mom skips through the door like an overeager child. "Baby!" She darts around the counter and wraps me in the biggest hug I've had from her in years.

"Hi, Mama." I return the hug. Her hand sweeps back and forth across my shoulder blades to settle the tension my body refuses to release without extra encouragement.

"I just heard the good news. Why did you keep it from me for so long?"

"What good news?"

She shakes her finger at me. "Don't play coy. I know you're living on the Sanchez's yacht."

"I texted you I couldn't live with Grammie anymore." Weeks ago.

She cups my cheek. "Dr. Sanchez is such a catch."

"Mama, no. It's not like that. Elena Sanchez invited me. I'm staying with her."

A little crinkle mars her smooth forehead. "But I thought ... you've never dated women before, but I guess if that's where your heart lies, I won't stop you."

"Oh, Mama. I'm not dating Elena. She's my friend."

"She's bein' awful generous to a friend. What's the catch?"

"No catch. Just a friend helping out another friend."

"If you don't want to tell me, that's fine. I know you like your secrets."

"What secrets?" Why won't she believe me? Why is it so hard to assume I'd have a friend who looks out for me?

"Sometimes you have to take the long path to the man you want. I get it. I was the same with your daddy." She hugs my arm. "It'll be good for you to be friends with your man's sister."

"Please, stop." She might be speaking to the dreams festering in my heart, but they aren't real. If I give in, they'll become nightmares. Nothing good lasts for me when it comes to relationships.

The only relationships that have lasted for me are with my siblings and a few rare friends.

Mama rocks on her heels. "What? I'm happy my baby's found someone to take care of her. You're so headstrong, I worried you'd never settle down."

I step out of her reach and tighten the strings on my apron. "I need to get back to work."

"Of course, baby." She kisses my cheek. "When you decide to share your good fortune, I'd love to meet his parents."

"Mama!"

She flutters her fingers and skips out the front door.

This right here is why I can't get swept away by Theo's charm. He can't take care of me. I will not put my well-being in anyone else's hands.

I have to be self-sufficient.

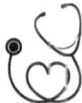

Theo

Shivers run down my spine as I step into the vestibule of Third Coast Regional Medical Center. It doesn't matter that I've only been here the one time Elena and I met with Keegan, it somehow feels familiar, like a favorite sweatshirt.

Maybe it's the lemon antiseptic smell, the constant seventy-two degrees, or the bright fluorescent lights at all hours of the day. Maybe it's the bustle of patients and staff moving from one part of the building to another or the hopefulness of the families in the waiting rooms.

Whatever it is, I stand just inside the door, taking it all in as the comfort settles into my bones.

I want to belong here, even if that desire is ridiculous given who I am and my destiny.

"Theo." Keegan raises his hand to get my attention. He's standing next to the elevator bank holding the door open.

I jog to him and shake his hand. "How are you?"

"Happy. You?" He pushes the button for the fourth floor, and the doors slide closed.

"Working on it." Trying to figure out what to do about Georgi. I can't go a day without the pendulum swinging from wanting to make out with her to wanting to fight with her.

At least there's passion in our relationship, right? We need to channel that intensity away from shouting and into kissing.

Keegan doesn't notice my silence and fills the air with questions. "How's your sister's shoulder? How's training?"

"Better. She's meeting with her physical therapist and training is going well. Your suggestions were the magic bullet she needed."

"Good to hear." The elevator dings, the doors open, and we step into the orthopedic waiting room. "Follow me." He badges through a security door and winds through white corridors to the physicians' lounge. A group of men sit at a table eating.

Keegan gestures to them. "Single men. As requested."

I clap him on the back. "Thanks." I explain the fundraiser and bachelor auction to the three physicians, four residents, three nurse anesthetists, and two OR techs Keegan rounded up. "The foundation will pay for and organize the dates, so you don't need to worry about that. We will also provide independent transportation to the date location if you or your date prefer. My mom's guest list is ..." I almost say *exclusive*, but that sounds elitist.

One of the cardiology residents, Wyatt Cruz, drums his knuckles on the table, saving me from finishing my statement. He reminds me of Superman, if Superman were the villain instead of the hero—lots of lean muscle, tattoos peeking out from under his scrubs, a mischievous, devil-may-care smirk on his face. "Are all of the bidders your mom's age? Are we cougar bait?"

Nora Montgomery enters the lounge. "You would ask that."

"Gummy Bear, are you jealous?"

Georgi's sister grabs a banana and chocolate milk. "Cruz, you need a warning label. Dangerous, even in small doses."

He tips his chair back on two legs and rubs his thumb along his bottom lip. "I do get your blood pumping."

Nora's cheeks redden like her sister's. "That's not ... whatever ... I have patients." She punches the door harder than necessary to open it and slams it behind her.

Keegan shakes his head. "You're playing with fire, man. The Montgomery women don't mess around."

Wyatt drops his feet to the floor. "I know what I'm doing."

Keegan elbows me. "Ask Theo. He's been after Georgi for a year and can't win her over."

We don't need to talk about my failed love life. "Back to the auction. To answer the original question. There will be some older bidders, but my mom's guest list encompasses women and men from all walks of life and socioeconomic statuses. If you're uncomfortable with that idea, you don't have to participate." I wouldn't if I didn't have to.

Wyatt waves away my statement. "No. It's cool. Just want to know what I'm getting into. You can count on me."

After a few more questions about logistics, all twelve men agree to participate.

Wyatt tugs on the stethoscope around his neck. "How about a wager, gentlemen? Losers buy the man who earns the highest bid lunch for a month."

Keegan chuckles and walks me to the elevator. "Should I tell him you're most likely to win that bet?"

"I'd trade him in a heartbeat."

Keegan rests his shoulder against the wall. "Still having problems with Georgi?"

"Always."

"Give her time. She'll come around."

How much does Keegan know about Georgi's situation? They grew up together, so I assume a lot. "She's too scared for her siblings and Tipsy to let herself have anything good."

"That's a caregiver's plight, but you know that. You'd do anything for your patients."

"True."

"I'll have Bridgette talk you up."

My eyes widen. "Don't. Your wife's awesome, but I don't need the matchmaker chain trying to convince Georgi to give me a second chance. That will make things worse. Elena's bad enough."

He rests his hand on my shoulder. "When Bridgette and I hit a rough patch, Jake Malloy put in a good word for me. It was the grain of sand that shifted everything. We could be your grain of sand."

"I'll think about it."

"Hey, do you know if anyone in your residency class is looking for a job? We want to expand our services and are having trouble recruiting anesthesiologists."

It's on the tip of the tongue to say I'll take the job. I doubt more and more that Dad will train me to take over and retire.

But I can't be both a physician and the man my family needs me to be, so I just say, "I'll ask around."

Chapter 17

Georgi

SHOPPING WITH CORINE ISN'T like any outing I've been on before. Theo drove their Jeep Wagoneer past the fancy boutique in Bubee and jumped on the highway to Houston.

Corine sat in the middle row and engaged Tipsy in conversation about every aspect of her life, leaving Elena and I in the third row for the two-hour ride. We arrived at a nondescript warehouse in the middle of town just after lunch. Theo opened his mom's door and helped her out. Elena was next.

As he helps me descend the tall vehicle, his thumb rubs a semi-circle across the back of my hand.

I frown at the tingles. What game is he playing? Last time we spoke, he yelled at me.

There should be no thumb caresses. There shouldn't be tingles.

Whatever. I didn't break Theo's heart, and I'm not letting him near mine.

The magic of the pantry and the beach was just that. Magic.

The sparkles are gone, and I need to turn back into plain old Cinder-girl.

But first, I'll try on dresses.

I follow the group through a rusty door, down a white hallway, into a room with a pedestal surrounded by mirrors. Four doors are open on either side.

Two satin chaise lounges sit in the middle of the room next to a glass and wrought iron coffee table and a bucket with champagne.

A young man, probably younger than me, greets Corine with kisses on either cheek. His light grey suit is impeccably tailored, and his sharp nose gives him a regal air.

"Thank you for fitting us in on such short notice, Frank." Corine squeezes his hands.

"Of course, madam. Everything is as you wish."

"Wonderful. Ladies, Frank is my designer and stylist. He's put a collection of gowns in each dressing room which we believe best suit your coloring, figure, and style. If you don't like any of the options, he will help you find something more suitable." She spreads her arms wide. "Enjoy." It's like Willy Wonka opening his arms to the candy garden.

I grab Elena's hand and yank her toward me. "Is this normal?"

Elena's eyes are as wide as mine, and her mouth gaps open. She shakes her head. "I know *of* Frank, but she's never done this before."

Out of the corner of my eye, I watch Corine pull Theo aside. She straightens his collar and smooths wrinkles from his shoulders. "Frank will measure you for a new tuxedo as well."

He steps out of her reach. "I don't need one, Mom."

She pats his cheek. "Indulge me."

He rolls his eyes but removes his suit jacket.

Why do I love watching the way his shoulders shrug out of his coat so much? I need to stop the butterflies. Someone grab the Raid. Sorry, pretty pollinators, for self-preservation, you need to die.

This isn't my life.

"Georgi," Corine waves. "Over here, darling." She opens the door. "You'll be in here, and Henrietta will be next door. Let yourself have fun." I blink at the blatant order.

Corine is right. I need to relax and enjoy this once-in-a-lifetime opportunity, right? It's okay to indulge and pretend for a minute.

I shake off the unease coursing through my veins. I can live in the moment.

The dressing room is as luxurious as the outer room. A floor-to-ceiling mirror fills one wall with a plush velvet chair tucked into the corner. Ten dresses in an array of gemstone colors hang to my left. Any undergarment I could want sits on a table next to them.

"Oh, my goodness." Tipsy bounces into my room.

My fingers run over the satiny, silky, sparkly gowns. "I feel like Alice falling into Wonderland."

"Or an episode of the Bachelorette." Her eyes are bright, and the gigantic smile adding a rosy blush to her cheeks can't be misinterpreted as anything but pure, unadulterated joy. She clasps my hands. "I want to see all your dresses."

Her giddiness infects me. Tipsy needs this. I probably need it too, but I'm not willing to dive as deeply into the pool of indulgence. "Me too. I want to see you in every one."

Tipsy closes my door behind her, and I'm alone trying to decide, Number One, which dress do I try first, and Number Two, how much is the crash into reality going to hurt when it's all over?

Only time will tell.

I immediately veto the dress with sheer beige lace across the bust and stomach—because modesty—and the mustard yellow one—because mustard and I do not get along in any form or fashion.

The other dresses are too divine to imagine wearing. What if I snag a sequin and rip the dress to pieces?

Stop worrying!

My eye is drawn to an emerald-green gown with a bell skirt and cap sleeves, but I don't want it to be the first dress I try. I might never take it off.

Instead, I pick an off the shoulder dress with a heart-shaped bodice. Black lace bleeds into a crimson skirt. When I step out of the room, Elena's on the pedestal in a white halter dress that shimmers like melting icicles. "Wow."

She shrugs. "I don't like the halter." She fingers the straps and runs her hands over her shoulders. "It makes my shoulders look too broad, and my boobs too flat."

She's beautiful. The lines make her trim waist look even tinier, but I see how she'd think she looks like a lopsided triangle.

Even if I think she looks amazing, it's more important for her to be comfortable and love the way she looks.

No one else's opinion matters.

She steps off the pedestal, and I take her place. "What do you think?" I turn to take in the beadwork down the back. "I feel like the villain in a cartoon movie."

Elena nibbles her thumbnail and nods "Not what you're going for?"

"Maybe another time."

Tipsy opens her door, and my jaw hits the floor. She's breathtaking in her strapless, pale blue dress. The skirt folds and cascades to her shin.

The corseted bodice makes her look more mature than I could have imagined.

I think of her as a little kid most of the time, but she's a woman. Almost eighteen. I'm not ready for that.

I give her the pedestal. "What do you think?"

Her fingers flutter over the material like she's afraid to touch it. "I've never worn anything so pretty."

Corine gently pulls Tipsy's shoulders back to straighten her posture. "Darling, you are the beauty. The dress just highlights your features."

Tipsy's cheeks flush. If only I could wrap Corine in a hug and thank her for the confidence she's imparting to my cousin.

Self-assurance isn't something that abounds in the women in my family. This day will go a long way to helping Tipsy realize how amazing she is, and how much she can accomplish if she takes the chance.

We try dress after dress. Elena decides on a pink floral gown with an empire waist and wide straps and Tipsy chooses an ombre silver and white tea-length gown with layers and layers of tulle. Corine takes them into another room to try on shoes.

I can't decide. The emotional weight of the Sanchezes' gesture builds with each dress I try.

I love the fairy tale, but it's too much. It's impractical. What am I going to do with a sequined mermaid gown after their gala?

I won't wear it on a date or to wash the dishes. What's the point? If Frank doesn't demand it back, the gown will gather dust in my closet and remind me of this one moment in time when I let myself dream bigger than I should have.

It won't be a happy memory.

It will be a reminder of everything I wanted but am never allowed to have.

I can't let Corine's extravagance make me complacent. This will end in a few weeks. The joy will be snatched away, and I'll be left hollow.

I'll be just like my mom. Instead of pining for my dad like she does, I'll pine for a life I never should have been exposed to. For Theo's soul-filled eyes, Elena's friendship, and the ease of someone sharing my burdens.

I'll ignore my present and live in my memories, pretending I can make them true again.

The clock ticks in the corner of the room. I can't procrastinate and wallow any longer.

I slip into the green gown. The satin grazes my skin, hugging my curves. I know it's perfect before I look in the mirror.

My cleavage strikes the perfect balance between modest and sexy. I need the bigger mirror to get the full effect, so I step into the main room.

Lifting the skirt, I step onto the pedestal. Alone in front of the mirror, I spin, taking in every angle.

My hair looks like autumn leaves, and my eyes sparkle, balancing tears of sadness with tears of joy. My cheeks are a beautiful, flushed peach without a hint of makeup. I've never looked or felt so beautiful.

Fantasy. Fairy tale. Fake.

I hide my face in my hands. I can't do this.

A door clicks closed behind me. I grind my teeth and surreptitiously wipe my eyes. When I blink them clear, Theo's leaning against the wall.

Perfect.

Of all the people to see me lose it over a dress, he's the last one I want to see.

I step down from the pedestal and half-sprint toward my room.

"Stop," he calls. His tone is soft, not commanding. Concerned.

I freeze, keeping my gaze on the ground.

"Why are you crying?" He's still next to the wall.

When I look up, I'm sure my eyes are full of sorrow. "This is too much."

"Why?"

I don't even have to roll my eyes. "You know why."

His mouth moves, and his eyes rake over me like he's looking for a wardrobe malfunction. "Is it the dress?"

I suck in a breath. "The dress is perfect." I bite the inside of my cheek and focus on the pain, so I don't cry harder.

He takes one step away from the wall and lifts his hand. "Help me understand."

I fluff the skirt. "The dress, your mom, Tipsy. All of this is overwhelming."

He chuckles on his exhale. Just a soft release of tension, not like he's laughing at me. "Sweetheart, when was the last time you were overwhelmed?"

I don't know how to explain why this feels so wrong. There's nothing wrong with my friend's mom inviting me to a party and going shopping with us to pick dresses.

But all of this ... how much do these dresses even cost? Can I afford the underwear it requires? Probably not.

I swipe the water from my cheeks. "I'm scared I'll get used to this."

It's a dumb admission. Why wouldn't I want to get used to this? Why do I feel unworthy? Like a fraud? Like someone's going to reveal cameras and shout, *Gotcha*?

Theo inches closer, holding his hands out in front of him. His fingers slide up my arms, and he wraps me in a hug.

I press my face to his shoulder and try to let his sweet sage smell calm my frazzled nerves. I shouldn't let him comfort me.

This is worse than the dress because I know without a doubt, his arms are the only place I want to be.

But the place I belong the least.

I shift back to step out of his embrace. He splays his hand across my shoulder blades, securing me to his chest. "You're okay." Theo's croons in my ear. I love how soft and gravelly his voice is when we're like this.

Just the two of us.

"There's no reason for my meltdown. I'm being silly."

His lips tingle against the shell of my ear. "We need to practice overwhelming you."

"It's nice to be taken care of. It's so rare that someone does, I didn't know how to react."

Corine clears her throat, and I flinch out of Theo's arms.

She raises her eyebrow. "Everything okay?"

I rub my thumbs under my eyes and scrub the wet spot I created on Theo's chest. "I'm overwhelmed by your kindness. Theo was helping me calm down."

Her eyes pinch ever so slightly. She doesn't believe me. "He does have a strong set of shoulders to cry on."

My smile barely reaches my lips.

She takes my hand and leads me back to the pedestal. "Is this dress *the one*?"

"Yes."

She twirls her finger, and I spin slowly, letting her evaluate my choice. Her eyes give nothing away.

"Perfect. Change. Shoes are this way." She steps through the door, leaving Theo and I alone. I step toward the dressing room. *Get it together, girly.*

"Georgi?" Theo catches my hand. He pulls me to his chest, wraps his arms around me, and kisses my temple. "I'm sorry."

"For what?" He has nothing to apologize for. I'm the one crying like a baby, unable to accept kindness in any form.

He whispers against my cheek. "For destroying your faith in me. I've screwed up in every way possible. I'm sorry I brought our guests to the coffee shop, and for their behavior. I'm sorry I wasn't the person I promised you I was. I ..." He licks his lips. "I'm sorry."

His eyes tell me so many things I don't want to see. We could have something priceless and precious, but I can't risk it.

My life can't be entwined with his. We never should have gone on that first date. I shouldn't have let myself hope for something more than my lot in life.

It's not fair to Theo. He believes I can be more than I am, but I can't.

I cup his cheek. "You have nothing to be sorry for. I jumped to conclusions and wouldn't listen. You're a great man. I'm sorry I didn't see it before. But ... I'm sorry. I can't."

I escape before I say or do anything I'll regret.

If I let him take care of me ... if I stay in his arms another moment, I'm lost.

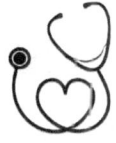

Chapter 18

Theo

HAVING GEORGI IN MY arms is addictive. How do I get my next hit? How do we get to the place where hugs are the expectation, not a rare gift?

She thinks I'm a great guy, but apparently not great enough for her to take a risk on us.

I saw the desire in her eyes. If only my mom hadn't interrupted. Could I have chased away her fears and helped her realize she belongs here? That she deserves good things in her life? Would Georgi have kissed me and let me love her the way I hope to?

I have to know.

The girls chatter about their dresses as we drive home. Georgi puts on a good face, but she's still shaken.

She doesn't believe she deserves good things.

We need to unwind her insecurities if I ever hope to win her heart.

Dad is with Viola and Lexie when we get back. Since the picnic on the beach, they have moved onto the boat full time. I'm waiting for the clichéd other shoe to drop.

Dad gestures for me to follow him into his office. "Theo, a word."

There's the shoe hitting the carpet. The thud echoes in my head.

Georgi skirts past us and disappears toward her room. Duty wars with my desire to comfort her.

I let duty win. There will be time to talk to her after I deal with whatever Dad has to say. Besides, chasing after her will only give Lexie another harpoon to throw.

Dad refills his whiskey and sits behind his desk. "Shut the door."

It's going to be one of *those* kinds of talks. Not father to son, but CEO to employee.

His calm demeanor makes me twitchy. I rest my ankle across my knee and do my best not to fidget.

He takes a sip. "I heard disconcerting news today, and I'm hoping you can clarify the rumors."

"What happened?" Lexie and Viola probably tattled on me, but I'm not throwing myself in front of the train if they're not what he's talking about.

He shifts forward and leans on his desk, skewering me with his eyes. "Are you accessing the Bubee factory financials and shadowing Ms. Tanaka after I explicitly told you not to?"

Sh ... I thought I'd have more time. "Yes, sir. I thought it best I learn more about our company."

"You don't deny your actions?"

I sit straighter in my chair, plant my feet on the floor, and my elbows on my knees. "No. As the future CEO, it's my responsibility to understand every level of our company."

"Ms. Tanaka's time is valuable. You're distracting her from her duties."

"She hasn't said as much. She was impressed with my initiative." I've learned more about managing people in the few days I've spent with her than in the three years since I completed my residency. She's brilliant at conflict resolution, time management, and fiscal analysis. She answers my questions thoroughly and then turns them around so she knows I've absorbed her lessons. She's the mentor I need since Dad refuses to fill that role.

Dad flicks his wrist. "You're my son. She would never tell you the truth."

"How can I trust her to tell me the truth when I'm CEO?"

Dad takes another sip. "You aren't ready to access the factory's financial information. You don't have the training to understand it."

"Then train me." I force myself to remove the desperation from my tone. "It's time I take my place and earn the respect and faith of our employees." No more margaritas. No more wagons with water and suntan lotion. The Employee Relations Liaison lunches have been good learning experiences, but knowing Tom in marketing's wife is having twins so he needs to extend his paternity leave doesn't teach me to navigate a hostile takeover

"Losing highly sensitive financial information is more likely to lose everyone's respect. If the wrong person obtains a copy, we will lose our shareholders' faith."

"Everything is on a password-protected laptop in my room. Perfectly safe."

He swigs the last sip from his cup. "You will not burden Ms. Tanaka with your naivety. You are done sneaking behind my back. Don't do it again."

"When do I get to do the job you've promised me? The one I gave up my career for?"

He rolls his shoulders back. "When I feel you are ready to shoulder the responsibility."

"I can save lives, but I can't run your company?" This is ridiculous. Why do I bother doing what he asks when it's a dead end?

His eyes narrow. "Others watched your back in the hospital. You were never independent. There are no such safety measures here."

His sucker punch tastes like rotten vegetables, the kind they used to throw at offkey performers and prisoners.

I choke it down.

He has no idea what my training was like. He doesn't know the lives I saved. He doesn't care. "If that's what you believe, you should mentor me, not exile me here." I jab my finger into my armrest.

"In time. Right now, I need you to focus on cultivating relationships with the men and women you host. They will be your contemporaries and future business partners."

Great! The speech that's been on repeat since he told me about the yacht weekends.

"Insulting your colleagues will not help our business grow," he continues.

At least that part's new. I huff out a breath and slouch. "Lexie told you what happened on the beach last weekend."

Dad glances at his watch. "Your unwise behavior proves you aren't mature enough to learn my trade." His tone is distracted. I'm losing his attention.

I flatten my hands on my knees, so I don't ball them into fists. "What do I have to do to prove that I'm ready?"

"At the gala, I want you to mingle, entertain, and get to know our guests better. Each and every one should consider you a dear friend. Then we'll talk."

In the hospital, we used S.M.A.R.T goals. Specific, measurable, achievable, relevant, and time-bound.

None of what dad asked of me can be measured. *A dear friend?*

I will never know if I'm good enough if the line in the sand can be washed away by fickle tides.

"If you want to earn my respect, you will serve this family as requested. This is not up for debate." He points to a piece of paper on his desk. "The medical personnel from Third Coast Regional were a great idea. High value. Related to the cause I'm impressed, but we need more bachelors for the auction. The gentlemen listed here are candidates. Tomorrow, please interview them and determine if they will be assets to the fundraiser. If they are, invite them to participate." Dad picks up his phone and scrolls across the screen. "Show yourself out. I have phone calls to make."

I feel like a dog who earned half a Milk Bone. I did good, but not good enough. Never good enough. Not anymore.

Since I was four years old, sitting on his knee during board meetings, I've known making him proud was the goal for my life. He'd ruffle my hair, ask for my childish opinions, and teach me why he was making the decisions he was making.

He was molding me into the man he wants me to be. A man respected by his family and his peers. A man who serves his employees and the company so it's profitable for everyone.

We were on track until the Olympic Trials. Then he abandoned me alone in a maze with no way out. Lost. Stumbling. Scared. I don't know how to find my way out and earn his forgiveness after ruining Elena's dreams.

I thought Party Host would be enough.

It's not.

At this rate, he won't forgive me.

Should I even keep trying?

I stand and move to shut the door behind me.

"Oh, and Theo."

I pause and look back at my dad.

He covers the mouthpiece on his phone. "Lexie will be your date to the gala. It will be your apology for your behavior on the beach."

"Dad—"

He moves the phone back to his mouth. "Hello, Jim." He spins his chair, so all I see is the cognac-brown leather. "Did you get Corine's invitation?"

Dismissed.

How can he treat me like this?

When did I become another commodity?

How do I explain my date with Lexie to Georgi after what happened this afternoon?

Georgi

I clear my plate—citrus sriracha salmon with broccolini and couscous. If heaven has food, I hope it's half as good as what Judah creates—along with Elena's and Theo's dishes.

"Put those down, dear." Corine wiggles her finger. "We have staff for that."

"I'd like to help." After their abundant generosity, it's the least I can do.

"Do we pay you?" Corine asks.

"No, but you've been so kind." Helping with something as simple as dishes feels normal, routine, not like a fairy tale I shouldn't have fallen into.

Corine smooths her perfectly styled hair. She extends her hand to me as she stands. "Let's have a chat, you and I."

I hope the fear boiling in my stomach isn't splashed on my face. I look first to Theo and then to Elena. Neither have expressions of dread.

"Umm ... okay."

She takes my hand. "Let's go to the back deck."

I precede her through the double doors onto the expansive deck. Lounge chairs surround the pool/hot tub. A retractable awning blocks the view of the stars.

Corine slides the doors closed behind her and takes a place at the railing. She inhales a deep breath. "I love Texas this time of year. No bugs. Minimal humidity. Crisp mornings and comfortable after-noons."

I join her and squeeze the railing. The breeze flutters my skirt. "Did you bring me out here to talk about the weather?"

After she caught me in Theo's arms earlier, I can only guess her motivations.

Most of my ideas mean the mouthwatering salmon was my last meal on this boat. I'm surprised they let me have a final dinner with them.

A whisper of a laugh crosses her lips. "I'm stalling. I'm not sure how to word what I have to say."

"I—"

She holds up her hand. "No. Me first." Her gaze travels across my face, through my hair and back to my eyes like she's looking for something specific. I hold as still as possible and try to hide my worry.

She exhales, and a little smile parts her lips. "I want to thank you for your friendships with my children."

Okay, not what I expected. "They're wonderful people. It's my blessing."

"We aren't a normal family." She gestures to the boat. "We can't even live in a normal house, but you help us feel like we could be. I haven't seen my daughter smile this much in years."

"I didn't do anything."

"Please, don't discount your efforts. Kindness and acceptance are more important than people think."

"Is there a *but* to this?"

"Yes. We should have had this conversation before last weekend's excursion, but I didn't consider it until I saw you and Theo earlier."

This is the part where she warns me away from a relationship with her son. My grip on the railing tightens, and I hold my breath. Disappointment is coming.

It shouldn't bother me if she doesn't think I'm a good match for her son.

I agree with her.

It will still sting to hear her say the words. Especially after the extravagant kindness of our shopping trip this afternoon.

I shore up the walls around my squishy middle.

She lays her hand on mine, pulls my fingers free from the railing, and holds my hand with both of hers. "Over the next few weeks, we will have hundreds of our friends, business associates, and investors aboard. I want you to prepare yourself. Some will accept you. Others will judge you. Some will assume you have ulterior motives. Before we subject you to that treatment, I want you to consider if you are up to the challenge." She raises her eyebrow. "If you aren't, we'll find you other accommodations until after the gala. If you are willing to stand by my children, I would like you and your cousin to participate in etiquette classes."

Wait, what? "Classes?"

She flutters her fingers. "They aren't as archaic as they sound. Silly things like which utensil to use. You'll be surprised how devoted people are to their fish forks. As you've already witnessed, there are ... people ..." Her gaze flicks toward the dining room. Lexie and her friends didn't join us for dinner, but I know they're who Corine is alluding to. "People who will exploit any differences we may have and label them deficiencies. I hope these lessons allow you a modicum of comfort as you persevere through the events I have planned."

"What if we don't want to participate in your classes?"

"They aren't required, merely offered. Either way, this is your home. You should be comfortable here. I don't want anything to upset you." She kisses my cheek. "Sleep on it."

Her motherly affection tingles my cheek and warms my heart. "I don't need to."

"Are you sure?" Her tone is full of surprise.

"I can't deprive Tipsy of this opportunity." I've seen firsthand how far something as simple as elegant manners can get someone.

She squeezes my arm. "You have such a protective spirit. It's a wonderful quality. Guard it."

"Thanks, I think."

She pulls out her phone and types something. "We'll start next Tuesday, if you're available."

"I am."

She types a few more words. "Wonderful. Judah will prepare a magnificent five-course dinner." She kisses my cheek again. "I'm excited for us." She returns to the main living area, takes her husband's hand, and they walk toward the other end of the ship.

Confusion and a weird feeling I can't describe settle in my chest as they disappear. It's this combination of warm fuzzies and ... joy? Happiness? Contentment?

Maybe it's just the lack of worry.

I don't know what to do with it.

Chapter 19

Georgi

YOU CAN BE FRIENDS with my daughter but stay away from my son.
That's what Corine was supposed to say. Instead, she wants to help
me fit in, to belong in this world where I've landed.

This is your home. She called their boat *my* home.

I stare at the moonlight dancing on the waves and fail to process
this new reality until a breeze pulls goosebumps from my skin and the
faint strum of an acoustic guitar floats to me.

The melody is sorrowful and haunting.

Curiosity gets the better of me, and I follow the sound upstairs.
Theo sits on the lounge chairs where Elena and I usually escape strum-
ming notes on his guitar. I don't want to startle or interrupt him, so I
hide in the shadows and listen.

The song reminds me of something my grandmother's dad once
played for us. I was probably five. My great-great-grandfather learned
to play the acoustic guitar as he built the railroad connecting Mexico

and Texas. He taught his son, who played for us at family events. Back when my family was something to treasure, not survive.

This explains why Theo has callouses on the tips of his fingers but not his palms.

"Are you going to keep lurking?" he asks.

I step out of the shadows. "I didn't want to disturb you."

"Are you feeling better?"

That's a loaded question. "I'm not sure." It's as close to the truth as I can manage at the moment.

He pats the chair next to him. "Tell me about it."

The part of me that is comfortable in the trailer park tells me I should just keep my mouth shut. Go to bed.

But as I watch the stars shimmer in Theo's open face, I realize I'm not that woman anymore. I don't belong in the trailer park. That doesn't mean I belong on this yacht.

I'm somewhere in the middle.

Will talking to Theo help me figure out where I belong?

It feels so weird to have a confidant who isn't one of my sisters. They understand where I'm coming from because they also lived through our dad leaving, our mom disintegrating, and our uncle taking over.

Theo has no first-hand experiences to help him understand how unstable I feel all the time.

But he has a compassionate spirit. He sees things in shades of gray I've never been able to grasp.

My insecurities haven't driven him away, so I tell him about my conversation with his mom, her concerns, and the classes. "I was so scared she was going to tell me to move out and stay away from you and Elena."

Theo sets his guitar aside and spins on his chair so his knees bracket mine. "Mom would never do that."

"I could tell her offer was about making me feel comfortable and not about impressing her friends."

Theo tugs at the hem of my skirt. "If you want to come to the gala in shorts and a T-shirt, she will stand behind you and dare anyone to comment."

"It's weird. My mom is like a teenager who never grew up. She doesn't know how to think past her immediate needs or see that other people need her help. Then here's your mom, willing to go out on a limb with her friends just so that I feel like I belong here."

"You do belong here."

My stomach pinches and a dull heaviness settles in my chest. "Why would I?"

He cups my cheek. "Because I'd like to think ... maybe you belong with me."

I lean back, out of his reach. "Theo, I can't."

"I'm sorry for all the dumb stuff I've done over the last year. I'm embarrassed by what my dad makes me do. I didn't know how to explain the parties in a way that didn't make me look foolish. I ... I don't know, I didn't think you'd like me for *me* once we spent more time together, so I let our guests tag along when I shouldn't have."

On what planet would Theo not be enough for me? Why would he have to prove himself?

He was perfect that first night. Playful, sweet, and spontaneous. Genuine.

I tuck my hands under my thighs so I don't reach for him. "Do you remember the first time you brought Lexie and Viola to the coffee shop? Viola looked drunk and pasted herself to your chest." I'll never forget the breathy way she asked him to take her to bed or the way it stole the oxygen from my lungs.

A sad smile tilts his lip. "Never take acetaminophen, dextromethorphan, and doxylamine during a juice cleanse."

"We didn't know each other beyond the one night we'd spent together the weekend before. I jumped to conclusions, but Lexie said something that resonated."

He shakes his head. "Lexie has ulterior motives."

"Even so, she told me I will never be able to compete with your dedication to your family. That anything or anyone who isn't them will always take a backseat."

He settles his hands on my bare knees. Their heat pulses and creates an entirely different kind of goosebumps racing across my skin. "Do you believe that?"

"Sort of. I know you will do anything for your family and if I try to get in the middle, you will choose them. That's what happened with the parties. You picked them over me." My stomach churns with the words I have to say. Once I say them, he'll pull away. I'll lose the heat between us, but I have to do this.

"How can I hold your loyalty against you when I'm the same?" I ask. "I might like you, but if you come between me and my siblings or Tipsy, I will always pick them. That's our problem. No matter how strongly we want to see where this goes, when things get hard, we will choose our families over each other." I lay my hands on his. He turns his wrists and interlaces our fingers. "You will take over Sanchez Biotech, make a pitstop in Hong Kong for a product unveiling before heading to Paris for an investors meeting. I have to be here to help Tipsy fill out college applications. Our lives intersect, but they don't overlap. I don't want you to feel stuck with me just because you're too kindhearted to let me go. I think that's what happened. You created a dream of me that I can't live up to. You need to realize it was just a dream."

He pulls his hands from mine and scrubs the scruff on his chin. "That was quite the speech." He stares into the harbor. "It sounds logical until you dig into the interior."

"It is logical." He has to understand that no matter how much we want each other—the attraction is real: he is the sexiest, most intelligent, most loyal man I've ever had the privilege of knowing—we can't have what we want. Life doesn't work that way.

He leans back on his elbow. "Tipsy and your brother graduate in a few months. What then?"

"They'll still need me. My sister's a fellow, and she doesn't remember to grocery shop regularly. If I don't take care of them, no one else will." Nora would subsist on stale hospital coffee and Pop Tarts if it weren't for me. The only reason I don't grocery shop for Angelina and Julietta is because they're too far away. They get care packages instead.

"You're breaking up with me before we start dating because you think we can't juggle the demands of our families with a relationship?"

"Yes." Family has to come first. They are my responsibility.

"What if things change?"

"They won't. It's safer this way."

"Safety is always your top concern?"

My fingertips trace where Hoyt hit me. The bruise is gone, but the memory still stings. "It has to be."

"Georgi, you are worth more than you give yourself credit for." I hate the anguish in his voice.

"I know where I belong. I know where I fit." *Even if I wish it were otherwise.*

Theo burrows his hands in my hair and cradles my face, so I have to look into his soul-filled eyes. His heart hangs by a thread in their depths. "I have never, never had anyone intrigue me or test me or force me to grow the way you do. There is not a version of my life—not one where I'm happy—that doesn't have you in the center of it. If you think I'll settle for just being your friend, you're wrong, and I have my work cut out for me."

Heat builds behind my eyes. "Please stop, Theo." He can't say these things. He can't let me watch his heart dangle there for me to pluck like a perfect, ripe apple.

His lips whisper across my cheek. "Or what?"

"If you kiss me, I won't be able to stop myself from kissing you back."

He pauses with his mouth next to the corner of mine. "You don't want to kiss me?"

I ache for him to kiss me. To finally close the space between us. "You know I'm attracted to you. That's not our problem. But kissing you … I can't. It's not smart." It will be my undoing. I'll momentarily forget all the sound reasons we can't be together, and I'll let emotion and attraction win.

I'll end up more broken than I already am.

His lip grazes the bone under my eye. "Kissing you is the smartest idea I've ever had, but if you want me to walk away, I'll walk away … tonight." His mouth circles to my eyebrow, the touch as delicate as a paintbrush before it touches a canvas. "But I'll try again tomorrow." He moves to the other eyebrow, a barely-anything caress that makes me want to lean forward and press his lips to my skin.

But I don't. I hold still.

If I move, I'm done.

I won't be able to keep myself from plunging into all he has to offer. Even when I know the outcome. He'll leave. I'll be here. There isn't a tomorrow for us despite his sweet declaration.

His lips move to the angle of my jaw. It takes everything in me not to tip my chin, so his lips will caress the sensitive spot on my neck.

He whispers. "I will pursue you the day after that and the day after that and the day after that. Just like I've done for the last year."

"I thought that was because you hate to lose."

He pulls his mouth from my skin and meets my eyes. His gaze darts back and forth as his pupils dilate, and I glimpse even farther into his heart. "It's because you matter, Georgi. You can have a life of your own. You don't have to settle for being the best supporting actress in everyone else's drama."

My stupid spine melts, and I lean into his embrace. "You can't say things like that."

"One of us has to tell the truth." His lips meet mine, and I can't stop myself from returning his kiss.

It's everything.

It's the sweetness of a first kiss and the comfort of an old friend.

It's the passion of completeness and the freefall of spontaneous unknowns.

He groans deep in his throat and pulls me into his lap. One hand stays buried in my hair and the other loops around my waist, securing us in this precious moment.

This is what we should have been doing for the last year. What my stubbornness and his embarrassment cost us.

Even though I doubt we can last, I give in to the sensation. I let my silly heart hope that everything Theo said will come true.

We *can* be together.

We *can* build a relationship that lasts.

The loyalty we give to our families can extend to each other.

We don't have to choose.

Chapter 20

Theo

YES!

I savor Georgi's taste as her lips slide across mine, her touch grounds me, and her breath fills my lungs.

My arms hook around her waist and haul her closer to my chest. I can't let a breath of air between us, or she'll dive into her insecurities, spook, and run away again.

Georgi doesn't trust easily, so the gift of kissing her like this is a treasure trove of intimacy and opportunity I don't take for granted. Her affection is hard-won and worth the fight.

It's not a long kiss, but I'm okay taking things slowly. It's taken a year to get back to this point. I'll let her set our pace. I'm not going anywhere.

She nestles into me, drapes her legs over my lap, and strums my guitar. "I didn't know you play."

"I don't pull it out often. My dad isn't a fan." To say the least. Playing it tonight after our "talk" is a selfish rebellion.

She rubs her fingers over the calluses on the tips of my fingers. "Your hands tell a different story."

I line up our fingers and spread my hand wide, pressing my palm to hers. "What other stories do my hands tell?"

She turns my hand to catch the light spilling from the cabin inside. "Your nails are clean, so you don't change the oil in your car or tinker with engines. There are no calluses on your palms, so you don't do manual labor like mowing lawns or swinging a hammer."

"Our chief at the hospital where I did my residency always told us to keep our hands 'doctor soft.' No calluses, perfectly trimmed nails. Moisturize every time you wash your hands. Always wear gloves when working outside. Patients are more confident in their physician when they shake a firm, smooth hand instead of a rough, limp one." It's a practice I continue.

She traces the lines across my palm. "Your patients know you're not doing anything but taking care of them."

"Exactly. I always have these callouses, though." I brush the tips of my fingers over her wrist. "They never go away."

"How long have you been playing?"

"Elena and I spent our summer vacations in Mexico City with my papa. He taught me when I was young." I examine my hands. "By the end of his life, rheumatoid arthritis made it impossible for him to play. His hands were hard and gnarled. His joints, frozen and painful. He was patient and encouraged me, even when I made mistakes."

She plucks a cord. "My dad always said, 'Soft hands, soft man.'"

"That's harsh." And untrue. Some of the best men I know pride themselves on good skincare.

"He was a harsh guy."

A man with harsh, hard hands uses them to hurt people. "He left you?"

She rests her head on my shoulder and continues to rub her fingertip over my hands. "Yeah, a while ago. We don't even know if he's alive anymore."

I kiss her temple. "I'm sorry." Heat and indignation smolder in my chest. What kind of man abandons his family? Who in their right mind would leave a woman like Georgi? She's precious and fantastic.

"Don't be. I'm surprised he stayed long enough to sire five kids." She bobs her shoulder. "Besides, it's easier without him. I only have to worry about one alcoholic instead of two."

"You should never have to worry about any." But it reaffirms why Georgi is afraid to be loved. If your parents abandon you, physically or emotionally, you can't learn how valuable you are.

Georgi is priceless.

Her friendship and love are all I want in life.

The revelation is as ridiculous as it sounds, but it's true. I've fought to help my dad build our company one party weekend at a time.

It's all been worthless compared to holding Georgi right now.

Take the yacht, the money, and Sanchez Biotech.

If I have Georgi and my family, I don't need anything else.

That's probably why my dad doesn't want to train me to be his successor. He knows my heart isn't dedicated to the company the way it is to Georgi.

Should it be?

Should I fight as hard to earn Dad's respect as I have to earn Georgi's affection?

Those aren't thoughts I should be thinking right now.

Georgi's here. In my arms. Letting me kiss her.

Now isn't the time to contemplate my loyalties and what I want after tonight.

I should be paying attention to Georgi spilling her heart. I squeeze her tighter.

"I don't have to worry right now," she says. "At least not for myself. Lee is keeping an eye on Tipsy."

Not a responsibility an eighteen-year-old boy should have either, but ... "How did she convince your uncle to let her go shopping today?"

"Mona at Love Bugs Tacos hired her to run errands for the day. We just neglected to tell my uncle the details of the errands."

"And for the party?"

"Sleep over with our grandma."

If their grandmother is helping Tipsy sneak out, why doesn't she help with her son? Or is this grandma related to Tipsy's mom? The Montgomery family tree is confusing, but hopefully I'll be around long enough to figure out the intricacies.

I kiss her temple. "We're turning your family into delinquents."

"As long as Uncle Hoyt doesn't crash the party, we should be fine."

The thought trickles ice water down my back. "Will he?" Will he demand his daughter? Will he blame Georgi? Will my parents protect them? Can I?

Georgi bobs her shoulder. "Harry might."

I wince. "I invited your cousin to participate in the bachelor auction. I was extending an olive branch. I haven't heard if he accepted or not."

"That was kind of you. If he shows up, we'll hide her. He'll be distracted by all the expensive breasts on display anyway." Georgi sits up and sticks out her chest like she's flaunting DD implants.

I'm a guy. I notice the way the top of her dress curves around her chest. The fabric pulls tight as she arches her back. I lick my lips and tighten my grip on her waist.

Someday, when Georgi's mine, I'll know what the rest of her creamy skin looks like under all that fabric.

But not tonight. Tonight, I'm content with my imagination and Georgi's flirty smile.

I clear my throat. "I'll let Dad's security know to keep an eye out."

She crinkles her nose. "Has your dad always been hard on you?"

"I made mistakes a couple years ago. I'm paying for them. It's been hard to earn his respect since I lost it. Sometimes, I don't think it's possible."

She swings her legs off my lap and moves back to the other lounge chair. "What did you do?" Deep hesitation and distrust fill her voice.

The distance makes telling her about the Olympic Trials impossible. Maybe if she'd stayed snuggled against me, I'd find the courage, despite her tone.

But with her eyes boring into mine and the cynicism in her voice, I can't find words that don't prove I'm the shallow, inconsiderate jerk she assumed I am.

Because that's what I was.

I was selfish.

I was inconsiderate and thoughtless.

"It's getting late." I stand and hold out my hand. "I'll walk you to your room."

She frowns at my hand. "That's it? You're not going to tell me?"

"I ..." I shove my hands in my pockets. I don't know why I did what I did in the first place, so I don't know how to explain it in words she'll understand.

"No. I get it. You're embarrassed. You screwed up but can't own your mistake."

"It's not that simple." I judged her dad for not being a man of his word, for destroying her faith in the people who are supposed to love her, and that is exactly what I did to Elena.

I promised I would be there for her when she needed me, but I wasn't.

There's no way Georgi doesn't see the reflection of her parents' failures in my actions.

Right now, while I'm earning her trust, the truth will do more damage than waiting. I don't know how to get her to see that.

She shakes her head and blinks rapidly. "Good night, Theo."

I try to wrap my arms around her. "Georgi, let me explain."

She shakes me off. "Theo, you have to get over whatever this is because you act one way, then say another. I can't do this." She bolts inside.

I chuck a throw pillow off the side of the boat.

Great job, Theo. Way to lose all the progress you've fought so hard to make. Stop being a chicken. Maybe she won't hold your decision against you like everyone else.

But what if she does?

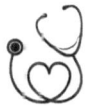

Theo

I jam my arms in my wetsuit. The flume won't cut it this morning. I need the Gulf of Mexico to work through the tumultuous thoughts cascading in my head.

I shouldn't have kept my mouth shut. I should have told her the truth.

She'll find out eventually. All she has to do is ask Elena, and my failures won't be secrets anymore.

Swimming until I can't lift my arms should clear my head and give me the words to fix the damage I did last night. I walk onto the dock and secure my goggles over my eyes.

"Theo!" Elena calls from the upper deck.

I drop my head back and groan. "What?"

"Give me two minutes, and I'll go with you."

"I don't want company." It's harder to berate myself and surrender to the burn in my chest when I have to make sure Elena's not drowning. Not that she would, but it's the principle of the thing.

She leans over the railing. "Too bad. It's not safe to swim by yourself, and I need the miles."

Her dark head disappears. I grind my teeth.

Sometimes caring about other people sucks.

She's right. It's not safe to swim alone unless you're towing a buoy, which I'm not. If she's excited about training, I won't deny her the opportunity to push her body to its limits.

While I wait for Elena, I stretch my triceps and lats. I pull my foot to my glutes and stretch my quad. Anything to keep myself moving and my brain focused on the task at hand instead of the redhead I can't stop disappointing.

Elena drops a towel next to my feet and secures her swim cap over her hair. "How far are we going?"

"Until I can't feel my arms."

"Hmm." She gives me a once over. Her eyebrow twitches with unasked questions.

"Are you ready? How's your shoulder doing?" I pull the sleeve of my wetsuit to make sure it's secure.

"Physical therapy is like magic, so lead the way."

I dive in and swim out of the yacht club, around the speed limit buoy into the bay. It's too early for most boats, but I angle toward the beach to be safe. We don't need to be run over by someone watching the sunrise.

One advantage to swimming is there's no way to chat as we work. Unlike running, when Elena asks unending questions, her face in the water, her focus on her breath, stroke, and positioning, not my grumpy attitude.

We swim past the pier to the end of the peninsula. Part of me wants to tread into deeper water, push all the way to the barrier islands, but that wouldn't be wise.

Despite my wetsuit, the chill seeps into my skin. If we don't turn back soon, hypothermia will set in. While I would welcome the numbness, I can't risk Elena's health.

My kicks slow, and my sister passes me. When she's a full body length ahead, she stops, treads water, and slides her goggles to the top of her head. "You okay?"

I nod the way we came. "Time to turn back."

She checks her watch. "It's barely been an hour." But her lips are two shades closer to blue than they should be.

"I have work to do."

Her nose wrinkles. "Like what? I heard Dad kicked you off the factory job."

"I'm doing the bachelor auction circuit again today." The last thing I want to spend my time on is talking strangers into donating their bodies and time to my mom's cause, but I'll do it. Until I reconcile everything with Georgi, it's my only course of action.

Elena splashes water in my face. "That's not why you're grumpy."

"Close enough." We don't need to get into what I *didn't* tell Georgi as my sister slowly freezes to death.

"You and Georgi were weird on the way home. What happened at Frank's?"

"Dinner was fine."

She lifts her eyebrow. "The dinner where Mom and Dad talked and you silently shuffled food around your plate? Where you pretended not to stare at Georgi like she was the salmon?"

"Yeah, that one." Guess I wasn't as covert as I thought.

"Theo, did something happen with Georgi?"

"It's nothing." I swim toward the boat. I'm not sharing my heartbreak with my sister any more than I already have. She's meddled enough.

Yes, I should thank her for getting Georgi to stay on the boat and giving me the opportunity to show her I'm not the man she thought I was.

But Elena's involvement adds a layer of confusion I can't escape.

If my sister weren't here, would Georgi have ever given me a second chance?

I haven't earned it on my own over the last year. The only reason Georgi gave me a chance was because of Elena's good word. Because I am a better brother to her now than I was three years ago.

How will Georgi react when she learns I'm not the good guy she thinks I am? I am the selfish, conceited jerk she decided I was when I took Lexie and Viola to the coffee shop.

Elena grabs my leg. "Did you kiss her?"

My sister is relentless. I have to give her something. "If I did?"

"Then I don't get why you're grumpy. Why aren't you happier?"

"She doesn't trust me. Heck, I don't trust myself."

"You need to have some fun."

I scoff and start swimming again "How will that help?"

"If you only measure yourself by your mistakes, you miss most of who you are."

"That makes no sense." My sister sounds like a broken fortune cookie.

She slides her goggles over her eyes. "You'll see." She swims toward the pier. "Race you home."

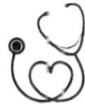

Georgi

Sunrise's soft orange tones filter through the curtain in my room. I stretch my arms overhead until I get a satisfying pop in my shoulders.

I don't work until this afternoon, so a lazy Saturday morning in my room is the perfect way to spend my time.

Some might call it hiding, but I prefer not to add that label.

I could go to the garage and talk to Uncle Hoyt, but I've decided to wait until after the gala to convince him to let me move home.

It has absolutely nothing ... almost nothing ... maybe a little bit to do with how much I love this bed and its fluffy pillows. The boat's gentle rocking is better than any medication to get me to sleep.

Besides, it will be easier for Tipsy to sneak out than for both of us.

My door flings open, and Elena hops on my bed. "Get up, sleepy-head." Her wet hair drips on my comforter.

I toss a pillow at her. "I am up."

She tugs on my arm and drags me to the edge of the bed. "We're having a fun day."

"You have practice."

She points to her wet hair. "I swam. I'll dive this afternoon."

"Theo's going to be mad at me for keeping you from training. I'm here to help with your stress, not let you to play hooky."

"No more arguments." She tosses the pillow back. "Get dressed. Meet me upstairs in twenty."

Elena can be so bossy. Why do I give in to her? Because we always have fun and I need more fun in my life.

I guess I don't get my lazy morning hiding from Theo.

Everything was going so well last night until I asked about his dad. Part of me thinks I should have left it alone. He'll tell me when he's ready.

But how is it fair for me to spill my guts and tell him all the painful parts of my life without expecting him to share in return?

Lasting relationships are built on open communication, sharing the happy and the sad. Our communication has been awful from the get-go.

If Theo won't share, then what are we building besides a house of cards?

Dressed and eating a piece of cinnamon-sugar toast, I plop on the sofa across from where Elena stands. "What's the plan? Where's everyone else?" Lexie and her squad are the last people I want to see this morning, so I need a heads up.

"I sent them shopping, so we can play games." Elena pulls several board games from the cabinet. "Pick one."

"How do you fit so many games in such a little cabinet?" I leaf through our choices. *Risk. Monopoly. Scrabble. Sagrada. Wingspan. Villainous. Settlers of Catan.* It's like we're ten years old. "I've never played any of these."

"Not even *Monopoly*?"

I shake my head. "Family game night wasn't a thing in our trailer."

"Then you, my friend, are in for a treat." She picks *Monopoly* and holds out the tokens. "Pick your piece."

I choose the dog. She picks the top hat and the racecar.

"Who else—"

"I call racecar." Theo raises his hand and jumps over the back of the sofa.

"I should have guessed."

He nudges my shoulder and smiles like last night never happened. "It's my lucky piece."

It grates on my nerves how easily he pretends we didn't make out then fight last night. Why is he happy-go-lucky all the time? Why can't he act like there are real emotions between us?

Or are they fake, and this is him being real?

Why won't he just make up his mind?

Elena sets up the board. "He's supposed to work too, but this sounded like a better way to spend our morning."

We roll the dice to see who goes first. Elena wins. She rolls a six and advances her token. We take turns, buy houses and hotels. Theo spends a lot of time in jail, which makes me laugh.

There isn't a hint of Elena's strain.

Some of mine melts away too. It's hard to worry about handsome doctors, proper utensil habits, and uncle's tempers when you're dealing for Tennessee Ave.

"I'll give you $200 and clean your room for a month." Theo says.

"My room is never dirty. That's a bad deal," Elena says.

"I'll drive you to practice."

"Nope."

"I'll pay for a masseuse."

I tap New York Avenue and St. James Place cards in the stack in front of him. "He wants the trifecta pretty badly. I wouldn't give it to him."

He shoos my hand away. "No opinions from the peanut gallery, please."

Elena rubs her thumb across her chin. "How many massages?"

"Three."

I punch his shoulder. "Cheapskate."

"Five."

"If you are going to insult me ..." She presses the property card into my hand. "Georgi gets it for free just to annoy you."

Theo runs his hand through his hair. "I never should have introduced you two."

"Too late now." I throw my arm over Elena's shoulders. "You're stuck with us forever."

Theo's eyes sink into mine. "Promise?"

Those blasted butterflies are back, swooping and swirling in my stomach.

They aren't allowed to be here. He can't be Mr. Flirty after refusing to talk to me last night.

Stop it, body. Do not react to the enviously long eyelashes or the perfectly stubbled cheeks.

I swallow the lump in my throat and press my hand to my stomach, but nothing helps. Did the heater just turn on?

"And that's my cue." Elena wipes her hands. "Mission complete. You kids have fun. I have back tucks to practice."

"Traitor," Theo mumbles.

I agree. I don't want to be alone with him. He owes me an explanation, but he won't give me one. Not a complete one. It will be more excuses.

If whatever Theo did is so bad he can't tell me, I know it will change the way I look at him. I was learning to like what I saw.

How do I go back to hating him with every fiber of my being?

Elena kisses her fingers and waves goodbye, a mischievous smirk on her face.

Escaping to my room is the coward's way out, so I stay and sort the money, sliding it into its container.

Theo puts away the property cards and tiny houses. "This was fun."

"Elena's seems to be doing well. She's happier."

"About last night ..." He drums his fingers on his thigh.

Small talk over. Got it. "Yes?" I won't make this easy on him. He can't act like last night never happened.

He takes the property cards from my hands and presses his palms to mine. "I'm sorry I didn't tell you the truth. You were right. I'm scared of how you'll react. Especially now that I know more about your dad."

I slouch against the back of the couch. "What does my dad have to do with any of this?"

He's been M.I.A. for seventeen years. I've lived more of my life without him than I did with him. The only reason he's an issue is because my mom can't let him go. She stupidly believes he'll come back one day. I gave up those delusions the day he walked out the door, and I prayed he'd never come home. Maybe I should have prayed a different prayer, but the past is in the past.

Mostly.

Theo brushes my hair off my forehead. "Your dad was supposed to be the first man you trusted. Who protected you, provided for you, and taught you the world is a safe place. But he failed you. He didn't keep the inherent promises being a dad requires."

"I—"

He presses his thumb to my lips. "Let me finish." He cradles my jaw, and I hate how much I love the way his fingertips scrape along my skin.

He licks his lips. "It was my job to get Elena to the Olympic Trials last time, and I failed her. I promised I would be there for her, but I wasn't. She would already be an Olympian if not for my selfish decisions."

"My dad is nothing like you." Every decision my dad ever made was about him, his wants. He never cared about us. Theo almost cares too much.

"We both failed the people we're supposed to take care of."

"I've never seen you do anything selfish." I point down the hallway where Elena disappeared. "Everything you do for your family, the career you gave up, it's all about helping other people."

"That's only because I learned my lesson the hard way when Elena suffered the consequences of my actions. That's why my dad doesn't respect me. I don't deserve it after what I did. It's why I host parties I hate and serve my family in whatever capacity my father deems most appropriate."

That's why he gave up medicine. He feels guilty about putting himself first, so he's decided he can't have what he wants. I guess we aren't so different after all. "I don't think you needed to give up being an anesthesiologist."

"There are millions of doctors in the world, and only about a hundred Olympic divers. Sacrificing my profession for her chance to win a gold medal is a small price to pay."

I don't understand how him not being a doctor will make Elena an Olympian. How does serving Lexie more margaritas help Elena be a better competitor? It doesn't. "Why can't you do both?"

"Have you ever sat in the driver seat while your sister bawled her eyes out, the goal she dedicated her life to no longer attainable because you couldn't be bothered to pick her up on time?"

I don't have an answer for him. I've held my sisters and Tipsy while they've cried, but I've never been the cause of their tears.

But I doubt what he did was because he was selfish. Was he stuck at the hospital? Was there traffic? A million variables could have caused him to miss picking her up.

Why was she his responsibility? Where were their parents? Why didn't she call an Uber when she realized he wasn't going to make it?

This can't just be on him.

I open my mouth to ask more questions, but the anguish in Theo's expression stops me.

He's already beating himself up over this. I don't need to pile on. I know enough about him to know he didn't intentionally hurt his sister.

Theo's not that kind of man.

Even if he thinks he broke his promise, he's nothing like my dad.

He's not selfish. He's too thoughtful and loyal to ever be selfish. He might not understand how other people will interpret a situation—like how I reacted to Viola asking him to take her to bed—but he can't control my assumptions. That's my fault for not asking the

right questions and letting my insecurities jump to the wrong conclusions.

Theo runs his hand through his hair. "My dad told me I have to take
Lexie to the gala."

Hello, subject change.

"That makes sense." Theo spends too much time with me. While
Corine may want me here, I don't get the same vibe from Sanchez the
third. Lexie is more likely to help advance their family business.

"I want you to be my date instead."

My pulse trills in my chest, but I bite the inside of my cheek to
squash the feeling. Kissing Theo last night was everything I'd dreamt
about for the last year, but we can't go back to our little bubble of
intimacy. His responsibilities and my commitments will pull us apart.
"I can't."

"Why?"

"You're smart. You don't need the list."

He drops my hand and scoots into the corner of the sofa. "I knew
I shouldn't have told you."

I place my hand on his knee. "Theo, stop. That's not why I'm saying
no. I'm glad I know the truth, but I still can't."

"Please," he pleads. "I won't survive a night with her. I don't want
to lead her on. She's not the woman I want."

"But the gala is business."

"It's not *only* business." The heavy innuendo in his voice worries
me.

I have to voice my fear. "Are you using me to get back at your dad?"

He tugs me toward him. "Never. I want to spend a magical evening
with the most beautiful, intriguing, sexy woman I know." He slides his
arm around my waist and dances feather-light kisses along my neck. "I
can't watch another man hold you when I know we belong together."

I push him away. Possessiveness is not sexy. "Think about the consequences. You said it yourself—you need to earn your dad's respect by doing what he wants. If your dad's respect is really what you want, I can't get in the way. I need to keep my eye on Tipsy anyway."

"She'll be with Elena."

"And your dad?"

Theo's shoulders slump. "I don't think it matters what I do. I'll never earn his forgiveness, so what's the point of sacrificing myself anymore? Please. You're great at saving everyone else. Save me."

The pleading in his voice is almost enough to weaken my resolve but not quite. Theo can't use me in this war with his dad, even if he says he's not. "You don't need saving. You need to decide what you want to do with your life. You say all you want is to earn your dad's respect, but taking me instead of Lexie—heck, coming to the coffee shop every Saturday for a year—that doesn't speak to the same motivations. You either want your dad's respect, to take over your family's company, and become the man your dad wants you to be, or you want to follow your own path. I'm not asking you to decide now, but you need to think about it before you do something we both regret."

Before my heart is demolished when he realizes I'm not part of his Sanchez Biotech CEO future.

"Will you buy me in the bachelor auction, then?"

I snort. "I can't afford you."

"I'll do anything."

"Like give me your American Express?"

"It doesn't have a limit, so Lexie can't outbid you."

"I can do that."

He kisses me to seal the deal.

Chapter 21

Theo

I SHOULD PAY ATTENTION to Keegan examining Elena's shoulder, but my mind isn't on my sister's health. It's back on the boat next to a *Monopoly* board replaying Georgi's ultimatum.

I've had the same thoughts: Will Dad ever respect me? Will he mentor me to take over the company? Are my sacrifices helping Elena achieve her goals?

Or has my dad shoved me out of the way and given me menial tasks so I can't do any more damage?

Is Bubee a gilded cage or a step in the right direction?

Do I know which path I'm on?

Does it lead to a life I love?

Where does Georgi fit?

Keegan shakes Elena's hand. "Keep up the good work. I don't want to see you in here again."

She giggles. "Sounds good to me."

"So, she's cleared?" I ask.

"Her shoulder is as good as we can get it through interventions. Any further improvement will come with time and proper training."

"Does Calum know what that means?"

Elena rolls her eyes. "Keep up, big brother. He's been at every physical therapy appointment." She waggles her eyebrows. "I think he has a crush on Debney. He kept tripping over his tongue when she asked him questions. It was so cute I have a future as a matchmaker." She playfully punches my shoulder.

"Let's focus on diving."

"What? I'm one-for-one. A little nudge, my perfect record will increase, and another happy couple can thank me during their wedding toasts."

"You're getting ahead of yourself there."

She hops off the exam table. "Nah. You'll marry Georgi within the year."

Keegan chokes and pounds his chest. "Sorry, swallowed wrong."

I don't like the smirk he gives me. It's too all-knowing. Like he agrees with my sister but also can't believe what he's hearing. "Do you have an opinion?"

He holds up his hands. "Georgi's been different the last few weeks."

"Do you think ..." I'm not sure what to ask. Our relationship floats in this weird space between love and loathing. She doesn't hate me anymore, but we have more reasons driving us apart than we do pulling us together.

Is what we have enough?

Is she my path?

Keegan pats my shoulder. "I know how you feel. Falling is scary and exhilarating, but the risk is worth it. You've spouted your love for

Georgi since I met you. If it's true, don't hold back. You'll never regret loving the person who makes your world make sense."

"See?" Elena smacks my side. "Told you. You and Georgi are meant to be."

I follow Keegan and Elena toward the front of the hospital. "How do we make it work when she won't leave Bubee and I have no idea where Dad will send me next?"

Elena stops next to the sliding glass doors. "Theo, you're not a kid. Dad can't make you do anything you don't want to do."

"That's easy for you to say. Diving is your dream. You get to do it every day."

"Is it?" She taps her chin. "I don't remember picking it to be the only thing I do with my entire life. I don't think I decided I'd only take online classes instead of immersing myself in the full college experience. I didn't pick punishing my body instead of going to medical school. You got to choose, but you gave it up."

This is not the place to have this conversation. "For you." I whisper yell.

"I didn't ask you to."

"You didn't have to. As your big brother, it's my responsibility to look out for you."

She gestures to the hospital's lobby. "Are you telling me you wouldn't jump at the chance to be back in an operating room?"

"That—"

"Don't say it doesn't matter because it does. Stop being a martyr, and be a man. You can be such a whiner, you know that?" She spins on her heel. "Thanks, Keegan. Your expertise has been invaluable. I can't wait to get to spend more time with you and your wife. See you around." She stomps out the doors into the sunshine.

Keegan crosses his arms as we watch her leave. "This is the most interesting appointment I've had in months."

"Shut up."

"She's right. If you want a job, we need anesthesiologists."

"I haven't worked in three years."

"It's like riding a bicycle."

Pfft. "While juggling flaming torches on a tightrope twenty feet off the ground."

"Yeah, like that, but it's totally worth it."

My shoulders slump. "I know."

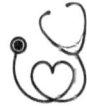

Georgi

Corine stands at the head of the table in an elegant dusty-rose tweed pants suit. "The gala will be a passed hors d'oeuvres event, but it is wise for each of you to understand proper table etiquette as well." She gestures for Elena, Tipsy, and me to pick up our napkins. "First, when seated, drape your napkin over your lap. If standing, drape it over your left arm and hold your plate with your left hand. This frees your right hand to greet guests."

"I watched *The Princess Diaries* last night to prepare," Tipsy leans to my ear and whispers. She gently shakes the folds from her napkin and gracefully lays it in her lap.

"Well done." Corine beams.

Elena follows suit with dramatic snap and flourish. Corine's mouth tenses, but she doesn't add commentary.

When my napkin is in my lap, Corine takes her seat and nods to Judah.

He arrives with the first course. "For the amuse-bouche, we have sourdough crostini with goat cheese, fig, and pistachios, finished with a drizzle of local honey. Bon appétit."

I pick up my bite, but it doesn't make it to my mouth. Corine scowls at me with enough vigor that I might melt into my chair. "Is this wrong?"

"These are slightly larger than a normal sourdough baguette. The wisest course of action is to cut it into two or three bites."

I put the yummy bite on my plate, pick up my fork and knife, making eye contact with Corine and waiting for her to nod that I'm not messing up again. She nods, and I slice it down the middle. The goat cheese oozes from the warm bread.

"Fingers or fork?" Tipsy asks.

"That depends on the situation. If a fork is available, always use a fork."

We eat our bites of crostini, and I want to beg Judah for seconds. The tart fig jam unites with the honey on my tongue like they are long-lost lovers meeting for a clandestine rendezvous. It takes everything in me not to capture the dropped goat cheese with the tip of my finger and suck.

Corine continues to coach us through our meal. Next is a minestrone soup with carrots, celery, kidney beans, spinach, and homemade noodles. "To get the last few bites, tip the bowl toward the center of the table and scoop away from you." Corine lifts the edge of the bowl closest to her and demonstrates the technique.

I was considering emulating the Beast and drinking from the edge, but this is less likely to smudge my makeup.

The fish course is shrimp cocktail without the tails removed. "Cut them from the tail. Don't try to get the part inside or you'll make a mess."

"Filet mignon with flaked crab, hollandaise, and roasted asparagus," Judah says.

"This is an exercise in patience. Cut one bite at a time." Corine demonstrates. "Place your knife on the edge of your plate, switching your fork back to your right hand."

By the time we get to the cheese course—please don't ask me to pronounce those French names—my attention is shot. My stomach wants to burst, and my head wants a pillow.

"Who knew a meal could be so exhausting?" I slouch in my chair.

Corine's eyebrow rises, and I assume the appropriate posture expected at a dinner of this caliber. Spine straight, shoulders back, jaw closed.

She nods her approval. "An upright posture demonstrates to your guests your respect for their time and thanks your chef for his wonderful creations." She claps for Judah when he clears the dishes.

"In our family, licking your plate is the highest form of flattery." Tipsy swipes a crust of bread through the remaining cinnamon hot chocolate in her champagne flute.

"Did we pass?" I fold my napkin and set it next to my water glass.

Corine dabs the edge of her mouth with her napkin. "Do you feel prepared?"

I glance at Tipsy. She shrugs. "I guess so," I say.

"Then it doesn't matter what anyone else thinks. This was for you, not them. In three days, enjoy yourselves and don't worry about the busy bodies whispering behind their champagne flutes. They're bored and looking to entertain themselves."

I wish I could take her encouragement to heart, but I'm too worried we'll make fools of ourselves and embarrass the family who's taken us under their wing.

Georgi

Tipsy arrives at the yacht shortly after lunch the day of the gala. She sits in the desk chair in my room and pulls up her legs to sit crisscrossed underneath her. Her hands twitch in her lap. "I can't believe we get to do this." The awe in her voice makes me smile.

"Just a few more hours. Corine has a hair stylist and makeup artist coming to help us get ready." My mouth drops open. "Did you ever think those words would come out of my mouth? We have personal stylists." I shake my head. This is Fantasyland, no doubt.

"Lucy at Storybook Styles will never do house calls." Tipsy props her chin on her hands. "At least not for our family. Too bad she and mom are still fighting over that bad dye job."

"Aunt Sally shouldn't have tried the DIY blue tips on top of her tiger-stiped highlights. Of course Lucy was offended."

"Mom looked ridiculous." Her eyebrows pinch together. "Do you think ..."

"What?"

"Is it silly that we're doing this? Will everyone look at me the way they looked at Mom?"

I gather her into my arms. "Tonight, you get to be a princess. There is no reason for you not to enjoy yourself. Elena is our friend. We're here to have fun with her. The fundraiser and all of Corine and Ted's guests don't matter."

"Are you sure?"

"Do you want to be here?"

"Yes." She doesn't hesitate to answer.

"Then hug that feeling tight, and don't let anyone take it away from you."

She lays her head on my shoulder and reminds of the little girl she used to be. Meek, timid, shy. I haven't seen this side of her since she met Elena.

Tipsy's become a little snarkier as she's gotten older, but she's growing into a curious, ambitious woman. She's breaking free of Uncle Hoyt's mental abuse and realizing she has power and strength.

I look forward to helping her grow into the woman she's destined to be.

I run my fingers through her hair. "How do you want to do your hair?"

"I don't know. Any ideas?"

We spend the next thirty minutes flipping through images on Pinterest until we find an updo she loves. With an asymmetrical part, braids, and a messy bun, it fits her personality to a tee and will make her dress look playful.

As she stares at the picture on the phone, contemplativeness settles in her expression.

I nudge her elbow. "Penny for your thoughts."

"Are you in love with Theo?"

I lurch back and almost fall off the bed. "What? Why?" That was not the direction I expected our conversation to detour. "What makes you think I am?"

"Elena."

"Elena?"

"She said if you didn't feel responsible for us, you guys would have fallen in love already."

"Honey, that's not true. My relationship with Theo is too complex to describe in one sentence. There are a lot of reasons why Theo and I don't work."

"Like what?"

Corine pops her head in the door. "Georgi, the stylist is ready for you."

I hold up a finger. "Can she wait a minute?" Tipsy and I need to finish this conversation. I can't leave this room letting her think she's a burden.

"Be quick," Corine says and walks down the hall.

"Tipsy, I like Theo. He's a great man. I'm attracted to him, and we have fun, but that's not enough to sustain a relationship. He doesn't know what he wants out of life, and my life is here."

She shakes her head. "Those are excuses. I don't know what I want to do with my life. Does that mean I can't fall in love?"

"No, but—"

She scrunches my comforter. "Aren't couples supposed to figure things out together? Why can't you do that?"

"I don't know. I just ..."

"He's perfect for you, Georgi. He makes you smile and laugh. He won't leave you. You should take a chance."

"I'm taking relationship advice from a seventeen-year-old now?"

"Maybe you can't see the forest through the trees and you need an outside perspective."

"I'm fine."

"No, you're not." She worries the edge of her shorts. "I think ... I think Dad kicking you out was the best thing for everyone."

A gaping hole explodes in my stomach. "What?" There's no way that's true.

"Lee, Elena, and I talked. We don't think you should move home. You need to stay here with Theo. It's better this way."

"How is it better?" Abandoning them is never going to be better.

"When you were there, you always defended me or distracted Dad. You always took care of me."

I squeeze her hand. "Yeah, that's my job."

"No, it's not." She pulls free. "I need to take care of myself. Elena too—she doesn't need Theo hovering like a helicopter. You need to have lives that don't revolve around us. We'll be fine on our own."

"But what if your dad gets drunk and tries to beat you up?" I try to keep my voice soft, but the way she flinches, I didn't do a good job.

"Then I run away or fight back. You don't need to be his punching bag. That doesn't help anyone."

I stare at her. My mouth opens and closes, but I can't find words. She doesn't want me to help her.

She wants to stand on her own two feet.

I respect that, but I'm not comfortable with this feeling growing in my chest. It's an empty hollowness, like wandering around in the dark with the boogie man taunting, invisible but too close for safety.

I need to protect her. I've spent the last seventeen years protecting her. I don't know how to turn that instinct off.

Corine walks into my room, grabs my hand, and drags me off the bed. "We need to get your hair done now or we'll be late."

I walk like a ghost and slump into the chair in Corine's bathroom. The hairdresser drapes a cape around my shoulders and fluffs my hair.

"What are we doing?" she asks.

I pull up the Pinterest picture I found. Since my dress has cap sleeves, I decided to style my hair in loose waves down my back. I hand her the velvet jewelry box that was delivered with my dress.

No note. No idea where it came from.

She flips the lid, and the lights around the mirror make the emerald and diamond comb sparkle. She winks. "Classic. I love it." She spritzes something in my hair and gets to work curling it.

I try to process everything Tipsy said, but I'm like a skipping record. The same sentences keep repeating.

You need to have lives that don't revolve around us.

You don't need to be his punching bag.

You shouldn't move home.

It's better this way.

If they don't need me, I'm free to do whatever I want.

Theo's free … if he can break away from his dad.

Is this what's best for everyone?

Can Elena, Tipsy, and Lee take care of themselves?

Do I need to let them go?

How do I let go?

Chapter 22

Theo

I peek in Elena's room where she sits on her bed, staring at her rose-petal pink gala dress.

I gently rap on the door. "The party starts in ten minutes. Are you going to wear the dress or just stare at it?"

"Why are we doing"—she waves around the room—"this?"

"To raise money."

"Why not take the money we spent on the party and give it away? Why make a show of it?"

"This is how Mom and Dad do things."

"But why?"

"I don't know." I wouldn't make philanthropy a public spectacle either, but I understand some donors need to feel they're getting something for their money, even if it's just a night out with friends. "You've never asked before. Why now?"

"I've been asking myself a lot of questions lately."

Time to be fashionably late. I loosen my tie and sit on the edge of the bed. Happy, *Monopoly*-playing Elena from a few days ago is gone. The sad girl who showed up on my dock a few weeks ago has kidnapped her. After yelling at me at the hospital, I'm not surprised.

Something has been eating at her from the beginning. I guess tonight is the night she finally feels like sharing. "What's bothering you?"

"Remember when you and Dad went to the Maldives two years ago, and Mom and I went to the diving competition in Syracuse?"

Images from that trip flip in my brain like a broken photo album. I thought we were going to learn to scuba dive. We didn't swim once. We didn't even leave the resort except to visit the local hospital. "I sat in the corner while Dad had board meetings." No more ruffled hair or asking my opinions. I was invisible.

"I sat in the hotel room shivering to death until it was time to dive. I lost so badly. And for what? Why did I give up vacations, prom, friends to chase a dream that doesn't matter?"

This is another iteration of the argument we had at the hospital. "It does matter. If it's important to you, it matters."

She rubs her eyes. "I'm tired."

I lift the edge of the comforter. "Go to bed. I'll tell Mom you don't feel well."

"An early bedtime won't fix this. My soul is tired. I don't want to compete anymore."

"At all?" This is new.

She shakes her head, but the action is slow, like it takes all the energy she has to make her head move an inch to the left and an inch to the right. "I love the free fall. Challenging my body to see if I can rotate a few degrees faster, angle my body a little straighter." She sags into herself. "But I hate to surface. I hate the scowl on Calum's face. The list of imperfections and mistakes I can't erase no matter how hard I work."

"Count the victories, not the mistakes. Isn't that what you told me?"

"I don't have any victories."

"You have hundreds of trophies. This isn't like you. Did something happen at practice today?"

"Nothing out of the ordinary. Calum wasn't happy with my twists. I kept hitting the water at a ten-degree angle and splashing."

"We can get a new coach." I'd love nothing more, especially if he can't teach Elena without destroying her spirit. Besides, sometimes new energy is the kick you need to make it to the next level.

"He's not the problem. I am. I don't want to go to Trials. I can't keep losing."

"You don't know you'll lose."

"The odds aren't in my favor. I've lost the passion I used to have." My little sister sounds so weary, it hurts.

"Mom and Dad won't like that." They've poured money and time into her chase. When our lives didn't revolve around Sanchez Biotech, they revolved around diving.

She tucks her knees to her chest. "They're why I haven't quit yet."

"What do you want to do instead?"

"College. Travel. I have some ideas, but nothing concrete."

"You need a plan before you talk to Mom and Dad, but I'll support whatever you decide." I'll be her bodyguard, if that's what she needs.

"I know. Thanks."

I lift her dress's hanger from the hook. "Are you coming to the gala?"

"This dress is too beautiful to waste away in a closet. I might as well wear it."

"Meet you out there." I give her a hug and shut the door.

Georgi stands with her head resting on her door. Stunning isn't close to describing how she looks. The dress is just as magnificent on her as it was at Frank's, but with her hair curled and the comb I secretly gifted her pulling it off her face, I can't blink or breathe. "Eavesdropping?" I shove my hands in my pants pockets.

"Small boat." She pushes from the wall and wraps her arms around my waist. "If I didn't know anything else about you except what I just heard, I'd know you are an amazing man. You know that, right?"

My cheeks heat as embarrassment floods my system. I settle my hands on her hips. "Thanks. We should go."

She doesn't release her grip. "Before we go, I'm sorry for the mean things I've said over the last year. I thought I was falling in love with you that first night, and I was embarrassed and hurt when you brought all those beautiful women into the coffee shop. I should have given you the benefit of the doubt."

I nuzzle her nose. "I shouldn't have brought them. I should have told you the truth. And for the record, I fell. Hard."

"Let's see if we can get back to that, okay?"

"I'd love nothing more."

I place a chaste kiss to her lips. Nothing more.

For right, now it's enough. The air is different tonight. The warmth from her body soaks into me, and the certainty that this is how things are supposed to be settles with heat in my bones.

Georgi and I belong together. I will love her until the day I die.

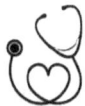

Georgi

I love Theo's caring soul. I love the way he takes care of his sister. I love how *seen* I feel with him.

I'm not sure if I'm safe, though. I know physically, he'll take care of whatever need arises. Exhibit A: letting me live on his boat.

But what about my heart?

If I fall the rest of the way into love, will he protect it?

If tonight, his parents make him choose me or them, will he choose me?

His loyalties might drive us apart

But I can't let what-ifs and worry stop me from trying.

Tipsy's right. I need to let go. I need to let myself love Theo with all of my heart, or I will always regret what could have been.

I clutch his hand as we ascend the stairs. His dad's eyes trace my face then linger in our interlaced fingers. His gaze drills into Theo. "Your date is upstairs."

His mom glances at Ted, but she doesn't betray her feelings. Corine extends her hand to me. "You look lovely, Georgi. Let me introduce you to the guests who have already arrived."

Theo squeezes my hand. "Save me a dance."

I nod and let Corine sweep me into the fray.

I don't kid myself. This is a battle of sorts. Corine said it doesn't matter, but tonight is more than a test of whether I know how to eat a crab cake without spilling pieces into my cleavage.

Can I fit in?

Do I belong?

Can I fake it long enough to make it?

Was Cinderella this nervous when she went to the ball?

She was expecting light snacks and pretty music. She didn't plan to win the prince's heart with one glance. A waltz to seal the deal.

Did she feel the weight of what his attention demanded of her?

Did she run because—even with how attracted she was to the prince—she wasn't ready to be a queen?

It's a complicated metaphor, but the children's story runs on repeat as I meet guest after guest. I know how a new woman feels when she comes to SUP club for the first time. Name tags are now a requirement. Even in the summer if we're in our bathing suits.

Corine stops in front of a broad-shouldered man with a handlebar mustache and full beard. He was part of the beach day two weeks ago, but we were never introduced. I don't know how he fits into the Sanchez Biotech puzzle. "Don, I would love to introduce Georgi Montgomery. She's a friend of my children."

Don clasps my hand and kisses the back with a slight bow. "I've heard about you." His tone is noncommittal. Who's talking about me? Did he hear good things or bad?

"All good, I hope."

He tips his head side to side, halfway between a nod and a shake. "Lexie is prone to exaggeration, but my daughter's a good judge of character."

I hide my cringe by itching the end of my nose. "She and I didn't get off on the best foot."

"It's hard to be friends when you're after the same man. Theo's a catch." He lifts his glass to Corine. "Tonight is the beginning of something special."

I swallow my tongue. I should have taken Theo's plea to save him from Lexie more seriously. If this is what we're up against, will Theo get a say in who he is with? Or will he continue to do whatever his dad tells him?

Corine hands me a glass of something with bubbles. I take a sip to regain my composure.

Champagne. It pickles my tongue and I cough to expel the tingles in my throat.

Not exactly the stellar performance I wanted for this evening. I didn't expect Don to be so blunt about Lexie's feelings.

Do Theo's parents support a Lexie-Theo relationship over one with me?

Has this been Corine's plan all along? Dress me like I belong, teach me to butter my bread one bite at a time, then throw me in the deep end to fight Lexie for Theo?

Corine rubs her hand up and down my back as I continue to choke on my spit. "Don, we aren't the Bridgertons. There won't be any arrangements made this evening."

But that doesn't eliminate the possibility in the future, does it?

She has to know Ted ordered Theo to be Lexie's date tonight. Is that the first step to a vow-bound alliance?

I've been reading too many novels with matchmaking aunties.

Besides, Theo kissed me in the hallway, and he's not the kind to kiss carelessly. The affection he gives has purpose and heart behind it. I didn't believe it before, but I do now.

Lexie may want to exploit him, drive a wedge between us by invoking my insecurities, but she's a spoiled girl who wants something that isn't hers to take.

I could tell her dad the nasty, childish things Lexie's done to me over the last year. Insults stream through my mind: Lexie treats servers like we're idiots, maybe you should have taught her manners. Lexie is vapid and only cares about her next spray tan. Lexie shouldn't treat people like property. Theo will decide who he wants to date.

But I don't say any of those things.

I stand tall, gaining confidence in my three-inch heels, and smile with as much authentic charm as I can fit into one facial expression. "Lexie is a smart woman. Beautiful, outgoing, I'm sure she has beaus beating down her door. I hope she finds someone who loves her as much as you appear to and doesn't settle for an arrangement to raise a company's bottom line. As Corine said, we aren't merging monarchies here." I wiggle my glass. "Sorry, Corine, but I'm not a champagne girl. I'm going to find Tipsy, Elena, and the sparkling cider. Please excuse me."

I glide across the deck into the living area before I chance a glance over my shoulder. Don's cheeks are a little rosier. His forehead twitches like he's trying not to scowl. I hit a nerve. Catching flies with honey is my specialty.

Tipsy and Elena are on the lounge chairs on the top deck, a plate of cheese, crackers, and salami between them. I sit on the end of Tipsy's chair. "Having fun?"

"You have to try this." My cousin shoves a stack of meat and crackers into my hand. "Judah is amazing. I want to marry him."

I giggle. "He is twice your age."

"Is he married?" Her eyebrow wiggles.

"No," Elena says.

"Then I don't see the problem." Tipsy shoves another bite into her mouth.

"Being able to cook isn't the only requirement for a successful relationship."

"It's a good place to start. He can teach me." She bats her eyelashes. "We'll bond over bearnaise."

I bop her nose. "You dream that dream, but maybe wait until you're eighteen. We would hate for him to end up in jail."

"It's never too early to plant seeds," Tipsy says.

The music changes from violin sonatas to Kid Rock's "Cowboy." I wiggle my finger in my ear. I can't be the only one hearing the screaming drum beat. "What is this?"

Elena sips her drink and bobs a lazy shoulder. "Theo bribed the DJ."

I stand and extend my hands to the girls. "Shall we dance?"

Elena and Tipsy look at each other and squeal in unison. We clasp hands and scurry down the stairs to the dance floor. This will be an amazing night, and no one's going to stop us.

Georgi

Ted and Corine covered the pool with wood and strung blue lights along the canopy. A disco ball is suspended in the middle by an invisible cord to look like it's floating.

Kid Rock flows into Beyonce's "Single Ladies" and Camila Cabello's "Havana." Tipsy, Elena, and I lose ourselves in the music. I lose track of time. We cha-cha and two-step. We sweat and sway. We dance like we don't care if anyone's watching—because we don't.

Intense heat warms my back. I don't have to look to know Theo's behind me. Close, but not touching.

"You like sneaking up behind me." I grab his hands and place them on my hips. His fingers bunch the fabric, and he pulls me close. We find our rhythm, swaying side to side.

When the song changes to Carrie Underwood's "Cowboy Casanova," he grabs my hand and spins me away from his body. Our eyes lock. Two beats pass. I read the desire in his eyes. I'm sure it's mirrored in mine.

He spins me back, and his arm wraps around my waist, trapping me against his body. He flicks a kiss along my collarbone.

My eyes flutter closed. I want to kiss him like no one's watching too, but I won't go that far.

Making out on the dance floor is one intimacy too many for this party.

I don't want to share Theo's attention with anyone. I don't want anyone to see what he does to me.

Not because I don't want them to know but because I know how fragile and special it is. I want to savor him slowly. I don't want him to worry who's watching, what his parents will think, or to embarrass his sister with my attraction.

I want him like I've never wanted anyone before.

My desire scares me. I said I would let myself fall. This is the moment when I have to decide.

He could shred my heart like a cat destroys a mouse when it hasn't eaten in days.

Nothing will be left of me if I let myself indulge in loving him and he decides I'm not who he wants.

If he picks Lexie or some other socialite his parents deem more appropriate, he'll break more than my heart. I may have told Lexie's dad Theo would make his own decision, but there's still that part of me that isn't sure.

If his parents want him to date or marry a Lexie-type, will his loyalty force his hand to a place his heart doesn't want to follow?

Frank Sinatra takes over, and Theo and I adopt a stiff-armed dance frame. He leads me in a simple box step. Tipsy and Elena find themselves partners as well. Tipsy throws her head back laughing. Elena's pink cheeks and the lip caught between her teeth are a dead giveaway that she likes the guy she's dancing with. The girls look so at home in this strange settling. I'm envious they don't have a million insecurities playing through their heads, threatening to destroy their night.

Theo's lips drop to my ear. "Having fun?"

I give him my most coquettish grin. "Isn't it obvious?"

His hand flexes on my hip. "Just because I think I know the answer doesn't mean I shouldn't ask. You might be hiding a blister or something."

I lift the hem of my dress and wiggle my bare toes. "I ditched the shoes a while ago. Don't tell your mom. Are you having fun?"

"I had to pull a prison-break-worthy escape, but it was worth the effort. This has been the best part of my night."

"Me too." I brush my lips across his cheek. "I thought being stuck on this boat with you was going to be the worst experience of my life, but you amaze me."

"I'm glad you don't hate me anymore."

"Let's not go that far. I mean, you're still on a date with Lexie."

"Am I? Seems like I'm on a date with you."

"Pretty sure I turned you down."

He closes our dance frame, wraps his arm around my waist, and presses his hips to mine. "It was implied when you kissed me outside my bedroom."

"I'll have to pay closer attention to my lips."

"I'll do that for you." He captures my mouth with tender intensity. His tongue darts against my lips, trying to get me to open and deepen our kiss. He wants to claim me here on the dance floor.

I pull away and suck my lips between my teeth. "Theo, we can't."

"Why not?"

I give him a pointed glare. "You're dating another woman."

He stops dancing and drops my arms. "No, I'm not. I never asked her. I never agreed to my dad's plan." We stare at each other as other couples spin around us. I feel their eyes, but they dance like we aren't interrupting their flow.

"Does she know that? She's glaring at us." Arms crossed, cheeks red, Lexie stands at the edge of the dance floor tapping her toe.

When she and I make eye contact, she straightens her arms, throws her shoulders back, and marches across the dance floor. Her fingers slide up Theo's arm until her hand rests possessively on his shoulder. "I believe the next dance is mine."

It could be said that this is Theo's moment to choose me, but it's not. His fight is with his dad, not Lexie. This is my moment to let what my heart's wrestled with come to light.

I feel Theo's eyes on me. The rest of the crowd stares. A few even have their phones out to record what could be an epic cat fight. People would love to throw a video on their social media feed of a socialite tangling with a townie. It's sure to get thousands of views.

But I won't stoop to Lexie's level. Just because she likes to throw stones doesn't mean I need to throw them back. She's as much a pawn in this as Theo.

"You look beautiful," I say. Her figure-hugging crimson dress is captivating. It's the most fabric I've ever seen her wear. The small diamonds tucked into her updo flash like fireworks. Half the men watching us have their eyes glued to her, but she's too focused on Theo to realize.

"Are you having a nice night?" I ask.

She cocks her head like she's not sure why I'm asking the question or why I paid her a compliment. "It was fine until you stole my date."

"Theo said he never asked you out. He's never lied to me before."

She's silent for a moment. Her fingers loosen on his shoulder. "His dad and my dad. They arranged everything. That's how it always is."

I place my hand in Theo's. "He's quite a guy. I understand why you like him. But that also creates a problem."

"Not if you leave. You don't belong here."

"Maybe." I look into Theo's eyes. Their deep hazel reminds me of liquid gold. The color of autumn leaves and a perfect beer. I read into their depths and know without a doubt the words aligning in my heart are the right ones.

I wink at him. "But I belong with him. He's my soulmate. I love him." It's like my heart and my head knew all along. I just needed to give myself permission to unwrap my squishy parts and let him have them.

Theo takes a sharp inhale. He moves to take me into his arms, but I hold him back. A crease divides his perfectly sculpted eyebrows.

Lexie and I need to finish this conversation before Theo and I deal with the bomb I just dropped on him. We have the rest of our lives to cuddle.

I look at Lexie. Her face is awash with misery. I take her other hand. "I'm sorry you had to find out like this." I keep my eyes focused on her.

"It's not fair." She sniffs.

"Nothing in life is fair. Some are born to billionaires who use their kids as pawns in their business dealings. Others have parents who are so self-involved they don't remember to feed them. But you get to choose where you go from here." I pull the bachelor auction flier from

Theo's breast pocket and hand it to her. "Maybe see if one of these guys is your soulmate. It's for a good cause."

She chuffs. "I want to hate you, but I can't seem to find it in me."

I slide my arm around Theo's waist, and he hugs me to his side. "I'm a likeable person. We just got off on the wrong foot."

"I heard what you said to my dad."

"It's the truth. You don't have to date the men your dad tells you to."

"But when I know they're after my money, it's easier to start a relationship."

"The right guy won't care if you have a trust fund. He'll see you're a sweetheart under all your crankiness. Take your time. Figure out what *you* want and go after it."

She twists her mouth. "You sound like a mom."

"When you have to raise your siblings and cousin, you get a lot of practice giving advice."

She wiggles the paper. "I guess I have some bachelors to meet."

"Check out number eleven. He might be the winner."

She glances at the card. "Thanks, Georgi." She moves into the crowd.

The DJ takes her exit as his cue to restart the music. The world starts to move again.

Theo drops his lips to my ear. "My turn?"

"Yes, Dr. Sanchez? What can I do for you?"

"Did you mean what you said? Soulmates?"

I press my lips to his, caressing his mouth with fervency. He holds me tighter and buries his hands in my hair. He angles my head slightly and deepens our kiss. Our mouths and bodies declaring our love for each other in a way words never could.

When I need air, I loop my arms around his neck. Even though I know he knows I love him, I need to tell him everything in my heart. "I met you and immediately felt seen. I never believed in love at first sight. I thought it was impossible. How can you know someone well enough to love them after only a few hours? But you changed that. You made me believe."

He touches his forehead to mine. "I love you."

My heart trills in my chest. "I know." I flatten my palms against his chest. "Can we really make this work?"

"We can." He kisses my forehead.

"What if ..." Doubts crowd into the door of my heart.

What if his parents don't approve? What if I can't let go of Tipsy or he can't let go of Elena? What if all the reasons that scare me come to fruition and I can't be what he needs?

"Never doubt that I love you. No matter what, we'll make it work as long as we rely on each other."

The waves are the only backdrop to my heart beating out of my rib cage. "I can do that."

Humor and surprise light his face. "Yeah?"

I shrug. "I love you."

He lifts my feet off the ground and twirls me across the dance floor.

Chapter 23

Theo

I SET GEORGI ON her feet and drag her through the crowd to the upper deck. No one is up here right now. Our little spectacle downstairs drew the crowd away.

I frame her face and stare into eyes as green as immaculate four-leaf clovers. I press my lips to hers and soak in the warm joy of kissing the woman I love.

Finally. Finally, she's giving me the chance to prove I can be the man she needs.

A throat clears behind me. Georgi stills. I run my hands down her arms and tuck her behind me as I turn to face my dad.

"Yes, sir."

"After your spectacle downstairs, I've removed you from the bachelor auction. It seems in bad taste otherwise."

I clear my throat. "I appreciate that."

"It's not like Miss Montgomery can outbid any of my guests anyway."

"Dad." My tone holds more warning and fire than I think I've ever used when speaking to him. He doesn't get to embarrass or degrade Georgi because she wasn't born with a silver spoon in her mouth.

Dad holds up his hands in supplication. "I didn't mean it as a judgment. Merely a statement of fact. You've broken enough hearts this evening, we don't need to add another to the pile."

"I didn't mean to hurt Lexie."

"But you did, and now I need to clean up the pieces." He looks behind me. "Georgi, if you'll give me a moment with my son. We have business to attend to."

Georgi's hand tightens around mine. I squeeze back. I don't want her to go, but I don't know what my dad's going to say. I don't want Georgi to hear him lay into me. "I'll meet you in the kitchen in ten minutes, okay?"

Her mouth twists like she's going to argue. Instead, she nods. "I'll check on the girls."

"They're with Corine on the stern deck," Dad says.

"Thanks." Georgi walks toward the stairs She glances back and I give her a reassuring nod. *I'll be fine*.

Dad waits thirty seconds, making sure Georgi has enough time to walk away. Since she's barefoot, we can't rely on the sound of her footsteps to know she's given us privacy. What Dad has to say can't be good. Not if he tailed us up here and demanded to speak with me alone right after we left the dance floor.

Whatever he has to say, I won't let him drive Georgi away. No matter what his plans, she's mine for the rest of our lives.

He steps closer to me. He lifts an eyebrow. "Her?"

I slide my hands into my pockets, so he doesn't see me clench them into fists. "What about her?"

"She's your match?"

"Why is that hard to believe?"

"You think you love her?"

"I do love her." Without a doubt or hesitation.

"Can you be what she needs?" Dad's voice is practically a low growl.

"I can try."

Ted Sanchez would never do something as plebeian as snort, but the sound he makes is close. "Like you tried for Elena?"

"I learned my lesson." I've paid for that mistake for three years. I've given up my career, my independence, and my life trying to earn back his respect.

His head shakes slowly, like a heavy weight prevents him from moving. "I wish I believed that."

"Dad, I've done everything you've asked."

He invades my space. "You disrespected our guests. This evening was supposed to be about the fundraiser. Now it's about the unknown redhead declaring her love for the Sanchez boy. It's romantic, but it takes the focus off what's important."

"My life is important."

"Not as important as the lives we serve with our company and our fundraising."

I don't step back. "People will still give you their money. They need to pad their tax returns."

"That is *not* the point. You've given gossips carte blanche to scrutinize our family."

"Their opinions don't matter."

"What about Lexie? She's embarrassed."

"I think Georgi handled things quite diplomatically. I was never going to date Lexie. You shouldn't have promised I would."

"You're right. I expected you to put the family first. I should have asked you before committing, but that doesn't discount that you went behind my back to secure a date with Georgi instead. If I can't trust you to come to me and talk through our differences, I'm not sure you're wise enough to take over Sanchez Biotech."

Sucker punch landed. I gave him the excuse he needed to shut me out.

"My personal life doesn't have any bearing on my ability to be a good CEO. You need to give me a chance to do more than plan fundraisers and host lunches and serve drinks at beach parties. I can do more."

"If you take over, the lines between personal and professional disappear. Your mother's friendships are just as important to this business as my negotiations, maybe more so. Your mom has faith that Georgi can take the mantle she bears, but I'm not sure."

I step back and raise my hands. "I've heard enough. Georgi handled herself with grace and diplomacy. She stepped into a situation she never should have been forced into and smoothed embarrassed egos and befriended the woman hellbent on destroying her. You can refuse to acknowledge me, but I won't let you discredit what she's done."

"Being a good kisser doesn't make you a good life partner. She needs to be able to trust you to put her needs before your own. With the way you've handled yourself, chasing her like a lovesick schoolboy while ignoring your responsibilities, I do not doubt there will come a day when you let her down. Who will pick up the pieces when you fail her too?"

Georgi

Theo's dad is a jerk.

There.

I said it.

Maybe just to myself, but the thought is in the universe. Who does he think he is?

Theo is a wonderful man. Dedicated. Loyal. Thoughtful.

Some of Ted's accusations are the same insecurities that played in my mind. The difference is I trust Theo to be the man he tells me he is—who he's shown himself to be.

He could break my heart, but I'm willing to risk it if being with him is the reward.

When Ted leaves, Theo slouches on the lounge chair with his head in his hands.

I sneak out of my hiding place on the stairs and kneel before him. "Are you okay?"

He sinks farther. "You heard that?"

"It was really hard for me not to jump out and yell at him."

"That would have been interesting to watch, but I'm glad you didn't. Dad's ... well, he's a hard man to win over."

I scooch onto the lounge chair and wrap my arm around Theo's back. "I don't understand how one missed ride led to this resentment. What else happened?" He has to tell me. The rift between father and son is a chasm we need to bridge if they will ever have a relationship.

He scrubs his hands over his face "It wasn't just that she missed competing. It's that she missed it because I was trying out for something I knew I would never actually pursue."

"Details, Theo. Give me details."

He stretches to his full seated height like he's preparing for battle. "Trials were in Indianapolis. Earlier in the week, a band I like put out an open call for guitarists, so I decided on a whim to tryout. I just wanted to see if I could do it. Their manager called me in for a second audition the morning of the Olympic Trials. It was supposed to take an hour, tops, but they liked my sound. I liked how it felt having people appreciate me. I lost track of time. My phone was off, so Elena couldn't get ahold of me. My parents' plane was stuck in Miami because of a storm."

"Theo, this doesn't make any sense. The coordinators wouldn't give you a grace period?"

He shakes his head. "It's the Olympic Trials. There were over one hundred divers competing for eight spots. We were two hours late. Her event had already started by the time I picked her up."

"That's why your dad doesn't like you playing the guitar." It's a reminder of his daughter's missed opportunity.

Theo stands and paces in our little hidden nook. "I was selfish. I sacrificed my sister's dream for a stupid hobby. I wasn't going to take the gig. Residency was almost over. My fellowship applications were ready to send out. But it felt good to be popular.

He sighs. "Accomplishments are everything in our family. Elena and I strove to do and be whatever it took to reach the next milestone, earn the next award. If we didn't reach it, it took too long, or we didn't surpass expectations, it was a mark against our acceptance. We hated to disappoint Dad. With every achievement or failure, my dad would set a new bar, and the cycle started over."

"Theo …" I see the echoes of that behavior in Theo's drive to prove himself to his dad.

"Even when I knew that cycle was wrong, I strove to be the best. There was always that deceptive voice in the back of my head whispering, 'Next time you'll be enough. He'll love you completely and you can stop striving for the affection and attention you crave.'"

"You'll never do something like that again," I say.

The sorrow in his expression. His hunched shoulders. The way he wrings his hands—I know he's learned his lesson.

It explains why he hosted the parties and let his dad use him the way he did.

"Dad doesn't see it that way, and I can see it from his point of view." He leans against the railing and crosses his arms over his chest. "Me wanting to date you instead of pursuing the women he knows will help grow the company is just as selfish. I spent a lot of energy hounding you that could have been put toward tasks for the business."

"Hounding?" I can't think of a less flattering way to describe his actions. Like he's a dog and I'm a rabbit. All he wants is to hunt and destroy me for his next meal. "What happened to all the crap you spewed ten minutes ago about fighting for us?"

He drops to his knee and clasps my hands. "Georgi, I don't agree with him. You have to believe that. We will make this work if you and I are in it together. I'm done pretending I want what he tells me to want." He licks his lips. "But that doesn't change that I'm supposed to take over Biotech—and I owe Elena. We have to make sure we don't compromise her dreams. She was distracted playing matchmaker and fixing my broken heart. She needs to focus on her training, not our relationship. If she had made the Olympic team three years ago, maybe she wouldn't be so stressed out and anxious right now. She would've already achieved her dream, and she wouldn't be afraid to tell my parents she wants to quit. She would have the satisfaction of that victory instead of her own heartbreak and my lack of dependability."

Theo's monologue twists around in my head. He's revealed so much that puts everything into perspective. But ... "Elena wants to quit?"

He rocks back. "That's the only part you heard?"

"No. But if we're talking about feeling responsible for people, then failing to drive a car when she could've called a cab or a friend—heck, where was her coach?—none of that compares to the pressure I'm under with Tipsy and my brother. I should have been in the trailer protecting them, whether they wanted me to be or not, but instead I'm here falling for you and getting used to this extravagant lifestyle that doesn't suit me."

"I'm not trying to compare the two."

"Maybe not, but the truth is still the truth. Tipsy may not think she needs my help, but she does. She needs positive role models and people who encourage her. What happens in a few weeks when Elena's done training and leaves Bubee? Who will Tipsy turn to then? Does Elena know you feel responsible for her like this?"

He doesn't answer, which is enough of an answer. They've never talked about his guilt. She knows he hovers. She started crying when she told me he let her down, but I doubt she knows the depth of his pain. He would have hidden it from her so he wouldn't be a burden.

Even if Elena is an amazing diver, the odds are less than eight percent that she would have made the team. How do they know she would have qualified if she had competed? Where would they be if she'd competed but failed to make the team? Would they still blame Theo because he's an easy scapegoat?

"What about your parents? I don't see your mom and dad wallowing in self-pity because their plane was late. Why weren't they at the competition already? Why is her success your responsibility?"

"*Pfft*. Way to pull your punches."

"You declared your love. I threw down with Lexie. You pleaded with me to trust you. I can count on one hand the number of people who have my back, and all of them are related to me. You have to give me more than this." He needs to work through his responsibilities and decide if he can be loyal to all the people who expect something from him.

He cups my face. "I'm doing the best I can. I'm trying to help Elena and you and your cousin and be ready for my dad to mentor. It's a lot of pressure."

I stand and step out of his grasp. "You don't have to worry about me. I can take care of myself."

"You don't have to." He spreads his arms wide. "All you've ever wanted is for somebody to put you first."

"Is that what you're doing? Can you tell me you're going to put me first?"

He drops his gaze to his shoes. "I'm working on it."

"Well, I'll leave you to think, then." I spin toward the stairs.

He grabs the back of my dress and pulls my back to his chest, wrapping his arms around me. "Please don't leave like this," he whispers.

I turn and kiss his cheek. "I'm not *leaving* leaving. I'm just giving you space. We both need it." I need to talk to Elena. Theo will never be free if his sister doesn't forgive him.

I walk out of his grasp and don't look back as I descend the stairs and re-join the party. Elena's in the corner flirting with a guy in a maroon suit. I catch her eye and wave her toward me. She holds up one finger to her guy friend and crosses the yacht to stand with me in the shadows.

Her eyes sweep over my face. "Are you okay?"

"Can I steal you for a minute? I need to talk to you about Theo."

"Did he propose?" She grabs my left hand and spins it to look at my fingers. Her face falls when she finds my hand empty.

"Did he tell you he was?"

"After the spectacle on the dance floor, I wouldn't put it past him."

I don't want to have this conversation where someone can overhear us. I grab her hand and lead her to her bedroom. I shut the door behind me and lean against it. "He told me about his guitar tryout and not getting you to the Olympic Trials."

She plops on her bed. "Yeah, that was a pretty sucky day."

"He entirely blames himself for your anxiety, for you wanting to quit diving, and I'm pretty sure your dad blames him for anything that goes wrong in your family."

"We all blame him." Her statement is so matter-of-fact that I blink at her in disbelief.

"It was an accident. Can't you forgive him?" Everyone makes mistakes. It's human nature. He can't be defined by one error in judgment. Not after he apologized and worked so hard to earn their forgiveness.

She stands and fists her hands on her hips. "If Theo's lifelong dream had been to be a rockstar, this would be a different conversation, but he auditioned on a whim. He knew how important diving was to me, and he still chose to stay to play his guitar."

"You're going to make him live with the guilt for the rest of his life?"

"I wish I could forgive and forget, but my life is defined by his ego. He wanted another feather in his cap to prove how cool he was. He was already the perfect son with perfect grades and more academic awards than I can count. He was a doctor. Why did he need another thing to prove he was better than me? Forgive me if I am not swayed by my brother's lack of chivalry." She storms out of the room.

I can't be another person Theo has to take care of, even if I like the idea. He deserves better than dealing with my broken family and inability to let someone take care of me.

To make our relationship work, we need to share that burden.

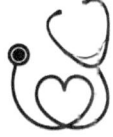

Chapter 24

Georgi

THEO ISN'T ON THE lounge chairs, by the buffet, or near the dance floor when I search the ship for him. The bachelor auction is underway in the Yacht Club dining room, so I make my way there.

The current bid for my cousin Harry is $1000. Clean shaven in his white polo and dark jeans, he doesn't look like the scruffy, unkind mechanic I know him to be.

Bridgette stands with her husband Keegan off to the side. "Have you seen Theo?"

"We've been distracted by the bidding battle over Harry." She points at Viola and Lexie taking turns raising their paddles to increase the bids $100 at a time. So much for bachelor number eleven. I guess now that Theo's off the market, they're desperate.

"I will never understand the allure of the bad boy," I say. There can't be anything else drawing them to Harry. He's not that cute.

Bridgette laughs. "Some women like projects. They think they can fix a guy. Or they're bored and want an adventure."

Keegan loops his arm around her waist. "Some men just need to love of the right woman to help them see the light."

She shoves his chest. "You were never a bad boy, so don't even pretend. You're a boy scout. A boy-next-door."

"And you love me for it."

She traces his jaw with her fingernail. "I do."

"You guys are too freakin' adorable." Theo and I will probably make as many people cringe when we up our PDA.

Bridgette points over by the stage. "Nora looks like she's trying to ignore her own bad boy."

Keegan chuckles. "That would be Dr. Wyatt Cruz. Her co-fellow. They have a pretty strong rivalry going according to the hospital buzz."

Nora's posture screams that she's fighting her reflexes, spine stiff, eyes fixed, and arms crossed over her stomach.

Other people would guess she's either trying not to punch him or kiss him. Being Nora's sister, I know it's the former, not the latter.

With shaggy hair flopping over his forehead in a way that begs to have fingers run through it, a black suit pulls across shoulders almost as decadently as Theo's, and the edge of a tattoo visible under his collar, the tall, muscular man is definitely not Nora's usual type.

Wyatt ruffles her feathers when they run into each other at Honey Beans, but she's never talked about him otherwise. He on the other hand has volumes to say about her. Things that make me curious where tonight might lead them. "Should I save her?"

"You might be saving him," Keegan says.

Shouts ring out from the entryway. I catch a glimpse of Tipsy struggling, desperation heavy on her face. Uncle Hoyt squeezes Tipsy's arm and drags her toward the front door. All thoughts of Nora and Wyatt vanish.

I run over and block their exit. "What are you doing?"

Hoyt flexes his fingers and shifts his grip, revealing angry red welts around her arm.

"I figured you were behind this." Spittle flies from his mouth. At least he doesn't reek of beer. "Filling my daughter's head with nonsense." His hand waves around his head to indicate the Yacht Club and guests.

"This isn't nonsense." He won't understand the opportunity being friends with Elena provides Tipsy. He can't. He's too lost in his own misery to see beyond the trailer park.

"She doesn't belong here."

"Why can't she? She's smart, driven, creative. She can be whatever she wants to be." Knowing "the right people" can open doors she never dreamed of.

"Girls like her—and you—don't get into places like this without compromising their morals."

Great, now he thinks I'm a whore too. "Why do you have to be so nasty?"

His fingers tighten on her arm. "I know my place—and my daughter's."

I point to the auction stage. "Harry's being bid on like a piece of Wagyu beef. How is that okay, but she can't come to a party?"

"You think I have a double standard for my children?"

I need to shut up, but my mouth doesn't care. Someone needs to tell Hoyt the truth. "You let Harry get away with whatever he wants."

"Harry knows how to deal with the consequences of his actions. Tipsy is too young to understand."

"She's almost an adult."

"Ha. Age doesn't matter when you're as naïve as she is."

"And me?"

"You were broken the day your daddy left and your mama lost her mind. If it weren't for me and your aunt—"

"You haven't done anything for me." I'm the one who takes care of everyone. I have for years. I sacrificed everything I could so they could be who they want to be.

I don't regret it for a moment.

Hoyt steps toward me. "What about the roof over your head?"

"Not much of a roof. It leaked."

Ted appears at my shoulder surrounded by security guards and police officers. "Excuse me, Mr. Buchanan, I need to ask you to leave."

Hoyt wraps his fingers around Tipsy's arm again and pulls her to his chest. Her hair falls out of its delicate style. "I'm just collecting my daughter. I'm sorry to cause trouble."

I spread my arms. "I won't let you take her."

"How are *you* gonna stop *me*?"

That's right. Hoyt's been the problem all along.

The police move behind him, and he bristles at the implied demand. A plan forms that might solve all our problems. The plan I should have set in motion months ago. The plan I didn't pursue because I was too scared to stand up to him. I didn't believe I had the power to make a difference.

I don't have a way to take care of Tipsy financially. I can barely take care of myself. I took shelter on Theo's yacht because I didn't have anywhere to go that didn't include geriatric nudity.

Being with Theo has been a distraction, taking me away from what I should've been doing all along.

But being with Theo has given me perspective and let me see the bigger picture. It's like a Magic Eye picture—I needed to lose focus in order to see the real image.

Tipsy's right. She doesn't need me to hover or take care of her. She needs me to stand up for our whole community and show everyone who Hoyt really is. No more trying to pretend our family isn't broken.

My gaze sweeps the grandeur of the room. The women dripping in sparkling jewels. The men in tuxedos that cost more than my entire wardrobe. They hide their gossip behind gloved hands.

I sink into myself. "You're right. I can't. I'm sorry." I step out of the way and sear a mask of contrition and sorrow to my face. "Uncle Hoyt, let me go with you. I want to come home."

"Ha," he barks. "No."

"I was wrong. You're right about me. I see that now. I got it in over my head. I should never have spoken to you the way I did." I glimpse Elena in my peripheral vision, but I don't make eye contact. "These aren't my people. Please let me come home."

I hunch my shoulders so I look as small and ashamed as I can. He needs to believe my rapid change of heart. He needs to think he's given me a grand revelation. This 180-degree reversal needs to seem real. "I can't pretend anymore. I need to come home and learn my place."

"I don't think you learned a thing." He rubs his chin. His gaze sweeps around the room at all the wealthy people in their expensive gowns with their fancy booze. His eyes land on Harry. My uncle's head slowly bobs. "But we miss your cooking. Your mama has been whining at me to bring you back, and I'm tired of listening to her."

My mouth drops open with a gasp. "Really? Mama did that for me?" If anyone else had said she spoke up, I wouldn't believe them, but Hoyt wouldn't lie about her.

"I'm not entirely as hard-hearted as you think I am. It's hard being the man of such a big house. She's my baby sister, and I don't like seeing her unhappy." He points toward the doors. "You mind your manners, do the chores like before, and we can try having you back. But we're leaving now."

It's as good as I'll get. A trial. A test.

Hoyt won't wait for me to say goodbyes or clean out my cabin.

And even though he needs my housekeeping skills, I won't be able to keep my mouth in check for too long. I'll bide my time until I get my plan underway.

Hoyt is the problem. He's the one who needs to go.

I need to focus on fixing my family before I can move on with the rest of my life.

Hoyt glares at the police ushering us toward the front doors.

Elena grabs my hand and yanks me back. "Where are you going?"

I wrap her in a hug and whisper in her ear. "Forgive Theo. The guilt is eating him up inside. Tell him not to give up on me. I have a plan."

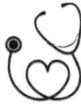

Theo

Georgi is gone. I told her the truth, and she left just like I hoped she wouldn't. She said she wouldn't, but she did anyway.

She was concerned about my loyalty when I should've been worried about hers. We've been at cross-purposes this whole time. She was looking for a way out, and I was looking for a way to keep her.

I slam the cabinet in my bathroom.

Another person I've let down.

Another person who can't forgive my flaws.

I strip out of my tux and stand under the icy shower until I can't feel my ears.

When I step out of the bathroom, Elena is sprawled on my bed flipping through a magazine.

"What do you want?" I grunt.

"Nice towel," she smirks. "Georgi says I'm supposed to forgive you for ruining my chances at the Olympics."

I wave her off. "It was my fault." We're past forgiveness. I haven't earned it until Elena competes anyway.

"You could also say it was Calum's fault. Or Mom and Dad's." She flips a few more pages. "They weren't even in town."

"The business needed their attention. You can't fault them for creating a legacy for us."

"If that were true, wouldn't Dad make you a vice president or something? I'm pretty sure he'll work until the day he dies, and we'll have to scramble to figure out what he's been doing all these years. I don't think Mom even knows."

"You worry about diving. I'll worry about Biotech." I open a drawer and pull out a pair of boxers and pajama pants.

She plops the magazine on the bed. "You know, no one ever asked me if I wanted to take over the company."

I freeze with my hand on the drawer pull. "Do you?"

"No." She grimaces.

"Then why bring it up?"

She taps her lips. "What if we sold it?"

I slam the drawer. "Mom and Dad will never go for that." Dad built the company from nothing. If he won't give it to me, he won't give it to anyone.

"They won't be around forever. It's worth a lot. We could sell it and then do whatever we want."

"Have you figured out what that is yet?"

She spins so she's sitting cross-legged. "Actually, I have. Tipsy and I decided tonight. We're going to apply to the University of Hawaii. I'll study sports psychology, and she'll be a marine biologist."

I slide my boxers under my towel, then toss it back in the bathroom. "And trials?"

She bounces onto her knees. "I'm giving it one more shot. If I don't make it, at least I know I tried my hardest. I won't have given up just because something was hard."

"That's quite a change of heart in one night. Before the party, you were done."

"Watching you and Georgi opened my eyes. The hard work is worth it."

"How do you think Tipsy's going to get to Hawaii?"

She points finger guns at herself. "She's best friends with a billionaire's daughter. What more does she need?"

"An acceptance letter would be nice." Elena has no idea how the world works if she thinks Tipsy only needs the right friends. They help, but she needs a good GPA, SAT scores, and financing. Not to mention getting away from Hoyt.

"Dad will donate a new library or something and make our admittance the binding clause."

"Why would he do that for Tipsy?"

"You might be the favorite kid, but he'll do it for me. That's all that matters."

"I am not his favorite. He'd return me for a different model if he had the chance." That's the part that stings the most.

"He'd probably return both of us. That's the problem. Dad pitted us against each other. We mostly get along, but I didn't realize until you were whining like a baby in the hospital that I've always envied the freedom they gave you. I felt trapped diving, and there you were living the life you wanted."

"But I'm not. I'm doing what Dad tells me to. I wanted to be a doctor, not a cabana boy."

She braces her hands on my shoulders. "Georgi will be back, you know."

"I doubt it. I finally showed her enough of the real me that she'll never come back." What I did to Elena was unforgiveable. I would have been better off keeping my secret.

"She didn't leave because of you. She left for her cousin. She said she had a plan and not to give up on her."

"That's a convenient excuse." I don't know where my lack of confidence is coming from, but all my insecurities, the fears I thought I had overcome, are right here, scraping against the inside of my head.

Georgi didn't say goodbye.

She hasn't texted to explain what's going on.

She ghosted me after I thought we'd finally overcome our last hurdle.

Elena smacks me in the face with my pillow. "Stop whining, you big baby. I'm taking control of my life. Do the same."

I grab the pillow and throw it on the floor. "I chased her for a year, and she left without a word."

"Doesn't loving someone mean chasing them for the rest of your life?"

I brace my hands on my hips. *Ack*. When did my sister become smarter than me? "What do I do?"

She throws my phone at me. "Call her, dummy."

I toss the phone back on the bed. "I have a better idea."

Chapter 25

Georgi

MY ROOM IN THE trailer hasn't changed, but that's not surprising. The same Barbie poster hangs by three tacks next to the window. We bought the plaid sheets at a secondhand store when Nora was a freshman in high school. The bunk beds are held together with duct tape and prayers.

Nothing around here ever changes.

But it's about to.

I slide out of my emerald gown and hook the hanger on the end of the bunk beds next to Tipsy's. My fingers run over the fabric. There's a smudge on the hip. Theo must have had something on his fingertip when we danced.

He's not going to understand me leaving. I hope Elena talks to him. They need each other more than ever.

"You shouldn't have come home," Tipsy says around her toothbrush.

"I need to be here." She told me before she didn't want me back, but for what I have planned, I need to live under Hoyt's roof.

She rolls her eyes.

I pull my pajama shirt over my head. "Your dad dragged you out of a party with more security than the White House and no one lifted a finger to stop him."

She spits out her toothpaste and grabs the floss. "I didn't ask them to. I knew my party was over as soon as Harry saw me."

"Why didn't you hide?" That was the plan all along. If she stayed on the boat and Harry stayed in the Yacht Club, we'd have finished the night snuggled under blankets on the lounge chairs.

But I also wouldn't have had my idea, so I guess being here is the best outcome.

She chucks the floss in the garbage can. "I shouldn't have to hide. We weren't doing anything wrong."

"Weren't we? We lied to your parents. You snuck out of Grammie's house."

She climbs into her bed. "Do you regret taking me?"

"No, never." I sit next to her and clutch her hands. "I just don't want you to get in trouble because of something I encouraged you to do."

She shakes off my embrace. "You treat me just like Dad does. I am fully aware of the consequences of my actions. I knew what would happen if I went to the party, probably more than you."

"What does that mean?" There shouldn't have been any consequences besides sore feet.

"I'm running away."

I scoff. "No, you aren't." She wouldn't get very far anyway.

"Why not? You did."

"Hoyt kicked me out."

"You found a place to live."

"Your dad won't let you live on Elena's yacht. He'll have Ted and Corine, maybe even Theo and Elena, arrested for kidnapping."

"Dad would never call the police. He hates them."

My grin is calculated. "We never thought putting him in prison was a real option. We've been working to get you and me out of the trailer instead." I point out the window. "But he's the one who needs to be gone."

Hoyt has always been the problem. The solution has to revolve around him, not us.

Aunt Imogen refuses to acknowledge how bad he's gotten, so she'll never see that he's too far gone and too stubborn for rehab and community service to be effective punishments.

Sally won't help. She's too afraid to live without him.

We all know how my mama is.

With all the preaching Grammie does about accepting the consequences of our actions, you'd expect her to be the voice of change, but she hates hard conversations even more. She'll never step up.

Tipsy and I have to force them to change.

Just like Elena forced me to see the real Theo.

Tipsy flips her covers and snuggles her feet underneath. "Dad's lawyer will get him off."

"What if he can't? What if Aunt Imogen stops giving Hoyt free passes to break the law and hurt people?"

"That will never happen."

"Yes, it will. He almost killed that little boy. He'll do it again."

"This is risky."

But every good thing is worth the risk. "Will you help me?"

Her eyes widen. "What can I do?"

"You're still Aunt Imogen's assistant. Help her send a couple emails to the judge saying she changed her mind about Hoyt."

Tipsy's face falls. "I can't pretend to be her. She talks with Judge Mayfield all the time. He'll bring it up and ask about her change of heart."

"We need to force her hand. Aunt Imogen needs to see that having Uncle Hoyt in prison is the best way to cure his disease."

"You think?"

"It's a long shot, but it's the best idea I have. That or get him in a fist fight with a cop, but I don't see us orchestrating that without more casualties."

Theo

Our dad sits at his desk with his glasses on the tip of his nose when Elena and I enter. He removes them and steeples his fingers. "Yes?"

I take a seat. "Dad, what's your long-term plan for Sanchez Biotech?"

Earlier Dad accused me of not being mature because I didn't talk to him about my relationship with Georgi. While the details aren't his business, I understand his concerns. If I'm to run his company—or he and I are going to rebuild our broken relationship—we need to have the same open lines of communication I'm building with Georgi.

His eyes pinch. "Why?"

My unease threatens to gag me, but I swallow it down. This is the conversation we need to have. We've been building toward this moment for months. I don't need to fear his reaction if I'm coming to him with a clear conscience and a thoughtfully conceived plan. "If I don't take over, what will you do?"

He replaces his glasses and picks up the spreadsheet he was looking at. "You'll assume the CEO position when I retire. That has always been the plan."

Elena scoots to the edge of her chair. "And me?"

"We'll find a place for you when you're ready."

Elena and I glance at each other. She nods. *I've made the right decision.* I straighten my shoulders and brace my elbows on my knees. "Dad, I don't want to run Sanchez Biotech. I've accepted a position at Third Coast Regional."

Technically, I haven't accepted it yet. It's midnight on Saturday. I can't call the chief of anesthesia and ask for an interview.

But I did send Keegan a text to get the ball rolling. His reply was enthusiastic and encouraging.

Dad opens his mouth, but Elena cuts him off. "I'm applying to the University of Hawaii and want to study sports psychology."

He rocks back in his chair. "Is that so?"

She gives a clipped bob of her chin. "Yes. I've battled anxiety and the beginning stages of depression over the last several months because I didn't have a healthy outlet for the pressure. I don't want other athletes to suffer like I have. I want to make a difference."

He fiddles with his wedding band. "Why is this the first I'm hearing of this?"

She gives him a gentle smile. "You brushed me off." She reaches across the desk and takes his hand. "You called it nerves. Told me to channel the stress into my training. It didn't work."

"I don't recall that."

"There are a lot of things about us you *don't recall*. You're too busy being angry at Theo and spearheading my diving career to be our dad. That stops now."

I expect him to grimace, argue, deny her accusations. Instead, he looks to me. "You don't want to follow in my footsteps." He says it as a statement, not a question.

"Dad, we both know you don't want to mentor me. Frankly, financial reports and shipping logistics bore me. The only thing I enjoyed about working with Ms. Tanaka was the human resources side of things. I'm not cut out to be your successor. I like working with people, not numbers." That's probably why he had me doing the parties and lunches in the first place. My dad may be mad, but he's strategic and good at reading people's strengths and weaknesses.

He rocks in his chair for a minute, and then two. His gaze sweeps over both of us. His expression slowly shifts from uncertainty to admiration. "I wish you both the best of luck. Let me know what I can do to help."

My mouth drops open. "That's it? You're not fighting us?"

"Why would I?"

I jab my finger into his desk. "You've spent years telling me it's my destiny and birthright to take over. You made me surrender my fellowship to serve the family. Now you're okay with me walking away? What's the catch?"

"No catch. If you don't want to be here, it's better I don't waste my time."

I can't decide if it hurts he's not arguing with me, trying to convince me to follow in his footsteps, or if I'm glad he's letting me choose my own path. I expected more questions. I thought Elena and I would have to defend our decisions. "Did you ever see me as a worthy replacement?"

"Why do you care? You don't want the job."

"I want to know what my dad thinks of me." If he ever thought I would be good enough.

He leans his elbows on his desk and squishes his mouth. His gaze analyzes me from head to toe—or what he can see of me above his desk. When his assessment returns to my eyes, he leans back. "Theo, I am not a good father. I know that. Your mother says my love language is gift-giving. I gave you this boat. I gave you the funds for your degree. I gave you everything you ever desired."

"I only ever wanted your respect."

"Your love language is words of affirmation. My failure to communicate is a shortcoming I'm dealing with. You have my respect and admiration. I apologize."

"Who are you?" I've never known my dad to talk about love languages or emotions.

He smiles. "After the gala, your mother cornered me and read me the riot act. She overheard our conversation and didn't agree with my sentiments. I assure you I'm the same person. My viewpoint is a little different after our conversation, but I'm still me." The harsh wrinkles in his face soften. "Your mom is correct. When the woman you love points out your deficiencies and errors in judgment, the stark contrast between the man you thought you were and the man you are is sobering. I was wrong. I apologize. I'll work to do better by both of you."

Elena scurries around the desk and throws her arms around Dad's neck. "I love you."

"I love you too, pumpkin." He holds his arm out to me. "Theo?" I join their hug.

I can't remember the last time my dad spontaneously hugged me, but it feels good to clear the air and know the future is brighter for us.

Now to fix things with Georgi.

Georgi

I'm supposed to unload a shipment of coffee beans from our farm in Rwanda while there's a lull in customers, but instead I'm in the back of Honey Beans staring at my phone. It's been four days since the gala and Theo hasn't returned my text. It was simple: *I'm sorry. Come to Honey Beans and I'll explain. I love you.*

He read it.

But nada in return.

I've been too busy meeting with lawyers and getting things ready to testify against Hoyt to get to the boat. I need to talk to him and explain everything.

I could have texted, but I'm worried Hoyt will see my phone and figure out what I'm up to. He can't know I'm working against him any sooner than absolutely necessary. He'll kick me out again and find a way to keep me from changing Imogen's mind.

The front doorbell rings, and I step through the swinging doors to the counter.

Elena's dripping sweat. She pulls headphones from her ears and waves. "Hey, stranger."

I swing around the counter and wrap her in a hug. "Training?"

"Always."

I point to the espresso machine. "Nonfat latte?"

"Not today. I just came to tell you we're leaving."

My heart jumps to my throat. "Leaving?" They can't be leaving. I need them.

She mops sweat from her face with the hem of her shirt. "Going back to Houston to pack. Trials are at the end of next month. Calum secured me time in the pool in Knoxville, so I'm taking advantage."

"All of you?"

A knowing smile crinkles her face. "Theo too."

"But he can't. I need him. What about ..." Why would he leave after he chose me? Did their Dad order him to go with Elena?

She tips her head and sorrow fills her eyes. "You chose to leave."

"I didn't *leave* leave. Tipsy needed me. I told him to come talk to me." Phase one of the plan is in motion. Tipsy upped her hours at Town Hall and is surreptitiously leaving information about alcoholism's effects on communities where Imogen will find it.

Elena braces her hands on the counter. "Theo took you leaving the gala early hard. I haven't seen him that low in years."

"I told him I love him. Why doesn't he believe me?"

She points out the front door. "I suggest you get your butt down to the boat and stop him."

I glance around the empty coffee shop. "I can't leave work. The afternoon rush should start in half an hour."

She swoops behind the counter. "I'll cover for you."

"Do you know how to use the espresso machine?"

"I'll be fine."

"Does he even want to see me?"

She takes my shoulders and steers me toward the door, giving me a not-so-gentle shove. "Do you really need to ask that question?"

Georgi

I run all the way to the yacht. I don't stop to say hello to Ted and Corine as they walk up the dock behind their driver, startled expressions on their faces. Theo's in his room, putting a laptop in his satchel.

I snatch the bag and hug it to my chest. "Don't go."

"Georgi?"

I brace a hand on my knee to catch my breath and make the world stop spinning. "Elena told me you're leaving."

"That was fast." He glances at his phone. "Elena said you were coming. I didn't expect you for another ten minutes."

"What?"

He brushes the sweaty hair out of my eyes, tosses the satchel on the desk, and pulls me to his chest. "Hi." He kisses the tip of my nose.

"What's going on?"

"Can't I kiss my girlfriend?"

"But Elena said …"

He searches my face. "What?"

"She said you're going to Houston then Knoxville."

"She's going to Houston and then Knoxville. I'm saying goodbye to her at the airport."

"Why didn't you return my text?"

"Were you worried?" He chuckles.

I shove out of his arms. "Why are you laughing at me?"

He leans against the wall and crosses one ankle over the other. "Sweetheart, what went through your mind when you thought I was leaving?"

The deep burning sensation in my chest builds and my eyes mist. "I was heartbroken. I thought you'd given up on me." I don't hide the sob that catches in my throat.

"That's how I felt when you left Saturday."

"So you wanted revenge?"

He gathers me to his chest and smooths his hands up and down my back. "No, sweetheart, never. After feeling like that, I never want to again. No matter what, you're it for me. I was going to come to see you later." He peppers kisses along my jaw and makes my toes curl. "Elena was just supposed to say her goodbyes. Knowing you understand my crushing desperation strangely makes me happy, though."

"Why? Why would you want me to feel like this?" My heart slams in my chest, trying to rebuild itself as we talk, fitting the jigsaw puzzle crumbles together.

He cups my cheek. "I don't want you to hurt. That's the point. We'll both do whatever we can to avoid feeling like we're being ripped in two. That makes us stronger."

"That was mean of her," I mumble into his chest.

"But it worked."

"Maybe ... yeah ... I hate you a little."

He tips my chin. "No, you don't. You love me, and you'll never let me get away."

He's right.

His eyes are filled with all the love he has for me. My soulmate.

While I don't agree with Elena's strategy, it had the desired effect. The ends justified the underhanded means.

I'm here.

The fear that raced through my body when I thought he was leaving burned on me like a brand. I never want to feel that way again. I'll never let him go.

I grab his collar and bring his mouth to mine. He just shaved, and I'm enveloped in his sagey-salty scent like a cozy bathrobe. Kiss after kiss draws us closer together.

His lips make my skin tingle and buzz, and I'm having a hard time keeping my hands from exploring his body.

He slows our pace and places one final tender kiss on the corner of my mouth.

I sigh. Content is an understatement. I rest my head on his shoulder and take in the room. Half-packed suitcases lay on the bed.

"You are leaving."

"I'll be back on Friday. Lexie and a bunch of her friends want to use the boat."

"You're still doing that?" It shouldn't surprise me as much as it does. I wanted him to be done hosting.

"For now. Until my Texas medical license is finalized, and I get permissions at the hospital."

I wiggle my finger in my ear. I can't have heard him right. Medical license? Hospital? "Hold on a second. What?"

He grins with the cocky assurance of a man who has everything he wants. "That's why I didn't get to the coffee shop the last few days. I took the open anesthesiologist position at Third Coast Regional. I maintained my license in California, so once I get everything transferred here and squared away at the hospital, I can start. I'll have a mentor for the first few months, but I'm okay with the safety net. It's better for my patients anyway."

I jab his chest. "Why didn't you tell me?"

"I thought you'd appreciate the surprise."

"I do. I love it. You surprised me." I lean in to kiss him, but he pulls back, so I can't reach him.

"Really? You're not just saying that so I let go and you can hit me again?"

"Do you want to live in Bubee?"

He leans in, still not letting me kiss him, nipping at my mouth. "I want to be wherever you are."

This man is my undoing, and I love every second of it. "Me too."

"Yeah?"

"You're all I've ever wanted. Even when I acted like I hated you, I wanted you. That's why it hurt so much." I reach for him again, but he denies my kiss. I grunt in frustration. "I'm sorry I left the party without telling you what was going on. I knew if I didn't leave with Hoyt, I would lose my shot at moving back into the trailer."

He flutters his lips over mine driving me even crazier with desire. "You don't need to be there."

"For the time being, I do. I have a plan, and I need your help."

"What can I do?"

"Your family has a lot of influence and knows a lot of other people with influence. I want to take advantage of that and pressure my aunt to put my uncle in prison."

He lets go of my wrists and steps back. "Will he retaliate?" His tone is serious. Our playful almost-kissing over.

"Hoyt ran over a kid. He deserves to go to prison for the rest of his life. Our family needs to learn to live without him. They'll be better off."

"We need to get my parents involved. They have more friends than I do."

"Does your mom need a new charity to partner with? Like the Bubee branch of Mothers Against Alcoholism?"

"That's something right up her alley."

Worry settles in my chest. "What do they think about you leaving the family business?"

He smiles with his whole body. "Strangely, me walking away has made them respect me more."

"I'm proud of you." I pull him close and finally get that kiss my lips ached for.

Chapter 26

Theo

GEORGI HAS SPENT EVERY day that I have known her swearing up and down that she doesn't need me. Having her storm into my bedroom and ask me to help put her uncle in prison feels like an invitation to the party of the century. A weird party, but still a party.

I wrap her in a hug and place a quick kiss on her temple. "Mom and Dad are about to leave. I need to stop them." I pull out my phone and send a text asking them to come back to the boat.

We meet them in the living room. "What's this about, son?" Dad asks.

I give Georgi a confident nod.

She squares her shoulders. "Last Thanksgiving, my uncle was drinking and driving and ran over an eight-year-old boy." My mom's hands fly to her mouth. "The boy survived. He's fine, but my aunt, the mayor, has used the boy's recovery as an excuse to convince the judge my uncle shouldn't go to prison. She keeps getting his trial delayed while she tries to talk the judge and prosecution into community service and rehab."

"That's …" Mom grasps for the right word.

"Horrible, manipulative, an abuse of power." Georgi ticks items off her fingers. "I'm sure I could fill a dictionary. The point is I need your help convincing her to stop enabling Hoyt's destructive behavior."

Dad slides his hands into his pockets. "Politics aren't our thing."

"But philanthropy is." Georgi holds her hands palms up. "You have done an amazing amount of good in Bubee, and my aunt recognizes that. If you sponsor an initiative against drinking and driving and get my aunt involved, she can't support Hoyt too. It would be the worst kind of PR for her not to help you."

Dad assesses Georgi with something new in his eyes. Pride? Confidence? It's the same look he gave me when I told him I was going back to medicine. It validates how amazing Georgi is and that we've made the right decisions.

"What's your timetable?" Dad asks.

"Trial is in two weeks."

"That's soon."

"I know I'm asking a lot. I've spent a lot of energy trying to figure out how to keep Tipsy safe. My attention should have been on how to keep the entire town safe. He is going to kill someone—probably not himself—and we need to stop him."

"You have our full support, darling. Isn't that right dear?"

Dad grasps Georgi's hands, cupping them between his. "I'm sorry I underestimated you."

She laughs. "That's okay. Most people just see my boisterous side and don't realize there's a brain underneath all of this flaming red hair."

Georgi

Corine and I arrive at Town Hall with brochures and invitations to the first annual Bubbles Against Alcoholism tea party.

Corine is amazing. Not only does she already have two hundred women from Houston and Bubee dedicated to the event, but most of the female business owners in town have donated time, food, or goods to an online silent auction to raise money for families impacted by drunk drivers in our area.

It's amazing what you can accomplish with enough money, integrity, and resolve.

Aunt Imogen gives us her politician smile and shakes our hands after she leads us into her office. "To what do I owe this pleasure? Tipsy put you on my schedule but didn't tell me what this is about."

I hand her an invitation. "We would be honored for you to be the keynote speaker at our event."

Her eyes travel over the details, and I can tell the moment she realizes the implications of what we have asked her to do. Her smile doesn't change, and neither does her posture, but panic overtakes the rest of her body. Her nose twitches like a rabbit and the fine lines around her eyes tense. "This is rather short notice."

"We apologize. It was a last-minute addition to the Sanchez family's philanthropic endeavors this spring," Corine says.

"I see."

Corine clasps Imogen's hand. "This is a cause dear to my heart. My father died of complications from alcoholism when my children were young. It's a great loss that they will never know their grandfather the way they could have because he couldn't put down his tequila." She turns to me with tears in her eyes. "He was teaching Theo to play the guitar when he died."

That explains why Theo loves it so much.

Corine turns her teary-eyed smile on Imogen. "I know we can count on you. Georgie speaks so highly of your devotion to this town."

"To serve is my greatest joy, but ..."

Corine stands. "We were so confident in your character, we went ahead and sent out the press release this morning. We'll see you on Saturday."

Imogen's mouth flaps. She can't say no to Corine. It would end her political career if she did.

Corine shakes Imogen's hand. "Thank you so much."

I wink at Tipsy as we walk past her desk but otherwise do not betray my elation.

When we are safe in Corine's car, she clasps my hand. "You are going to be an amazing addition to the Sanchez family."

"It's too soon to assume—" Her soft smile makes it impossible for me to finish my thought.

"I don't think so. At least I hope not." She wraps me in a motherly hug that threatens to make me cry.

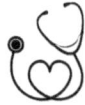

Georgi

I wanted to have the tea party at Honey Beans, but Corine outdid herself. We have over five hundred guests. The maximum capacity at Honey Beans is 126.

Thankfully, one of my best friends owns a barbecue restaurant on the beach. We set up a massive tent on the sand behind Jake's BBQ, cooked enough roast chicken and pulled pork to feed an army, and made one hundred Bayou Goo pies. My taste buds tingle every time I think about the layers of sweet cream cheese, chocolate, pecans, and whipped cream.

But that's not why we're here today.

Corine and I stand at the hostess station welcoming guests. I hand the next group of women—Corine's friends from Houston—their welcome bags. "Inside you'll find a nametag of sorts. Please use the provided pen, and instead of writing your name, please write how you've been affected by alcoholism."

Asking our guests to share something so personal is risky, but their honesty will add intimacy and gravity to what we are accomplishing.

My name tag says Orin, my dad. His alcoholism started my branch of our family tree down the path we're on. If he was sober and devoted to his family, we never would have lived with Hoyt. Protecting my siblings never would have been my responsibility. I might have gone to college or moved away from Bubee.

I'm not saying I would rather have that life. If I'd left, I never would have met Theo or befriended Elena. We wouldn't have SUP club and the Bubbles. I love Honey Beans as if it were my own.

But the *what if* always itches at the back of my mind.

The women chitter with excitement and take their bags. They make their way through the exhibit in the main dining room toward the stairs to the tent. We created a maze of posterboards with data about the effects of alcoholism and drunk driving on families and communities.

The statistics are depressing.

Their faces fall as they see pictures of families ripped apart.

That's where we need their emotions to be.

This isn't a fun tea party.

This is an intervention of sorts.

Hoyt and alcoholics like him need to be stopped.

My uncle has to pay for the people he's hurt.

Judge Mayfield and his wife, Gina, enter holding hands. He reminds me of Colonel Sanders from the old KFC commercials, white mustache and beard, slightly rotund stomach, but a friendly grin and hearty handshake for everyone he meets.

He'd make a good mayor if he ever decided to run against my aunt. If this works, maybe that will be my next initiative.

Judge Mayfield shakes Corine's hand. "Pleasure to meet you, ma'am."

Corine beams. "The honor is mine, your honor. We are so excited to have you both with us today. May I show you to your table?" She waves a hand toward the exhibit.

My feet want to follow them, but we decided it would be best for Corine to take the lead with the Judge and his wife. It looks less conspicuous if I'm not whispering in his ear asking him to toss Hoyt in prison and throw away the key.

Corine is in her element. Statuesque and intelligent, she holds their attention, drawing them through emotions that will hopefully aid in a conviction next week.

Aunt Imogen is the next to arrive. Did she stop the Judge outside and have a conversation about Hoyt? Would she be that bold and two-faced?

I honestly have no idea.

I've never understood why she stands by Hoyt the way she does. With all he's done, it doesn't make sense. He's a liability to her political career. There has to be something we don't know. Maybe something happened when they were younger, and he's been blackmailing her.

"Hi, Aunt Imogen." I hold out a gift bag for her.

She pastes on her politician smile. "Georgi."

"Are you ready to give your speech?"

"I didn't know you were the type to organize fundraisers. I would have utilized your skills in my last campaign had I known."

I scrunch my shoulders. "This is all Corine Sanchez. It was her idea. Theo played the guitar one night, and it sparked something inside her. You remember she told you her dad was teaching him to play when he died, right?"

"The timing is coincidental."

"To what?"

Her scowl creases her makeup "Georgi, you aren't a dumb girl. I've known you my whole life. I know your work when I see it."

"Aunt, I don't know what you mean." My politician smile spreads across my face. I will never confirm her theory. What would be the point? She's still stuck speaking against the behavior she's secretly supported all these years.

The alarm on my watch buzzes. "Time to get started. Follow me."

I don't rush through the exhibit, but I don't dawdle either. She reads the statistics and sees the pictures. She knows most of the devastating stories already, so there's no reason for her to stop and immerse herself.

Downstairs, Corine calls the party to attention. "Ladies and gentlemen, thank you for joining our event on such short notice. At the gala we hosted a few weeks ago, it came to my attention that Bubee doesn't have a strong organization supporting local families affected by alcoholism. This town has become a second home to me, and I thank you for helping me rectify this oversight today.

"Many of you know my son, Dr. Theo Sanchez. When he was young, he spent his summers in Mexico City with my father. During their first visit—Theo was ten—my dad was sitting on his veranda plucking away on his guitar. Theo sat enraptured for hours listening to the beautiful melodies Papa coaxed from the lovely instrument. The next day, Dad presented Theo with one of his old guitars." She gestures to the guitar sitting on stage. "He began teaching my son the techniques his dad had learned from my great grandfather, passing on their traditions."

She thumbs a lonely tear from her cheek. "My father was a vibrant man. He loved good food, good conversation, and unfortunately, good tequila. When Theo was fourteen, my father was diagnosed with stage III liver disease. You might know the disease better as cirrhosis. He irreversibly destroyed his liver. The stubborn man refused to stop drinking and seek medical treatment. While I miss my father, the greater tragedy is that he deprived my son of the opportunity to know his grandpa. They never finished their guitar lessons."

She makes eye contact with everyone around the room. Pausing to let the story sink in. My heart clenches. Poor Theo. No wonder he loves his guitar so much—and that the only melodies he plays are sorrowful.

Corine tips the edge of her mouth in a sad smile. "Daddy's guitar sits in the corner of Theo's room as a constant reminder of what we've lost. It is my greatest hope that no other families feel this emptiness.

To that end, we set up an online auction to raise money to promote awareness and assist families devastated as ours was. The URL is in your bags and on the centerpieces. Bidding closes at midnight tonight. Now, I would like to invite Mayor Buchanan to the stage. She's a staunch supporter of our cause." Corine steps from the podium and claps for my aunt.

Imogen graciously takes the stage, hugging Corine on the way to the microphone. Now is the time she will either call us out or give in to peer pressure. Tipsy slides into the seat next to mine and clasps my hand. I hold my breath. I wish Elena and Theo were here too, but she's training in Knoxville, and he's attending mandatory orientation at the hospital.

Imogen flexes her hands around the podium and blinks at the crowd. She clears her throat. "It appears Mrs. Sanchez and I have similar stories." She sips her water. "I didn't expect to be so affected by hers. I had a speech prepared, but I think ..." She scans the crowd. Her eyes come to rest on a spot in the corner. I crane my neck. She's looking at my grandmother. "Mom, I'm sorry. Can you ... We need to tell the truth."

Grammie rises from her seat and walks to the podium. She squeezes my aunt's hand. "It's okay, dear." Grammie turns to the microphone. "Many of you know me. For those of you who don't, my name is Dotty Buchanan. Imogen is my daughter. The truth ... the truth is my husband August was a wonderful man. Sweet, kind, a pillar in our community until he died." She drops her gaze and swallows hard.

When Grammie regains her composure, she sweeps her gaze across the crowd. "The reason Imogen can't speak is because my husband was also a high-functioning alcoholic. It's hard to reconcile the boisterous, fun-loving man you knew with the version we saw behind closed doors. He was the king of backhanded compliments. Statements like,

The roast would be wonderful if you hadn't added so much salt. How much prouder would Imogen feel of herself if she'd earned a perfect score instead of a ninety-five on the test? While on the surface there was nothing wrong with those statements, they were stated with a hurtful edge."

Tipsy and I stare at each other. "Did you know that?"

She shakes her head. "He always snuck me lollipops."

But that explains why Imogen protects Hoyt.

They grew up protecting Peepa's secret, and when Hoyt started drinking, that habit transferred to him.

It also explains why Hoyt is the way he is. He's not a jerk just because he's a jerk. Alcoholism has a genetic component, and if our grandpa passed that gene to him while making him live under unattainable expectations, I can see why he would drown his learned self-loathing in alcohol.

It doesn't forgive his behavior—he still needs to go to prison—but it explains it.

Grammie turns to Corine. "The hardest part is wanting to help but not knowing how. Thank you for investing in resources so the next generation has tools to combat this disease."

Corine opens her arms and engulfs Grammie and my aunt in a hug. Imogen's shoulders shake. Grammie runs her hand over Imogen's head and whispers in her ear.

When they finish the hug, Corine steps to the microphone. "I think we can all use a cup of chamomile and some chocolate pie, don't you?"

Laughter trickles through the room.

Tipsy, Bridgette, Corine, and I place warm teapots in the table centers while the wait staff serves the meal. Gina Mayfield clasps my forearm when I deliver their pot. "I'm so sorry. I never knew that about your grandpa."

I crouch between the judge and his wife. "Neither did I, but we need to stop the cycle." I meet the judge's eyes. "My uncle is sick."

Tipsy joins us. "Dad's getting worse. Aunt Imogen doesn't want to believe it, but he is."

The judge holds up his hands. "We can't talk about open cases."

I grasp Tipsy's hand. "I'm testifying Tuesday. You need to hear the whole story."

He nods. "I'll see you then."

Tipsy and I leave the tent. The ocean breeze washes over me as I blink back the emotions threatening to leak from my chest.

"Do you really want to testify?"

"I need to. I should have a long time ago. I'm not scared of him anymore." We all hold a little blame for keeping the secret, enabling Hoyt's destructive behavior, and not stopping him.

If I'd stood up to him earlier, maybe he wouldn't have been driving on Thanksgiving. Maybe that little boy wouldn't have been in his path.

Hoyt will never hurt anyone again. I just never realized how much I needed support to see this through.

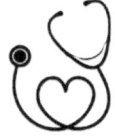

Chapter 27

Theo

I SQUEEZE GEORGI'S HAND as we walk into the County Courthouse. She's gorgeous in a knee length pencil skirt and white blouse she borrowed from Nora. Her hair's piled on top of her head in a messy bun. "I'm proud of you." I kiss her knuckles.

"Thanks." She swipes her other palm on her skirt. "I didn't expect to be this nervous."

"I'm not going to talk you out of testifying. You've got this." She does. We've reviewed her testimony so many times, I could tell the court her answers.

She drops my hand and wraps her arm around my waist. "Thanks. It's easier with you here."

I kiss the top of her head and open the door. Mom, Dad, and the rest of Georgi's family fill the small vestibule outside the courtroom.

Hoyt paces in front of the door. He glares at her, but my family forms a protective barrier between them. I'd like to see him try to intimidate her.

Harry shakes his head in disappointment until his mom leads her children into the courtroom with Hoyt.

Imogen and Dotty aren't even here.

My family and I sit behind the prosecutor's table with the little boy's parents, standing when Judge Mayfield enters the courtroom.

"Let's put this matter to bed, shall we?" He bangs his gavel. "Madam prosecutor, you may begin your opening statement."

The district attorney stands and tells the jurors about Hoyt's accident on Thanksgiving. She tells them about the bottles of beer found on the floorboards of his truck and his history of DUIs.

The jurors are hard to read, but I guess that's the point. They need to be impartial in order to deliver the fairest verdict.

It doesn't stop me from flexing my hands and digging my nails into my pant leg as she describes the trauma Hoyt's inflicted.

The defense attorney takes his turn. He doesn't deny Hoyt's actions, instead he states that Hoyt can't be held responsible for his actions because at the time of the accident, his mental disease made it impossible for him to understand that what he was doing was wrong. He informs the jury that Hoyt's disease needs treatment, not punishment.

My stomach turns at the sincerity in the defense attorney's tone. There comes a point when some diseases can't be treated. My professional opinion is that Hoyt has reached that point.

The first witnesses are called. Dr. Jeremiah Thompson testifies to the boy's injuries, and nurse Rachel Adabi talks about the fight between Hoyt and the boy's dad in the Emergency Department on Thanksgiving Day.

One witness at a time, the prosecutor paints a picture of Hoyt's behavior and the lack of consequences.

Georgi's knee bounces faster and faster as the number of witnesses dwindles.

It's almost her turn.

I massage the back of her neck to impart calmness. I have faith she'll do well, but it doesn't stop me from worrying.

Stressful situations manifest physically as elevated heartrate, labored breathing, and difficulty following a train of thought. Georgi needs to have her wits about her when she takes the stand.

"The prosecution calls Georgiana Montgomery to the stand."

Her face pales, and she inhales a shaky breath.

I kiss her cheek. "You can do this."

She nods, stands, and moves along the aisle toward the front of the courtroom. Her Aunt Sally grabs her hand and pulls her down to whisper in her ear. I can't hear what she says, but Georgi makes eye contact with her aunt. She stands straight, throws back her shoulders, and strides with purpose to the witness box where she takes her oath and sits.

"Miss Montgomery, please state your relationship to the defendant," the prosecutor says.

"Hoyt Buchanan is my uncle. I live in his trailer with my mom and brother." Her voice rings loud and clear.

"How long have you lived in his home?"

"Seventeen years."

She and the prosecutor go back and forth establishing her history with Hoyt.

"I'd like to enter prosecution exhibit twenty-seven." The prosecutor hands a photograph to the judge and clicks a remote to display the same picture on a screen in front of the jury. An ugly purple bruise and bloody lip stain Georgi's beautiful face.

My mom grasps my hand, blinks at me with tears caught in her eyelashes. Georgi's mom whimpers.

I will never forget walking into the coffee shop and seeing the bruises. If I was a violent man, I would have tracked Hoyt down and taught him a lesson.

But I don't solve my problems with my fists.

The prosecutor gestures to the image. "Miss Montgomery, tell us about this picture."

Georgi's cheeks are a bright crimson. "That's me the morning after Hoyt hit me. My sister took the picture."

"Did you provoke him?"

"Yes."

More gasps.

"Tell the jury what happened."

"Every Saturday night, my sisters, cousin, and some friends meet for drinks under the pier."

"Your cousin?"

"Henrietta Buchanan." Georgi points to Tipsy.

"You serve alcohol to your underage cousin?"

Georgi laughs. "No. We always bring grape juice or fruit punch for her."

"What made this night unique?"

"When we got home, Hoyt was drunk."

"And that was abnormal?"

"No. He's usually passed out when we get home. We try to plan it that way because he emotionally bullies Tipsy and me. This time, he woke up and yelled at me for taking Tipsy to the beach." A hesitant, forced laugh trickles past Georgi's lips. "I mean, Henrietta. Sorry. She's had the nickname for so long, I forget to use her given name."

"That's all right. Will the court reporter please indicate in the record that 'Tipsy' is Henrietta Buchanan's nickname. Continue, Miss Montgomery."

"Anyway, he was mad I kept her out past curfew, and then I called him a drunk and a bully, so he hit me."

"Had he ever been physically abusive before?"

Georgi's bun wobbles as she shakes her head. "Never."

"Do you feel this was a one-time occurrence?"

The defense attorney stands. "Objection. Calls for speculation."

"I'll rephrase. Miss Montgomery, are you afraid for your safety?"

"No." She points to the photograph. "I can take a punch, and I'm not afraid to defend myself if I need to." She inhales and looks at the jury. "I'm scared for my cousin. What happens if he decides to take his anger out on her? She's a kid."

The prosecutor looks confused. "How old is Henrietta?"

"Seventeen. I know that makes her almost an adult, but no one should be afraid to go home because they're worried their dad might beat them up. He's been calling her garbage, stupid, and worthless her whole life. Those aren't the actions of a caring father."

The defense attorney stands again. "Objection. What does this have to do with the events of last Thanksgiving?"

The prosecutor gestures toward Hoyt. "Your Honor, I'm demonstrating a pattern of behavior. If his family doesn't feel safe, his actions on the day in question aren't the result of a onetime mental break caused by a disease."

The defense attorney jabs his pen into the table. "Will the judge instruct the prosecutor not to provide her own testimony?"

"My apologies. I thought you wanted me to answer your question."

Judge Mayfield raises placating hands. "Madam prosecutor, do you have any more questions for this witness."

"No further questions."

The judge gestures to the defense. "You may cross-examine the witness."

The defense grills Georgi—why didn't she press assault charges, why hasn't she talked to the police before, why does she still live in an environment where she doesn't feel safe—but she holds her ground. She details her search for a new home, her fear for her family and the community.

When she steps down, the prosecution rests.

Georgi sits next to me. I kiss her temple and hug her tightly. "Good job."

"I don't know if it will be enough."

"It will be. Between what you said and the rest of the testimony, they can't be lenient."

The defense presents their evidence and experts, and by three p.m. the jury is given the case to decide Hoyt's fate.

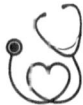

Georgi

Theo hasn't let go of my hand since I left the witness stand, and I love it.

His calm, unwavering support fills me with joy and peace. We walk through the vestibule into the sunshine and gather with the Sanchezes on the lower stairs.

Corine wraps me in a hug. "I'm so sorry for what you went through, my dear."

"It was worth it if puts Hoyt in prison."

Theo shoots a glance over his shoulder and squeezes me against his body. "He's not happy."

Hoyt, Sally, Harry, and my mom are talking to his lawyer. He runs his hand around the back of his neck and stares at the ground. He's nervous. "He should learn to be an adult and face the consequences of his actions."

"What did your aunt say before you took the stand?" Theo asks.

I shake my head. "Thank you."

"Really?"

"Yeah. She knows. She always has. She's just as scared as the rest of us."

"Georgi?" My mom steps away from Sally. "Can we talk?"

Theo meets my eyes. "You don't have to."

"It'll be fine." My mom and I haven't really talked since I moved back. She's been busy at work, and I was preparing for the tea party and trial.

It's not a great excuse, but I don't know Mama's reaction to me testifying. I didn't tell her ahead of time. I didn't need her voice whispering in my ear that I shouldn't do it.

She pulls me around one of the columns, so we have a little privacy.

Mama fiddles with the strap on her purse. "I'm glad you worked things out with the Sanchez boy. He'll take good care of you."

My stomach clenches. "That's what you want to talk about?"

She tucks a hair behind my ear. "I'm proud of you."

"Because I have a rich boyfriend?"

"Don't say it like that." She twists her wedding ring. "That's not what I meant. I know you like him for more than his money. It's nice to see you picked a nice boy to care for you."

My mouth drops open. I testified against her brother, hoping to put him in prison for the rest of his life, and she's excited I'm dating. The anger and frustration of her misplaced priorities builds until I can't contain it anymore. "Mama, you are something else."

Confusion settles on her face.

I point toward the courthouse doors. "That was one of the hardest things I've ever done, but you only care about me dating a cute boy." I throw my hands in the air. "Theo isn't even a boy. He's a man. He has been for a long time. I don't love him because he can take care of me. I love him because he has a sweet spirit. He's kind, thoughtful, resourceful, dedicated, persistent. While I doubt he will ever leave me, if he does, it will be because of him, not because I'm deficient. I'm sorry Dad left you, but that's on him, not you. He couldn't see what an amazing woman you were because he was selfish. You deserve better, Mama. I wish you'd stop living in the past."

My tone is harsh, but I know in this moment I will never be like my mom. I don't know why I was so afraid of that idea for so long or why I used it as an excuse not to love Theo.

Who I am will never be determined by anyone besides me. I won't worry if I'm making someone else happy enough to stay with me.

I can keep my family safe without sacrificing my life and what fills me with joy.

I am a little cooky. A little bossy and short-tempered, but I'm who I want to be.

If other people don't like me, their loss.

Mama blinks at me. Her chin wobbles. She sniffs like she's going to cry.

I wrap my arms around her and pull her in for a hug, feeling more like I'm the mom and she's my kid instead of the other way around.

She sobs into my shoulder.

I bite my cheek and pet the back of her head. "Shh. Shh. It's okay, Mama."

I shouldn't have yelled, but someone has to help her snap out of this. Dad is never coming back. Just like Hoyt, she needs to grow up and live the life in front of her, not the one she wants to pretend still exists.

My world doesn't revolve around Theo the way my mom's revolved around my dad.

Theo and I are partners. Side by side.

My dad treated my mom like a dog he led on a leash. When he stopped pulling her where he wanted her to go, she was lost.

She needs to realize she doesn't need the collar or the leash. She can run free.

"Mama, you are a great woman. Don't let an idiot define you."

"I am proud you testified," she mumbles into my shoulder.

"Thanks."

"What are we going to do if Hoyt's locked up?"

"We'll be fine. We can take care of ourselves."

"You can. You always have." She straightens my collar. "I admire that about you."

"I'll teach you, okay?"

"Thank you, Baby." She sniffs and hastily brushes tears from her cheeks.

Footsteps echo behind us.

Theo's hand settles on my low back. "The jury has their verdict."

That was fast.

I nod, but I don't release my mom. Not yet. I soak in her scent and say a silent prayer that the trial gives her the shove she needs to be the mom we want her to be.

She forces me to let go, and we follow the rest of our family into the courtroom. The judge runs the jury through the procedure and the foreman declares Hoyt "Guilty on all counts."

A mixture of cheers and sobs fill the room.

I know the judge says something and bangs his gavel, but the only sound I hear is air rushing from my chest. I bury my face in my hands and cry happy tears.

I did it.

My family is safe.

Hoyt can't hurt them anymore.

Hopefully he'll learn his lesson.

If he doesn't, by the time he's released, Tipsy will be settled into her life. She won't have to live under his roof, by his rules, or put up with his rollercoaster temper.

Theo locks his arm around my shoulders. He kisses my temple. "I'm so proud of you."

I'm proud of me too. I return his hug. "Thank you for supporting me."

I could have done it without him, but I'm glad I didn't have to.

Chapter 28

Theo

ELECTRIC IS AN UNDERSTATEMENT to describe the energy in the Knoxville dive center. Tense. Stressful. Excited. All of the emotions overlap as we watch Elena climb the platform for her final dive.

She needs to be nearly flawless in her back tuck to earn enough points to qualify for the Olympics. Only the top two qualify, but I know she can do it.

She's put in the time. Her heart and her head are ready.

Mom grips my hand on one side and Georgi grips my other. I'm the middle link between my parents and Georgi and her cousin. We hold our breath.

Elena steps to the edge of the platform and takes her position.

I don't remember when she started diving off the 10-meter platform, but the confidence it takes to fly thirty feet through the air amazes me.

Elena lifts onto her toes and pushes off. She rotates, twists, then stretches perpendicular to the water, entering perfectly.

I jump to my feet and cheer. That had to be good enough. It just had to be.

We watch the scoreboard. 73.3 lights up the marquee.

She's in second place with three divers left.

Tipsy jumps into Georgi's arms. "She did it!"

"Not yet."

We take our seats and wait.

The next diver makes a big splash and doesn't pass Elena.

But the next two are flawless.

My heart tumbles in my chest. She finishes the competition in fourth place.

Elena isn't going to the Olympics. All her hard work was for nothing.

Mom cries into my dad's shoulder. Georgi rubs Tipsy's back.

We meet Elena at the athletes' exit. My feet slow when I see her. She has a gigantic smile on her face. It seems cold-hearted to want her to be upset, but that's what I expected to find.

Mom brushes past me and envelops my sister in a hug. "Good work, sweetheart."

"Thanks, Mom." She lets go and hugs Dad. He's been softer, kinder these last few weeks since our discussion in his office. He is trying to be a better dad. He beams at my sister, and I feel the radiated warmth even though Elena's demeanor confuses me.

"Now what?" Mom asks.

"French fries." Elena gives a clipped nod.

Dad takes Mom's arm, and they lead the way toward our car. I pull Elena back. "Are you okay?"

"Yeah. Why?"

"You didn't qualify."

"I know."

"I thought you'd be upset."

"I am. A little." She shrugs. "But I'm done. This doesn't make me happy anymore, so it's time to retire." She sways her hips in a hula move. "Hawaii calls."

"That's it?" After the years of training, the injuries, the sacrifices she's made, I don't know how she just walks away.

"Everything doesn't have to be like pulling teeth without anesthesia," she says.

"You're funny."

She puts her hand on my elbow, and we stop walking. "Don't blame yourself for me not qualifying. I did everything I could, but I wasn't good enough. I'm okay with that. Thank you for helping. I appreciate everything you've done."

"As long as you're really okay."

"I am." She tucks her chin to her shoulder. "I'm relieved. Now I don't have to wait until August to retire and can start classes instead."

I rub my knuckles on her wet hair. "I'm so proud of you."

"Ditto." She turns and starts walking. "So, when can I call Georgi my sister?"

"Slow down. We've only been a couple for a month."

"Why waste any more time?"

"So much has changed. I want to give her time to adjust." Between Hoyt going to prison, Harry taking over their family garage, me starting at the hospital, and Tipsy and Lee graduating high school, Georgi and I have barely had a moment to ourselves since the trial.

"You're being silly. Why adjust when you guys will just have to change it all again in a few months?"

Georgi and Tipsy reach the car. She steps up on the running board and waves. "Hurry up."

Elena elbows me in the ribs. "Yeah, hurry up."

Georgi

"This feels weird." I step out of the cabin toward the lounge chairs and hand Theo a glass of iced tea. He takes a sip and places his cup on the side table.

"How so?" He pats the spot in front of him, and I snuggle between his legs, resting my head on his shoulder like a pillow.

"The boat feels like a ghost ship with everyone gone." We took Elena and Tipsy— excuse me, she's all grown up and wants to be called Henrietta now—to the airport with Ted and Corine this morning for their flight to Hawaii and gave the crew two weeks of vacation.

Theo kisses his way down my neck. "It's nice to be alone."

I purr like a greedy kitten soaking up his attention. "This is nice."

"Does that mean I can convince you to move back?"

I sit up and spin to face him. He's asked me multiple times over the last months to move back onto the boat, but it didn't feel right.

I love him.

He's it for me. My soulmate. The love of my life.

But there's an old-fashioned bone in my body that wants us to be married before we cohabitate.

Most people think I'm weird, but that doesn't stop the feelings from being there. I was the result of an "accidental pregnancy." Sometimes I wonder if my dad freaked out because he felt trapped. Theo and I aren't in the same position as my parents, but I need the commitment.

"Theo, I'm not ready."

He picks up an envelope from the ground and hands it to me. "But I need your help with a decision that affects us both."

I unfold the paper. It's the certificate of title for the yacht. My eyes scan the page. My hand flies to my mouth. "The boat is yours?"

It's there in black and white. The owner of the *Midnight Star* is Theodore Esteban Alejandro Frederick Sanchez *IV*.

My Theo owns the mega yacht, not his parents.

"Dad handed this to me when they left. He always referred to the yacht as mine, but I thought he meant in a familial way, like Biotech is mine because he owns it. But he actually meant the title is in my name. I've owned it since they bought it."

"Why does this affect me?"

"Do you want to keep it?"

I fold the paper and hand it back to him. "That's not my decision."

"It is. As my wife, you and I decide together where we live."

My brain breaks. "Your wife?"

"What do you think?" He runs his thumb over my ring finger. "Do you want to live on the yacht or buy a house in town?"

"Are you bribing me with real estate?"

He pinches the bridge of his nose. "I didn't think I'd need to bribe you into marrying me."

My heart speeds up and thrums in my ears. "Oh, my word. Are you really asking me? Like right now? Or are we talking hypothetically about the future when we might someday get married?"

"Did I mess this up that badly?" He cups my cheeks and stares lovingly into my eyes. "Georgiana Montgomery, I'm asking you to marry me. Please, will you be my wife?"

I fling myself against his chest and wrap my arms around his neck. "Yes. Of course. Always. Yes." This is the best day of my life. Holy cow! I get to marry Theo and spend the rest of my life with him.

He kisses the side of my head. "Way to make a guy worry."

I pull away from his chest and playfully smack his shoulder. "I didn't expect you to propose with the title to a mega yacht. Usually, guys are down on one knee with a ring."

"Nothing about our relationship has been normal. Most couples don't fall in love on their first date and then spend a year trying to get a second."

I rest my forehead against my fiancé's. "I'm glad you didn't leave me alone."

"I know." He tips my chin and kisses me, slow and sweet. our lips dancing and caressing like we have all the time in the world to savor each other. Because we do.

"So smug," I whisper against his mouth.

"I love you."

"I love you too." Forever.

Epilogue

A month ago, at the Gala

Nora

"HEY, GUMMY BEAR, ARE you okay?" Wyatt Cruz tries to hand me a champagne flute as my sister, cousin, and uncle leave the gala with a herd of police and security guards.

Part of me wants to chase them, but I don't know what good it would do. Georgi has everything under control anyway. She's always been the fixer in the family.

I don't accept Wyatt's drink. Leaning deeper into the shadows by the bachelor auction stage, I breathe to calm my nervous energy. "Why are you still here? Don't you have an heiress to charm?"

Wyatt's part of a bet to see which bachelor can earn the largest bid. He undoubtedly believes he'll win. With an ego like his, he believes everyone loves him.

I do not. Have not. And never will.

Wyatt slides behind me "Nah. You didn't answer my question. I'm worried about you."

"Go away, Wyatt." My co-fellow never listens, so I'm not sure why I waste my breath.

His scent of salt, sand, and something distinctly Wyatt makes my eyes want to flutter closed it's so delicious. Like the beach after a storm. But this is Wyatt. Hulk-shaped body and ego. He leans his mouth by my ear. "You should bid on me. We'll have fun. Promise."

I bat him away. "I spend all day actively avoiding you. Why would I purposefully trap myself on a date with you?"

"You have a paddle. Who else are you going to bid on?"

"That's none of your business." Because I know the ridiculing I'll receive for thinking anyone could be more attractive, smarter, funnier, or wittier than Wyatt. My palms are sweaty enough as it is without Wyatt's opinions destroying my nerves.

"Good thing I'm second-to-last. I'll hang out here and make sure a creep doesn't bother you."

I stop responding to him. It doesn't matter what I say or do. Wyatt's like a wart you can't remove no matter how much acid you pour on it.

My cousin, Harry, sells for $2,000 to Viola Rothchild. If that's the kind of money these guys are earning, there's no way I can buy the guy I'm hoping to win.

The next bachelor only sells for $500 and the one after that for $300. Maybe I do have a shot. My guy's new in town, so hopefully that works in my favor.

Wyatt hovers at my elbow. He whistles along with the background music. I hate to admit that his tone is melodious. His voice makes the little hairs on the back of my neck stand up, and unfortunately, it's not in irritation.

Wyatt has a deep, crooning voice that should be whispered in ears on a feather bed with silky sheets. *Ugh*. That is not the image I want in my head.

Yes, Wyatt is gorgeous. Sexy. Until he opens his mouth that is.

The MC steps on stage. "Our next bachelor this evening is Dr. Beckett Kemp. He's an internist recently relocated from Tampa, Florida. Let's give him a round of applause."

My breath stills in my chest as Beck steps on stage. He was in the class ahead of mine in medical school. His gorgeous blue eyes melted me every time he looked my way.

He never saw me. He looked right through me most days, but that didn't stop my tender, young heart from wishing someday he'd see me.

Today will be that day. If I can afford him.

Bidding starts at $100. I raise my paddle.

"Him?" Wyatt sneers in my ear.

"Shut up."

The bid rises to $200, then $400. I raise to $500. I'll be eating beans and rice for a year, but if I win a date with Beck, my dreams will finally come true.

"You don't want to date him," Wyatt says.

"You don't know him."

"I know enough. He's a tool."

"Shut up." I raise to $800.

"Save your money."

"I never asked for your opinion."

Wyatt's hand slides around my arm. "You can do better."

I jerk from his grip. "What, like you? Ha. In your dreams."

"This will blow up in your face."

I raise my paddle to $1000. It's not just about winning Beck anymore. It's about proving Wyatt wrong. Who does he think he is dictating who I date?

He spends every day irritating the bejesus out of me just because he likes to watch me lose my temper. That's not the kind of man I need in my life. Beck was always helpful to his classmates and kind to patients.

He's the type of man I want to end up with. The boy next door.

Not the tatted up bad boy who disdains following the rules and doesn't care about other people's feelings or opinions.

The auctioneer bangs his gavel. "And the winner is Nora Montgomery for $1200."

Beck's eyes land on me, and the gigantic smile that shines from his face is worth every malnourished meal.

"Gummy Bear, you're breaking my heart." Wyatt whispers in that crooning voice.

I spin to face Wyatt, pop to my toes, so I don't have to glare up as far. "That would require you to have a heart, and as far as I can tell that place in your chest is vacant."

Gack. Wyatt is the only person who turns me into this wicked witch. I hate who I am around him. If he'd just leave me alone, everything would be great.

He clutches his hand to his chest. "Ouch." He leans close enough for me to practically taste the mint on his breath. "Gummy Bear, just wait." He brushes the back of his finger along my cheek. "You'll go on your date with Beck, be bored out of your mind, and realize he's not man enough for you."

"What does that even mean?" My voice is traitorously breathy.

His lips brush the shell of my ear, and my body shivers. "It means you're full of fire and passion and you need a man who lets you burn bright. Beck won't appreciate you the way you deserve."

"Let's put our hands together for Dr. Wyatt Cruz," the MC calls.

Wyatt stands to his full height and winks. "Miss you already, Gummy Bear."

I squeeze my hands into fists and bite my lower lip to keep it from trembling.

I do not want a man like Wyatt. Even if his crooning voice makes my knees wobble and my throat tighten. Even if I didn't know he could be so tender to caress my cheek. Even if somewhere along the line he learned my favorite song and hums it when I'm having a hard day.

I want someone sweet like Beck. I want someone kind and loyal like Georgi found with Theo. I want someone dependable like Bridgette found in Keegan.

Wyatt's a bad boy. He doesn't just bend the rules. He runs over them with his Harley, laughing.

A man like Wyatt can't be what I need.

The first paddles rise, and bids for Wyatt climb higher and higher. He slides his jacket from his shoulders and rolls up his sleeves one agonizing crease at a time to display the intricate tattoos covering every inch of his forearms.

I lick my lips.

A woman about my age, with diamonds the size of grapes in her ears, wins him for $3,500.

He leaps from the stage and wraps her in a hug, whispers in her ear, and pulls a bright crimson blush from her cheeks.

I'll never admit it out loud, but the emotion roaring through my veins is jealousy.

But I don't have a crush on Wyatt Cruz. No. Never.

Beckett Kemp is the man of my dreams.

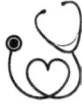

Want more?

Georgi and Theo's wedding will be the event of the year. They need you to help them plan it! You have flawless taste after all, so who else would they ask?

Scan the QR code to participate in an exclusive Choose-Your-Own-Adventure style bonus epilogue.

Fake Dating the Cardiologist

I'M AWARE I'M AN idiot and my plan is poorly conceived, but you can't blame a guy for trying to make all his dreams come true when the opportunity of a lifetime presents itself.

The director of our cardiology program won't write me a letter of recommendation, so I can apply for my dream job in London unless I clean up my act, stop embarrassing him in front of our patients, and learn to play by the rules. No one plays by the rules better than Nora Montgomery, so she's my ticket out of this little Texas town with too many sad memories to make it home.

Nora, my gorgeous, goody-two-shoes Gummy Bear hates me. I have irritated her especially well during our fellowship, so I deserve her ire. She's head-over-heels infatuated with her former medical school classmate, but the dude doesn't give her the time of day until I flirt with her.

If I can convince her to be my fake girlfriend and help me clean up my reputation, she'll earn crush-boy's attention.

It's a win win.

But as I get to know Nora, I realize she might be the dream I should have been chasing. Rules are meant to be broken, but can I risk breaking my heart if I can't convince Nora I'm the man she deserves, not her crush?

Treat yourself to Nora and Wyatt's fake dating, enemies-to-lovers medical romance, the next book in the Third Coast Medical Romance Series, today.

Afterword

Darling Reader,

Oh, Theo. That man had some hard lessons to learn. Loyalty is a tricky thing. Sometimes it saves us and sometimes it's a millstone dragging us down.

The good news is he decided to follow his heart and that is what he needed to do to earn his father's respect.

I'm glad Georgi was able to see past her bruised ego to the real chance at love Theo offered.

And I love she did it barefoot in satin;)

I hope you have strength like Georgi to be yourself even when other people are screaming you don't belong.

We all belong.

We all have a seat at the table.

We all have voices that need to be heard.

Thank you for spending this time with me and my characters. I can't wait to see you on our next reading adventure.

Happy reading,

About Daphne

Lover of baking and running, Daphne spends her days imagining ways to mend broken hearts for happily ever afters. She currently resides in Texas, but was raised in Las Vegas (yes, that Vegas) and has the stories to prove it. Her kids make her a little crazy, as does her husband, but she wouldn't want to explore this beautiful world without them.

Visit her at www.DaphneDyer.com, Facebook at Author Daphne Dyer or Instagram at Author Daphne Dyer.